BADLANDS

JO SCHAFFER LAYTON

OWL HOLLOW PRESS

Owl Hollow Press, LLC, Springville, UT 84663

Badlands
First Edition
Copyright © 2024 by J. Schaffer Layton

Library of Congress Cataloging-in-Publication Data
Badlands / Jo Schaffer Layton — First edition.

Summary: When 17 year-old Jaqueline is dropped off in the middle of the Idaho Badlands with other problem teens, what starts as an adventure in wilderness survival becomes a real life-and-death ordeal as kids and counselors start turning up murdered.

Paperback: 978-1-958109-62-5
ebook: 978-1-958109-63-2

Dedicated to all who have wandered and to all who provide good maps for the way back.

To my parents who provided me the opportunity to find myself in the Badlands, and to "Big Jim," Vanessa and Patty who patiently led a motley crew of troubled teens through the rugged terrain of the wilderness of their own pain.

CHAPTER 1

JAQUELINE COLE CRUSHED an empty beer can in her hand and dropped it to the ground. She pressed against the stone wall. The moon cast the long, slanted shadow of a tilted cross onto the pavement. She held back a belch and smiled as warmth spread through her. The whisper of Sean's breath from where he stood beside her was all she heard over the beating of her heart. He squeezed her hand hard.

She found his face in the dark. "See anyone?"

He raised a cocky brow. "Nah. You've never done anything like this before... don't worry. I have." His breath was a waft of fermented, malted barley.

"I learn fast." Jaq told herself the goosebumps on her arms were from the chill in the air. But a sense of danger and fear prickled along her spine. This was the next bad step in a series of angry, determined strides forward. The chaos inside had leaked out and swirled through her life like a tornado—and that was okay.

"About time you totally drop that good girl act," Sean breathed. His hands slid hot around her waist and pressed into the small of her back. "Jaq... there's other ways to be bad."

Jaqueline's inhale stuttered. "Knock it off." Despite how he made her pulse jump, she pushed away from the wall and slipped out of his arms, unsteady on her feet for only a moment. "Let's get this over with." There was time enough for fooling around later. But this place creeped her out.

Of all the places her dad's cleaning crews took care of, this one was his favorite. He'd married her mom here, though that hadn't turned out so great. He'd been taking out his failed marriage on Jaq ever since Mom left.

A stray dog ambled across the dim courtyard of the church. Nobody seemed to be coming from any direction. She gripped the cold, heavy crowbar tighter in her hand. A large wooden door with an iron ring for a handle stood between her and the ultimate "screw you, Dad."

This place mattered to him—so he couldn't ignore this. She jammed the crowbar into the crack between the doorframe and the wall. The old wood splintered a little on the first crank. Too easy. Jaq smirked. *You'd think that ruining your life would take more effort.*

"Gimme that." Sean pushed her aside. His sexism irritated her, but he was so hot when he was assertive. Besides, she'd get him back later and he wouldn't even know why.

The muscles in his arms bulged and after a few loud cracks the door swung open with a heavy creak. "Sweet." Sean pushed into the dark interior of the small gothic church.

All hesitation evaporated in the heat of her excitement. "Let's go."

A shiver skimmed across Jaq's skin as she stepped inside. Shadows crisscrossed the stone floor, thrown there by moonlight that came through stained glass windows. Dim lights glowed on the stone walls, casting just enough light for their purposes. Inky clouds gathered in the peaked arches of the ceiling like a storm. Lightning might strike them at any moment.

"Okay. Make Daddy proud." Sean's whisper echoed in the mausoleum of hope and prayers. He reached into his backpack and then handed Jaq a can of spray paint.

She took it, thrumming with anticipation. This was her protest. To her dad's ambivalence, to her mom's abandonment, to authority, to being the perfect child... to everything that made her feel futile and small. She sauntered forward. *Where to start...*

The reverent air of the church smelled of candles and graves. The peace and quiet jarred in contrast to how Jaq felt inside. She walked down the aisles and hummed the wedding march. It vibrated bitterness in her throat. She'd never promised to take care of her dad and do the dishes until death do we part. It was never her job to stop being a kid because there was a household to run and a kid sister to take care of. She never signed up to be anyone's surrogate spouse.

So what if she wasn't the perfect daughter anymore? It was her life. She'd made mistakes and gotten into trouble... but not once had he even tried to understand why. Then he'd gone too far and grounded her from seeing Sean and took away her cell phone. Enough was enough. He had to understand he couldn't control her.

Jaq hiccupped and it echoed in the empty church. "Shhh..." She waved a hand at Sean who had given her a startled glance.

Something moved in the rows of wooden pews. She froze and glanced around but the darkness seemed to move like smoke. Nothing there. A few more steps and she stood at the altar draped in white cloth. Jesus looked down at her in agony where he hung on a gold cross that stood behind the altar. Blood ran down his face and body. *So creepy.* A flicker of guilt made her lungs catch.

"Ugh. Total nightmare in here." Sean startled her from behind.

"After I finish, we're making out right here." Jaqueline kicked the altar. The thump almost stopped her heart.

Sean grabbed her wrist. "Then let's hurry." His scratchy voice made her stomach zing.

She pushed him away and shook the can of paint. The sound echoed like breaking glass. *Clean this up, Dad.* Red paint hissed out onto the white altar cloth.

"Looks like something got sacrificed on it," Sean whispered.

FORGIVE ME dripped red on the altar. Sean snickered. Jaqueline continued around the chapel and Sean started in the other direction with his own can of paint. Her pulse skipped; it was hard to get a full breath. Benches, walls, statues of bearded dudes, weird paintings of angels—each split open and bled under her hand in the soft yellow glow of electric candlelight that flickered against the walls.

It would take a miracle to get this all cleaned up. Jaqueline tried not to think about what she was doing, pushing away the notion that there might be a God someplace who saw every-thing. She found herself back at the altar and looked up at Jesus. Jaqueline held the can high and hesitated.

Sean chuckled. "Not like he isn't already bleeding. Do it. Hurry up." He sat on the altar and watched her in the way that always made Jaqueline feel weak and wild at the same time.

She lowered her arm. What if this went too far?

"Do it. Then get over here." Sean's eyes seemed to swallow her from head to toe.

Jaq gave him a slow smile. She wanted to impress him. Anyway, what had Jesus ever done for her? Where had He been when she needed saving? She dropped the paint and put both hands on the cross and shoved. It tilted and went down with a loud crash. The crown of thorns skittered across the floor. Jaqueline stared in excited horror at the bloody, broken body of her Divine victim. Her stomach constricted and she blinked back a sudden sting in her eyes.

"Woohoo!" Sean's voice soared into the vaulted ceiling.

The bright ceiling lights flashed on, illuminating the room streaked with their crime. Jaqueline's heart dropped. Two men in dark clothes stood at the back of the church. Sean automatically reached for the air with both hands. He knew the routine.

"Don't move," one man's voice barked with authority.

"I'm so busted." Jaqueline whispered. She forced a smile. This was what she wanted.

Sirens sounded from outside as Jaq followed Sean up the aisle, hands raised in the air. The two men stood alert with hard expressions on their faces. She hated how they looked at her. They didn't know the first thing about her life.

———

By the time Todd Cole showed up, Jaqueline sat on the sidewalk beside Sean with her hands cuffed behind her back. Colored lights from the cop cars flashed across her father's angry face.

"Hi, Dad." She smirked at him.

"What the hell," he muttered, shaking his head. "Defacing the inside of a church?" His voice climbed with each word. "Do you know how hard this is going to be to fix? How this reflects on my company? On me? If they decide to press charges, do you have any idea what this could mean for you?"

Jaqueline shrugged. The metal cuffs dug into her wrists. Her heart beat fast and she tried to maintain a mask of indifference...but the laugh broke out of her. It was all so funny. She hid her face in Sean's shoulder while the giggles shook her. When she finally looked up, her dad stared at her.

"You're drunk."

"Barely." She had been worse. Many times.

Her dad took a deep breath. He seemed to struggle with what words to say next. "I don't know what to do. I don't know how to help you. Sneaking out, drinking, shoplifting..." He ran a hand through his messy hair. "Now this. I'm going to beg them not to press charges, but you're going to clean this graffiti up yourself even if it takes you a month."

Jaqueline glared. "Not likely."

"This is your mess. I've evidently failed to teach you anything about personal responsibility." Her dad rubbed his face, his shoulders dropped in defeat.

My mess? The *world* was a mess. And it definitely wasn't her fault that mom left. "But I'm a minor." She pursed her lips. "I might have to do some community service, but the cost to repair this is on you."

He shook his head, meeting her defiant gaze with his defeated one. "I know. I can't do this alone. I don't know how to be a dad and a mom and—"

Sean stifled a laugh beside her.

"This is funny?" Jaq's father's face turned red, and any vulnerability in his expression vanished. "Punks like you make parenting so much harder. What're you doing for my daughter other than leading her into trouble? I never want to see you around her again," Dad barked, face hard.

Sean grinned. "Oh, you won't see me."

"Stay away from her," her dad warned, stepping toward Sean.

"I'll decide," Jaqueline said, her voice brittle. She suddenly felt ill. How many beers had she drank?

Dad grimaced and swiped a hand over his eyes. "You'll decide? Like you just decided to get drunk and deface a church?" He shook his head and looked up at the sky. "I can't do this. I can't help you if you won't help yourself. I don't know what to do with you. It's obvious that I can't give you what you need. We have to find some place better for you to live."

His unexpected words struck Jaqueline with force. Was he kicking her out? *I can't give you what you need.* She'd overheard her dad say that to her mother with the same level of exasperation in his voice. Her shock turned to fury.

"Good! I'm glad," she yelled. "Mom was right to leave you!"

Her dad just looked back at her with pain etched on his face. Then he nodded and turned away.

CHAPTER 2

IT WAS SO hot that the inside of her mouth felt like Arizona. Jaqueline opened her bottled water and took a drink. It was nice and wet in her sticky mouth—too bad it would just end up in her pits. She tossed the bottle into the back seat. Flower was probably thirsty too. Her sister sighed a thank you from behind.

Jaqueline had gone numb after days of raging against her dad's decision. Even after she spent a week scrubbing red paint with chemicals that burned her hands, her dad hadn't changed his mind. Banished to her weird aunt's house in Idaho: a punishment worse than all kinds of horrible deaths.

The hot vinyl seat stuck to her legs. The booger-green station wagon smelled of baked foam, plastic, and old metal. She gazed out the window, taking in the small town as they passed through. Boring. People who lived in places like this must stare at their dying lawns for excitement.

She noted her chipping blue nail polish. Being on the road, stuck in the car with her dad for days, sucked. All she could do was sit, sweat, and think about how unfair and screwed up her life was.

"Give me those, Jaqueline." Her dad sighed and held out

his hand for the cigarettes she thought he hadn't seen tucked into her cutoff jeans.

Sweat trickled down her back. "Fine, Todd," she snapped and handed the contraband over. He wouldn't be happy until he'd taken everything from her.

Jaqueline's dad shook his head. "Why do you do all the things you do?" He rubbed the reddish stubble on his chin.

"Guys ... come on," Flower muttered from behind.

"And smoking will destroy your health," Dad grumbled as he rolled down the window and tossed the cigarettes out.

Jaq watched in the mirror as they bounced on the road and disappeared behind them.

"Gee, thanks. Didn't realize that."

"You better not have spent my money on those coffin nails."

"Heaven forbid we should spend your money." She glared at her dad when her stomach grumbled again. Their last meal had been last night in Reno, where they stayed in a scary cheap motel. If her dad didn't munch on corn nuts and sunflower seeds to stay awake, they probably wouldn't even have those.

Sweat beaded on her forehead. He wouldn't run the AC either; he said it wasted gas. Open windows caused "dragging," and that also wasted gas. Somewhere in Nevada, Jaqueline had freaked out and rolled down her window anyway, which helped about as much as somebody blowing a giant hair dryer in her face.

She despised her dad's weirdness about money. It was what motivated most of his decisions—even after what happened with Mom. Jaqueline squeezed her eyes shut and pushed away the image of her mother throwing clothes into a suitcase.

"What in the world is that?" Flower spoke from the back seat. Jaqueline glanced up to see what her sister had spotted.

A large tree grew on the side of the highway. Hundreds of shoes dangled from the branches like some sort of deranged

Christmas ornaments for cobbler elves. There were even shoes piled on the ground around the trunk. The car slowed down and her father gave a low whistle.

"No, Todd." Jaqueline slumped and pressed her head against the seat's back.

He pulled onto the shoulder and parked before turning toward her and pushing his nerdy glasses up the bridge of his nose. "Don't call me that—it's disrespectful. Anyway, they don't belong to anyone."

The car filled with tension like an unopened Dr. Pepper with a Mento inside.

Flower, likely sensing the oncoming fight, got out and leaned against the car. Jaqueline turned to her father and gave him her best look of disgust. He chuckled with a look of genuine delight at her distress.

He spit another sunflower seed shell into a paper cup that was nearly full. "Lighten up. There's nobody here to be embarrassed in front of—no peer pressure. You can stop acting like a rebel. You don't have an audience out here." He gestured to the middle of nowhere around them.

Jaqueline's face flashed with heat. She hated how her dad thought everything she did was because of peer pressure. The smoking, cutting school, and, well, okay—the vandalism may have been influenced by her friends, but more than likely it was the beers and not the peers. But they were her decisions. He had no idea how she felt—how could he? Jaqueline flipped her dad the bird to enlighten him, but he just gave her a condescending smile and got out of the car.

She stared at the wavy blur of heat rising from the black road that stretched to the horizon. If anyone looked at her right now they'd probably see the same thing floating up from her skin. Her blood simmered as her father shopped for his size on the strange shoe tree.

Dad grabbed a pair of small pink Keds and tossed them to Flower. Then he yanked down a pair of hiking boots. He sauntered around the tree, kicking at the pile of shoes on the ground, then stooped to pull up what looked like black biker boots, holding them up to Jaqueline with a grin. *Very funny.* She scowled at him and pinched her nose as if she could smell the nasty things from where she sat.

Scavenging used shoes just because they were free was low. But he'd done worse on this very trip. He'd pillaged some toys from a roadside shrine to a kid, leaving only the flowery cross and candles. His argument was always, "Nobody is using them. It's a waste."

What her dad didn't realize was that he was a waste of perfectly good oxygen.

Jaq's eyes were drawn to the tree. It seemed petrified in the merciless sun. Discarded journeys and paths once walked by faceless people dangled from every branch. It struck something deep inside. It was like a message... an omen. She shook off the uneasiness.

Flower and Dad got back into the car with his harvest after what seemed like a class period of math. "Are you done scavenging? Can we go now?" Jaqueline wiped sweat from her forehead.

Her dad nodded, satisfied. "These are good quality." He gave his hiking boots a squeeze as if they were actual produce. "Like yours, honey?" He glanced in the rearview mirror at Flower.

"Yeah. They're great. Thanks, Dad." Flower had a soft voice. She knew how to pick her battles.

———

Jaqueline woke when the car stopped again. Another nightmare had her heart thumping. She glanced down at her hands. No blood. Just the faint stain of red paint.

The crunch of sunflower seeds brought her back to reality. Dad looked over, eyes dark behind his glasses. "She's awake."

"Where are we?" Jaqueline croaked, still coursing with adrenalin from the familiar slasher dream. There was always some psycho chasing her through the woods or a barren and rocky canyon. Sometimes the killer had her brother's face. Jaqueline rubbed her wrists as if to erase Brian's phantom grip on them.

"We're going to eat here." Dad removed his glasses and rubbed his eyes.

"Finally." Jaqueline was happy to see the rundown diner with the blinking sign. She could eat anything at this point. She looked over at her little sister. Flower was petite for a fourteen-year-old and fair-haired, with big brown eyes like her mother. It was hard to imagine what went on in the quiet, possibly empty rooms of her mind.

Her sister smiled. "I'm starving!"

It was late and every table was vacant. The smell of fried food and cigarettes reminded Jaqueline of the first time she'd taken a smoke at a carnival with some of her friends. She could totally use a cigarette right now. She searched the menu for the cheapest possibilities. Her little sister's stomach growled.

They sat at a table with a stack of menus. Her dad rubbed a freckled hand over his face and let out a deep sigh. Flower flipped through the menu, her finger tracing the options.

"What can we get?" Jaqueline leaned her face into her hands, her elbows on the orange laminate table.

"Whatever you want." Her dad checked his watch, then pushed up the sleeves of his worn plaid shirt.

"Really? Cool." Flower bounced in her seat, her blonde hair

swinging. Somehow, she stayed bubbly most of the time. It was as if she had no idea that everything sucked.

Jaqueline wondered if her dad planned on shooting down their orders in front of the waitress to teach them some kind of lesson about entitlement.

As if Jaqueline thought the waitress into existence, she appeared in a brown apron, holding a notebook and snapping gum. "Hi. What can I get ya?" Her heavily made-up eyes drifted shut as if waiting for their answers tried her patience.

"Cheeseburger, curly fries, raspberry Italian soda, and mudslide pie." Flower smacked her lips and wiggled with excitement.

"Italian what?" The big haired waitress grimaced and clicked the back of her pen several times.

"Soda. Right here." Flower pointed to the menu.

"Hm. Not sure what that is."

"It's... on the menu. You take soda and flavored syrup and cream..." Flower motioned as if mixing ingredients.

"Oh. Yeah, I'll ask about that, And you?" Miss Clueless ignored Flower's incredulous eyes and squinted at Jaqueline.

Frowning she said, "Um. Tater tots. And... the club sandwich," she let out a breath and waited for her dad to cancel the order.

"I'll have the spicy chicken wings with steak fries and a slice of chocolate cake. You girls want anything else?" Dad clapped his menu onto the table and raised his brows at his daughters.

"No, we're good." Jaqueline bit her lip, puzzled by her dad's casual spending.

The waitress strode away before anyone could change their mind. Flower leaned against her big sister with a happy sigh. "Thanks, Dad."

He nodded and then said to Jaqueline, "Well?"

"Thanks." She drew her brows together, waiting for the punchline.

"What? I can't get my hungry girls a meal?" Her father checked his watch again.

"It's the money—you hate spending money." Jaqueline felt her sister stiffen. She didn't like upsetting Flower, but some things just had to be said.

"Hey, things have been really tight. But I put money down when it matters. Lots of money." Dad locked eyes with his oldest daughter. The lines on his face and the hunch of his shoulders betrayed his fatigue. It wasn't just the drive from California. The last six months must've been hard on him. Mom left and then her psycho older brother, Brian, ran off to be with her, plus all the trouble Jaqueline had gotten into. The stress of it all showed on her father's face. Guilt snaked its way from Jaqueline's stomach to her chest, but she hardened against it with a glare. He deserved to be worn out. It was his own fault all of this had happened.

The savory food went down fast and easy. It almost put Jaq in a good mood until she remembered the reason for their trip. She hadn't seen her aunt in years. Jaqueline had the dim recollection of flowery blouses, cats, and a lot of Jesus talk. It was going to be the worst thing ever.

Dad seemed distracted. He got up and mumbled something about using the bathroom. When he'd lumbered away, Jaqueline reached over to his plate and plucked up an abandoned fry and took a bite. It was cold and too salty.

The waitress dropped off Flower's Italian soda, unapologetic for its lateness, and then sauntered away. Flower looked at it critically before taking a sip. "Ew! What the—is this Pepsi with milk in it? Why is it even on the menu if they have no idea what an Italian soda is?" She stuck out her tongue.

Jaqueline laughed. "That's so weird." She leaned back, full

and sleepy now, and thought about what her life would be once they dropped her off in Idaho. Maybe she should miss Sean more than she did. She tried to conjure feelings but came up numb.

"I'm gonna miss you," Flower said softly.

Jaqueline looked at her sister, a little surprised. They had been so distant since everything happened. "Yeah?"

Her sister nodded and glanced away. There was probably something Flower wanted to say but Jaqueline wasn't sure she wanted to hear it, so she pushed scraps around on her plate with a fork.

"Well, you have your friends and that cute Tyler guy to keep you company."

Flower forced a smile. "He is really, really cute."

"Kiss him yet?" Jaqueline raised her brows.

Her little sister blushed. "Not yet."

"Get in there." Jaqueline elbowed her sister.

They sat in silence poking at their plates. There was a time when they could chatter nonstop and knew each other's secrets. But that was in the days of dollies and Kool-Aid. They seemed to have less and less in common every year. Flower seemed to be fading into a mousy thing with nothing interesting to say.

Their dad returned from the restroom and checked his watch, then checked it again before giving his girls a nervous smile. He grabbed the check from the table and scanned the numbers for too long. He pulled his wallet out of the pocket of his outdated cords and searched inside, fingering the bills out once, twice, three times.

Todd stood and walked over to the counter carrying the check with him. He bent close to the waitress in conversation. Jaqueline shook her head. He was probably trying to get out of having to pay for some of it. The waitress's eyes widened as she nodded her head.

The door to the diner opened and two men appeared. The waitress, half asleep until now, scurried to meet the newcomers, and Dad returned to the table. He sunk into his chair, exhaustion replaced by some kind of nervous energy. All this over money?

The waitress came toward them with two men following. She sat them at a round table nearby, handed out menus, and wandered away. She looked over her shoulder, right at Jaqueline, with an apologetic side smile and then disappeared into the kitchen. Jaqueline scrunched her nose. Maybe she felt bad about the Pepsi-milk. She should.

"We going, Todd?" Jaqueline flicked a straw wrapper across the table.

"Give Flower a minute. She's still working on that drink."

Flower stuck out her tongue and took another bite of her dwindling piece of pie. "It's not very tasty."

The newcomers both looked over, their menus untouched where the waitress had placed them. One of the men was bulky, shaved bald, and had the beginnings of a short, sandy beard. He wore a dark blue t-shirt depicting an eagle in flight clutching a mouse in its talons. The other guy, much younger, had dark, shoulder-length hair and a pitted face, as if teen acne wasn't too far in his past. Sinewy arms poked out of a red shirt with the same picture on it as his companion's.

Jaqueline's dad straightened in his chair and seemed to examine the men with a mix of dread and anticipation. Flower blew bubbles into her gross drink, oblivious.

The bald man inclined his chin at her dad with a questioning twist of his mouth. Dad swallowed, dropped a few bills onto the table, and looked at Jaqueline without meeting her eyes. He leaned across the remains of his meal and kissed her cheek. She thought she saw tears shining in his eyes.

Jaqueline only had a moment to register surprise when a sudden loud scrape of chairs on tile made her jump. Big Bald Guy and Pock Face loomed over her and had their hands on her before she knew what was happening. Her bottom left the seat as python-like arms slid under her armpits and pulled up hard. Jaqueline's mouth opened, a scream trapped in her throat. Her chair hit the ground with a crack. Flower let out a sharp yelp.

"Hey!" Jaqueline could hardly breathe.

"You're coming with us. You won't get hurt." The gruff voice grated into her ear.

She looked with wild desperation at her father as the two men dragged her toward the door. Why wasn't he doing anything? Her dad stood still, with a clenched jaw and balled fists at his sides as strangers took her away. Beside him Flower screamed, eyes huge with terror she lurched forward as if to run after Jaqueline. Only then did her dad move—to hold his younger daughter in place.

"No!" With legs climbing the sky, Jaqueline thrashed in pain. "Dad! Daddy!" The words burst out of her with the force and heat of fireworks before a hand clamped over her mouth and rough fabric was forced over her face, turning everything black.

JAQUELINE STRUGGLED until her strength gave out. She heard the metallic whine of a door opening just before the men tossed her limp body onto a scratchy, thin carpet. She rubbed her backside and cried out again. At least they hadn't tied her hands together. Heavy metal doors slammed with finality. Jaqueline yanked the black wool beanie from her face.

She sat on the floor in the back of a dark van with no windows. A hopeless terror made her hollow inside. The engine roared and the van vibrated. She pulled on the locked door lever and screamed until her throat hurt and the helplessness took over. What was happening? Her dad had done nothing to stop these men from taking her. It was as if he had planned it with them. Nobody was coming to the rescue. The bastard. The money-loving monster.

Her captors sat in the front of the van with a metal screen separating them. They sped out onto the highway into the darkness while Jaq screamed and kept driving when she stopped. Jaqueline hugged her knees as her body trembled. She scanned her mobile prison. There were no seats—just a big empty space with low pile carpeting and nothing to bludgeon anyone to death with. She stared at the back of the two heads at the front of the van, her hand itching for something heavy and blunt.

What was happening? Where were they taking her? Anger and fear combined until her breath came in spasms and gasps. The long-haired, wiry man turned to look at her with unreadable eyes.

"Perverts! How much did you pay? Huh? What did he sell me for?" Jaqueline tried to clench her chattering teeth. She had heard about things like this but never dreamed it could happen to her.

The younger man pushed his long dark hair away from his face and raised his brows. He smiled as if at an inside joke. "You're just fine. Calm down."

"Oh, you were pricey." Bald Guy's shoulders shook as if he silenced a deep chuckle.

Revulsion somersaulted in Jaqueline's stomach. Oh, dear God. They were taking her somewhere to rape her—or auction her off. Sex trafficking. She hadn't even technically gone all the way with Sean yet. Sean, with his intense mahogany eyes and warm hands. If Sean had been there in the restaurant, he would have fought for her. She pictured the tattoo of a skull with three cracks on Sean's muscular arm. Each crack represented a guy he'd put in the hospital. What Jaqueline wouldn't do right now for the gun Sean kept in his locker. Her eyes teared up, and she dug her nails into the heels of her hands.

Her mother had abandoned her—escaped without her. Jaqueline closed her eyes and saw her mother throwing expensive luggage into her new convertible. Mom, with her bleached golden hair and heavy makeup, grinned like Barbie as she flipped off the house and squealed away into a Malibu sunset—to find happiness and freedom elsewhere. Jaqueline's mom seemed to wake up to her misery about a year ago, and the metamorphosis from dowdy, depressed homemaker to glittering desperate housewife seemed to happen overnight. Six months of screaming fights over money and standing up to Jaqueline's dad, followed by makeover, boob job, clubbing, and finally, six months ago, an Oscar-worthy diva departure.

Jaqueline regretted not leaving with her. Especially now. She choked on tears and let out a piercing scream from deep inside her gut.

The van swerved, tires screeching on the dark road. The bald guy huffed. "Don't do that again. My ears are still ringing from the first fifteen minutes." He twisted a finger in one of his ears. "Want to get us all killed?" His voice was gruff, but it sounded like someone talking to a naughty child.

"What difference would that make?" Jaqueline spat.

"Aw. Poor you. You've had it so rough. And nobody understands." Baldy glanced over his shoulder, mockery glinting in his eyes.

"Screw you." Jaqueline leaned against the wall of the van. "You won't get your money's worth. Sorry to disappoint."

"Sheesh," the man muttered. He leaned over to his companion, and they spoke low for several moments. The rattling and roaring of the van made it impossible to hear what they said.

Jaqueline clasped her hands together and brought them to her forehead. Her anger only substituted for bravery so much. Her insides quivered. Where were they going? What would they do to her?

Through the windshield there were fewer lights than before. She couldn't calculate with her foggy brain how long they'd been driving. A half hour? The road was bumpier now. She had to balance herself with her hands pressed to the floor. The headlights revealed dirt and emptiness. No houses, trees, or cars—a secluded place to do whatever they wanted to her and then hide her body.

Jaqueline's mouth watered just before the contents of her special last meal with Daddy splattered onto the floor of the van. She retched twice more, spitting the sour taste from her mouth, wiping her lips with a shaking hand.

"Oh boy. That's appetizing," the driver muttered.

"Not as tasty now, am I?" Jaqueline croaked, her throat burning.

"We'll get you cleaned up. We're almost there," the long-haired guy said, almost sounding concerned. Jaqueline crept closer to the front of the van and heard him say, "I hate this job. She's really freaked." The big man only nodded.

Hope unfurled inside of her—weak as vapor, but it gave her strength. Maybe these two were just delivery guys. She might be able to get the younger one to sympathize with her.

"Please." She scooted closer to the metal screen. "Please let me go. Right here. I can find my way back. Just don't take me wherever you're going." Jaqueline couldn't keep her voice from breaking and heard her own pathetic whimpering. "Please," she whispered again.

"Can't do that. Sorry." Baldy didn't even look back or slow down as they drove too fast down the dusty road.

The other one frowned and looked back at Jaqueline, and she caught the look that flickered across his face. Pity. She pounced on that, giving him a small smile while begging with her eyes.

Jaqueline knew she was pretty. In fact, she'd rebelled against her own beauty for a while. She'd gone through a metamorphosis of her own this last year. From bouncy, popular cheerleader to pissed-off anarchist. Being a babe was how she was able to first date Eric, the cute quarterback—then after choking on that cliché when she finally figured "it" all out, she captured Sean, the angry and wicked-sexy troublemaker. Even the friends she'd lost during her transformation couldn't deny that he was hot. They'd all had bad girl fantasies about him shared late at night during sleepovers. Jaqueline knew they all talked trash about her now—they just wished they could break the act and get real too.

But this was too real, even for Jaqueline. The long-haired guy with the bad complexion continued to stare at her. She bit her lip and ran her hand down one leg suggesting any reward he chose for helping her, which made her stomach roil. He cleared his throat and shifted in his seat, hissing into the driver's ear.

"Well, then don't look at her." Baldy chuckled.

Jaqueline blushed and lay down in defeat. She thought of Flower and how terrified she had looked. What if her dad sold her too? Rage surged into her tired limbs, and she leapt up, her feet apart for balance as the van bounced over large rocks in the road. Jaqueline beat her fists and feet against the back door of the van.

"Let me out! Help! I'll kill you!" Jaqueline shrieked, trying to smash through the door. Her lungs worked with jagged ferocity and pain burned her hands.

The van stopped with a sudden lurch and Jaqueline was thrown to the floor with a sharp cry, hitting her head and bruising her hip. Her cheek rested in her own vomit. She moaned and curled up into a little ball, sobbing.

After a moment, the high groan of the doors opening stopped Jaqueline's heart. The two men stood silhouetted against a moonlit sky.

"We're here, kid. Craig, go get R.J. and bring a towel or something to clean up this mess," Bald Guy grumbled. Craig ran his hand through his hair, nodded a few times, but seemed glued in place. He looked at Jaqueline with a grimace that seemed apologetic before turning to jog into the darkness.

Jaqueline crept closer to the open doors of the van, waiting for her eyes to adjust. There was a small cabin outlined on a ridge to the right, but before she could get a good look, Baldy stepped in front of her.

"Don't try to run," he warned, standing with fists on his hips.

"Where would I go?" Jaqueline let her shoulders droop in submission. Maybe he'd let his guard down if she cooperated.

There was little hope left. The rancid smell of her vomit and the dusty, weedy smell of the wilderness evoked a barren desolate feeling that threatened to swallow her from the inside out.

Pounding feet approached and Craig reappeared, breathing hard. He tossed a towel at Jaqueline. "R.J. is with the others. He said to bring her up."

Baldy grunted in acknowledgement and waited while Jaqueline wiped her face, hands, and thighs with the towel that smelled like mildew and synthetic flowers.

"C'mon." The burly man wrapped a large hand around one arm and Craig grabbed the other, pulling Jaqueline out of the van. She stumbled along as the uneven ground rose toward the tiny wood cabin. A dim yellow light came from a small window beside the crooked door. A wolf-like, white-and-gray dog stood in front of the entrance as if to challenge them. Jaqueline was struck by the dog's startling ice blue eyes when it looked up at her.

"Hey, Always. Stand down." Craig reached out with his free hand and scratched the dog's head. The dog made a small whine in its throat and lapped at Craig's hand with a glossy red tongue then relaxed onto the ground.

Great. A guard dog called Always. Sounded permanent. Jaqueline held her breath, heart thumping, as Baldy pushed the door open.

"Craig, Mick, bring her in." A trim man with black hair

lightly sprinkled with silver welcomed them with a gravelly voice. He was dressed in a long duster coat and cowboy boots. He squinted at Jaqueline and extended his hand. "I'm R.J."

Jaqueline glared at his hand. This must be the guy who bought her. She looked beyond him and noticed three guys about her age sitting on a cot behind him. Jaqueline shivered and took a step back toward the door.

"Sit." R.J. lifted his chin toward a cot on the opposite wall. Other than the two cots, a small wood burning stove and a table with a lantern on it, the cabin was just bare wood. Jaqueline resisted when Craig pushed her forward but soon gave up and sunk onto the cot, feeling all her new bruises. Her head hurt and she was only one rough word away from crying again.

The three men huddled, conversing in low voices. Jaqueline kept her head down as she examined the three boys sitting silently on the other cot. One lanky boy had a shaved head but for rusty bangs that hung over one eye—he wore army boots and a plaid shirt. His arms crossed over his chest, shivering, his eyes cast down to the floor. The boy in the middle leaned against the wall as if asleep. He had spiky blond hair and wore a football jersey and jeans. The third boy with tan skin, brown hair in need of a cut, and a black t-shirt leaned forward, elbows on his knees, watching Jaqueline. She studied her fingernails, struck with the thought that earlier that day the need for a manicure mattered. She chipped some dark blue away, then felt sad to see it go.

The cabin door creaked open, and a dark-haired young woman entered carrying a red duffel bag. "Hey guys." She grinned at the men and dropped her bag to hug the burly guy.

"Ready?"

Jaqueline couldn't make sense of it. The chipper girl looked wholesome and neighborly—like a college student just arriving on a camp-out with friends. Her heart contracted as she wondered how she was involved.

R.J. checked his wristwatch and cleared his throat. "Katie, you're late. Alright, let's get going or you won't make it to Number One tonight."

Katie clapped, turned to the boys on the cot and Jaqueline, and raised her brows. "Orientation, Mick?" she questioned Baldy. Mick shook his head, rubbing his fingers over the sandy stubble on this chin.

R.J. turned to face the room, his long coat swinging at his sides. Jaqueline half expected him to flick back one side of the duster to reveal a gun at his hip. When he spoke, he sounded hoarse and gravelly. "Alright, kids. We're all here. I'm gonna ask you to remain silent and seated while I explain what happens next."

R.J. had a scar on one cheek and looked like a character in a movie. All three boys sat forward, alert now, fear and respect showing on their faces. R.J. smiled with teeth like blades, reaching down to grab the red duffle bag that Katie had dropped to the floor. The unzipping sound broke the silence like fingernails on a chalkboard. He pulled out a wad of army green fabric and tossed a t-shirt at each of the kids. "Welcome to IBSA–that stands for Idaho Badland Survival Academy. Where failure is not an option, losers."

Jaqueline's mouth dropped open as she held up her shirt. The eagle clutching the mouse stared back at her. Like a million bats disturbed in a cave, her mind swarmed and fluttered in confusion. What was this and where the hell was she?

CHAPTER 4

IT TOOK a few minutes before Jaqueline could form any kind of rational thought. She stared at R.J. as he droned on about rules, discipline, and goals. All of Jaqueline's fear and desperation crumbled away, leaving only rage. Rage at her dad and these crazy people. They had no right to take her the way they did. She leaped off the cot, trembling with fury.

"You mean, I wasn't kidnapped or sold? I was scared out of my mind for this... summer camp for delinquents? I'm going home—don't touch me!" Her voice came out shrill, and she pulled away from Craig's reach.

"Sit down." R.J. whispered, pinning her in place with his icy gaze.

"Gonna make me? Now that I know who you all are, I know damn well I'm not in real danger. There's got to be a way to sue jerks like you!" Jaqueline faced R.J. but could not meet his eyes again.

Everyone else in the cabin was silent. The boy with the long red bangs frowned and muttered something under his breath. He had sweat on his forehead, despite the way the temperature had dropped with the sun. He scratched his arms and rocked on the edge of the cot. *Drugs,* Jaqueline realized with pity and revulsion. She did not belong here.

"You can't leave. You've been completely signed over to us," R.J. stated. "You're miles from anywhere and have no survival skills—yet." Even as intimidating as the man was, the challenge in his eyes did something to Jaqueline. Although defiance reared up inside her, the rational part of her mind accepted that she was stuck. They wouldn't drive her anywhere—and she doubted she could make it alone. A city girl on the far side of Boonieland had no chance without water, food, or a compass. Even with a compass—who knew how to use one? Plus, it was dark and cold, even for late August.

She hated her dad.

"So, my dad finally found a way to get rid of me. Awesome. Three down and one to go." Poor Flower—what was in store for her? "Well, at least I'm one less mouth for him to feed." Jaqueline snorted with a bitter ache in her chest.

Mick gave Jaqueline a lopsided grin. "This ain't saving him any money, kid."

The blond jock on the cot across from Jaqueline sneered. "Yeah. We're all here at a high price. I guess getting rid of us is worth a lot to our parents."

"Getting you help is worth a lot to your parents. *You* are worth a lot to them." The college girl, Katie, spoke up, her tone at once warm but firm.

Katie's words made the room rock and Jaqueline had to sit down. It made no sense. Her father didn't spend money; it meant more to him than people. At least that was what her mother always said.

R.J. spoke again. "You will hike to the first site tonight and bed down. In the morning you'll be given a journal, a curriculum booklet, provisions, and more instructions. Time to move." With a loud clap, R.J. made everyone in the cabin jump.

"Alright, boys—it's dark outside, so the search will take place in here. Please turn your faces to the wall." Mick sauntered across the cabin and folded his meaty arms across his chest. The boys didn't seem to know what he was talking about, but they all turned to face the wall, throwing their legs over the other side of the cot. Mick faced the boys' backs as if standing guard. "Do not turn around," he commanded.

Jaqueline glanced around in confusion. Only Craig made eye contact with her. His dark eyes stared and flashed as if taking a snapshot of her, then shifted away. He dipped his chin at Jaqueline before slipping out the cabin with R.J. Outside R.J.'s gravelly voice sounded muffled through the door.

A sharp whistle and then, "Always, down! Come."

An answering bark followed, and the sounds of R.J. conversing with Craig softened as they moved away.

Katie stood before Jaqueline with a gentle expression on her face. Her words came out in a careful and steady cadence. "Jaqueline, I need you to remove all of your clothing, please."

Jaqueline sat back on the cot. "What?" A hot prickling covered her scalp and face.

"Be happy it's not our winter term and in the daytime—or we'd be doing this outside in the snow." Katie smiled apologetically and fidgeted with the hem of her t-shirt.

"I'm not taking my clothes off for you. Sorry." Jaqueline pressed her back to the wall and wrapped her arms around herself, crossing her legs. No way.

Katie stepped into a wider stance and nodded. Without looking behind her she raised her voice "Mick, take the boys outside."

"I'm not watching all three of them outside in the dark by myself," he huffed, glancing over his shoulder.

"Then get R.J. and Craig to help you."

A distant engine started and quickly retreated. "They're heading to Station One to drop off our stuff," Mick said.

Katie held up her hands in apology. Jaqueline's bubble of hope thinned and popped.

"She'll have to avert her eyes while the boys do the same." Mick gave a shrug that could have lifted the ceiling if he were any closer to it. He turned his back again.

Katie pushed her hands into her pockets. "Go ahead."

"This is a strip search?"

"Yes."

"You can't make me do it."

Katie crossed her arms. "We rely on your cooperation. Your cooperation gains ours. Otherwise, you could starve out here. Or stay out here longer. It's in the agreement with your dad."

With no energy for anger, hopelessness hollowed her out. Jaqueline's knees wobbled as she stood up and moved palsied hands to unbutton her jean shorts. Her eyes flew to the opposite side of the room to make sure she saw four solid backs. The sound of her zipper in the quiet cabin was like the cracking noise under your feet on a frozen lake. She swallowed, trying not to cry.

"It's okay—this will be quick," Katie said.

"I can't do this. I swear—I'm not hiding anything." Her voice trembled. It was worse than the stage fright she used to get before cheering a new routine at a football game. Way worse.

"W-wait," somebody said.

Jaqueline sniffed back tears and looked up, pausing with her thumbs hooked over the denim waistband.

"We won't r-run," the dark-haired boy in the black t-shirt said with a quiet, halting voice that bounced off the wall just inches from his face. He cleared his throat. "Just let her do this with some p-privacy."

Mick put his fists on his hips and sighed out long and slow. "Fine. You all agree?"

The other two boys, with their faces still to the wall, nodded and muttered that they would cooperate.

"Okay. But I warn you, do not run. If I don't catch you, the coyotes will." Mick turned toward the door.

Jaqueline pulled her shirt down over the top of her shorts and wiped her tears with the back of her hand.

Mick opened the door and waited for the boys to follow him. They shuffled toward the door and filed by Jaqueline with their heads down. She watched them go with relief. At the last moment the boy in black flashed her a quick look from under long dark lashes. Jaqueline tried to smile at him and then the door swung shut.

Okay. Jaqueline pretended she was at home just undressing with her sister in the room. Shorts down, shirt off, bra undone... the illusion helped until she was asked to turn around and drop her underwear. Her face burned and she waited forever memorizing the ceiling until a stranger finished the thorough scan of her body.

"I have to inform you that if you have anything hidden, we'll find out and we will confiscate it. And steps will be taken to punish you—including prolonging your stay with us. Is that clear?" Katie said. It sounded memorized.

"Hidden where? Inside? Ew. Yes, I understand." Jaqueline shuddered and yanked up her teal underwear with the lace edging.

"Now is your chance to give it up without punishment," Katie clarified. She looked very uncomfortable when Jaqueline faced her.

"Got it. No. I have no drugs up there. Or anything else for that matter. Sick."

Katie's cheeks reddened. "Well, it happens, and we have to

ask." As matter of fact as she tried to be, it was obvious that it pained the friendly looking college girl to embarrass anyone.

After Jaqueline dressed it was her turn to wait outside in the cold with Katie while Mick searched the boys. The scattered deep muttering inside the cabin told Jaqueline they were all required to fess up or deny any internal stashes of their own. She cringed, hoping every one of them said no.

After a few minutes Mick emerged from the cabin, carrying the bright lantern from the table inside. The boys followed him, not speaking, still in shock from their pop quiz of nakedness, no doubt.

They were instructed to put on their new t-shirts, with the I.B.S.A. logo and the predatory bird. Everyone pulled the shirts over what they wore—it had gotten colder. Soon, they all trudged in a line behind Mick and his lantern, with Katie following at the back with a flashlight.

Everyone silently stumbled along the rocks and dirt, skirting the sagebrush and ragged bushes shadowed by night. The stars poked bright pinpoints of light, like sequins all over the deep indigo sky, which had lightened from black with the moon's full rising. It reminded Jaqueline of her prom dress on a perfect night when she was still a cheerleader, with Eric the quarterback in his dark tux. Everything had been a sort of normal. Her mom was still a mom and her dad—what was he back then? Jaqueline couldn't remember. It didn't matter. Those days were not all that great. Eric was shallow and her friends were all fake kiss-ups and her mom didn't really want to be her mom. At least now she knew where everyone really stood.

Time seemed different in the dark, and Jaqueline was so exhausted. Her legs moved robotically, and she was past conscious thought as her inadequate shoes found footing again and again on the uneven terrain. The strong smell of the sage and dirt surrounded her like a fog. A distant howling made Jaqueline's skin tingle. They were out in the middle of nowhere —but not alone.

"We're here." Mick announced, holding up his lantern so they could see.

Where? Just a cleared area against the side of a huge rock with a fire pit in the center. No cabin. Jaqueline thought she would cry again, but she was too tired. She dropped to the ground, every part of her body heavy and sore. She wanted to put her face down into the dirt and sleep for a thousand years.

The beam of Katie's flashlight disappeared behind the wall of reddish rock. She returned with several folded, gray wool blankets. Mick went behind the rock and returned with a large, framed pack. He pulled out a few items and busied himself at the fire pit.

A blanket was tossed into Jaqueline's lap, and she pulled the warm scratchy material around her, resting her chin on her bent knees. Sitting felt good—even on her bruises. Red-bangs Guy dragged his feet through the dust and sank to the ground beside Jaqueline, sweat glistening on his forehead. His ragged breathing filled the space around them. The other two boys followed Mick like shadows, observing him as he did something to a rock that caused sparks.

"I'm Finn." The boy's voice was reedy and weak.

"I'm Jaqueline." She knew why he was here. And even though some of her friends partied, that didn't mean she'd be making best friends with a tweaker—even if they were stuck in this reality TV nightmare together.

He sniffled several times, just an undefined inky blob, like a Rorschach test at her side. "Is it okay if I call you Jackie?"

"No. Some people call me Jaq though."

"Nice to meet you, Jaq. I'm so thirsty," he croaked.

She was cotton mouthed too. And her stomach growled.

She'd emptied it in the van ages ago. She shut her eyes and thought about food. What was the procedure out here if you got thirsty or hungry?

She opened her eyes when an orange glow lit up her eyelids. Like a magician, Mick had made a decent-sized fire out of nothing. It was oddly comforting. She dug her heels into the dirt and scooted herself forward until she came close to the fire pit. The heat spread through her like beer.

"Is there anything to drink?" Jaq asked nobody in particular.

The other two boys looked across the fire pit at her where they stood beside Mick, who chopped at some thin logs with a small hatchet. The big man paused to raise his chin to the right. "Over where that scrub brush is clustered, there's a stream."

Jaq looked in the direction he indicated, already night blind from the fire. The faint outline of some tall bushes came into focus about twenty yards away. As much as she wanted to say something pissy, it just seemed futile. She hugged her blanket closer and stood. Mick materialized beside her, handing her the lantern. "Here, Jaqueline. This way you can see where you're going and so can we."

"It's Jaq." She snatched the slender metal handle and sneered. "Thanks."

Jock Boy whined, "Great. I'm not drinking dirty water."

"The water here is fine. But after tonight you will routinely boil your water before using it. Should become habit—just in case." Mick lumbered back to the fire.

Finn sprawled in the dirt, casting a longing glance in the direction of the stream, but he didn't move—aside from the trembling of his body that never stopped. Jaq tripped along toward the bushes, straining her ears for the howling she'd heard earlier. About halfway there, she realized someone was with her. A glance back showed the tan, dark-haired boy. She concentrated on the ground again, his footsteps heavy behind her.

Soon, she heard the trickling of water. A small stream wove itself over the rocks in a narrow bed. Jaq set the lantern on a rock, mesmerized by the shining liquid that called to her dry throat. It was strangely natural to kneel and scoop handfuls of the cold water from the earth to her lips. *Yay for water.* She washed her face and hands to clean off the faint sour scent of her vomit.

The dark-haired boy used both hands to gulp down a drink, then he sloshed some all over his face. The lantern accentuated his square jaw and his long lashes, made thicker with water. Then he peeled off his I.B.S.A. shirt revealing the black one he still had on under it. His lean muscles, underlined in shadow, flexed as he dipped the army green shirt into the water until it was soaked. Jaq shook her head. It was cold—why would he want to do that?

She grabbed the lantern, and they headed back toward where the fire lit up the figures of the others huddled around it. Jock Boy was mouthing off to Mick about not wanting to sleep on the ground. Katie hummed while looking through a second framed pack, and Finn coughed hoarsely, still in a prone position not far from the fire. Pathetic.

"Dude. Open your mouth." Black T-shirt Boy hunkered down beside Finn. He held his soaked top over the shaking boy's face and twisted it, sending a stream of water into his mouth.

Finn sputtered and swallowed. "Thank God. More?" After he'd had enough, he took the shirt in his own hands and wiped his face with it. "I'm burning up, man. Thanks. What's your name?"

"No problem, bro. I'm Russ," he answered before retrieving his own blanket and coming to the fire near Jaq.

There was a scuffle from the other side of the fire pit.

"Daniel. Enough. Don't touch my things," Mick barked at Jock Boy.

Daniel scoffed, stomped to the fire, and dropped down, muttering complaints to himself.

"Alright, guys. We bed down now. In the morning, we'll hand out your supplies and further orient you with this program." Mick stood over the fire, small hatchet in hand. In the firelight, he looked more like Thor wielding a hammer. "Find a spot and settle down. Silence begins now."

Everyone crawled to their own spot near the fire, and the lantern went out.

"Goodnight." Katie whispered. Nobody answered, not sure they were allowed.

Jaq curled herself into a ball and rested her face on one arm. She knew she was covered in dirt. The ground was hard, and the air was cold. Mick, Katie, Finn, Daniel... Russ and R.J. —the new faces and names swirled in her head like characters from a movie that wasn't her life. Jaqueline Cole didn't exist here. That thought struck her with a mixture of fear and relief. Everything faded and blurred the more she tried to think. So tired and hollow.

The silence of the wilderness was only disturbed by the quiet groans of her fellow prisoners trying to get comfortable on the hard ground, the snapping of the fire as it consumed the small branches, and then the forlorn and spooky howling she had heard before. The alarming chorus floated like a far-away lullaby for the damned. Jaq plunged into a sleep filled with nightmares. She was too burned out to resist them.

CHAPTER 5

THE KILLER STOOD over Jaq with his gory ax dripping in the dim starlight. The surrounding woods closed in as if to watch. Her heart pumped hard. Somehow he always knew where to find her. But wait... the killer had no face, just a blurry, flesh-colored, featureless mask. And the ground was scattered with her old stuffed animal collection... a rainbow of furry innocence.

The whole scene evaporated, and Jaq blinked up at a dark, starry sky. Another dream. Relief came over her like warm water. No more scary movies. The nightmares were becoming too regular of a thing.

The muffled sound of violent retching bounced off the cottony insulation of Jaq's exhaustion. She rolled over, aware for a blurry moment that Finn had crawled into the bushes. He spit several times to rid his mouth of the inevitable flavor.

"No-no-no-no—Oh, God, no," he groaned just before heaving again.

"It's okay, man. This is good. You'll feel much better tomor-row." It was Russ, his low voice soft with reassurance.

It was still too dark to see more than their outlines. Jaq

turned away and lost awareness, unable to fight the heaviness of sleep.

"Get up." A deep voice rumbled. Jaq wanted her dad to just shut up and let her sleep. Was the sun even up? Jaq groaned and shifted in the dirt. A gong went off inside her headache when she remembered everything.

"Time to get up," the voice said again.

Jaq sat up like she had lead for a brain. Her head pulsed. Her whole body was sore, and her hands felt like they'd been crushed. Then she remembered pounding on the door of the van the night before. Great. She slowly flexed them as she opened her eyes to the dim gray of predawn. Mick grinned down at her, his white teeth standing out fang-like from his scruffy face.

"Morning." He sauntered over to the pile on the ground that was Daniel and gave it a soft kick.

Daniel growled. "Argh. You gotta be joking!" He threw his blanket off in a fury, cursing to himself.

"Not usually." Mick stifled a yawn and then smiled at a tree as if sharing a private joke.

"How did you sleep?" Finn asked quietly.

Jaq looked over at the vomit boy. He sat on his blanket not far from her, one hand tangled in his long red bangs, his eyes deep and dark with misery.

"Like a rock. In the dirt. I feel really awesome." Jaq stretched and her back crackled. She frowned.

"Did I keep you up?" Finn's voice was hoarse, and his pale face tightened with embarrassment.

"Nah. I was dead to the world." Jaq shrugged, distracted as Russ walked by, his blanket rolled up under his arm. He engaged in a conversation with Mick that she couldn't overhear. The desire for him to turn and look at her flickered, but she shook it off and freed herself from the blanket that wound around her legs.

"Okay, you have five minutes before we gather at the fire pit. So do what you gotta do," Mick announced.

He meant go pee or something. Jaq had a full bladder but had no idea how to go about relieving it. "Do we have toilet paper?" she grumbled without hope into the dark morning.

"Nope." Mick sat by the fire pit as if expecting everyone to take a squat.

"Sucks for you." Daniel smirked at Jaq. "Guess you can't shake it off like we can."

Jaq snorted in disgust. "Thanks for that visual." She couldn't remember why she'd ever liked jocks.

Katie came out of the cluster of trees where Jaq had found water the night before. She smiled as she got closer and gave an exaggerated sigh of relief. "That's better." She winked at Jaq. "Drip dry," she whispered as she passed her.

Oh, wonderful. Jaq stalked away from the clearing, her face burning. They all knew she was going somewhere to pee on the ground. Nice. She found a spot out of sight. Squatting low to avoid the shorts around her ankles, she relieved herself to the sound of the small stream nearby. Amazing how just peeing could make her feel so much better.

She stayed crouched, waiting to feel dry. It didn't work. Irritated, she yanked up her shorts and wrinkled her nose at the uncomfortable sensation. She wondered if she would ever get used to not wiping. What about poo? Use leaves? Of course, if they starved her, maybe there wouldn't be much of that anyway. Jaq shuddered and stomped back to where the group gathered at the fire pit. The boys all glanced up at her with brief, curious looks. Daniel looked smug, and she narrowed her eyes at him.

"Survive that?" Mick raised his brows and continued

without waiting for an answer. "You're all about to learn how to survive a lot of things. We'll teach the skills you'll need to empower you and enable you to overcome your environment. You'll each complete the curriculum in this booklet"—he held up a small orange spiral bound book—"keep a daily journal, and accomplish several goals. That is, if you want to get home. Ever."

Jaq swallowed her dread. What would they make her do? Crawl inside dead animals for warmth or drink her own pee like that survival guy on TV? This was ridiculous.

Katie handed each of them their own copy of the curriculum book along with a mechanical pencil. "This program will be one of the most demanding things you'll ever experience. Your success will depend on your effort and your attitude." She paused to smile at each of them. "The course is designed to end in twenty-one days. But if you don't master the requirements, we'll keep you for as long as it takes for you to be successful. The diploma that you earn at trail's end will be hard earned and well deserved. In the end, you'll have more choices and the ability to be happy and successful when you return home."

They opened their books and read over the contract on the first page. Jaq squinted in the dim light. A pledge to complete the program and obey their "competent trail leaders." Jaq felt her hand shake. She hated feeling forced to bend her will. Surrounded by nothing but dust, rocks, and sage brush, and with no food in her belly, there was no other option. She had no choice if she ever wanted to go home. She signed, and the scratch of pencil on paper meant the boys had come to the same conclusion.

"We'll give you provisions that you're responsible to care for. If something is lost, stolen, loaned—you'll have to learn to do without. Especially take care of this booklet—it's your ticket out of here. Either me or Katie will have to sign off each requirement in here. And you'll notice there are a bunch of blank pages at the back. Those are for your daily journal. It's a requirement for you to write every night before going to bed."

"This is bullshit." Daniel dropped his book into the dust, his hands in tight fists.

Katie picked it up and flipped a few pages, then read aloud, "Requirement number five: 'I have gone six consecutive days using only acceptable language. I have excluded from my language any swearing or other foul language.'"

"Redundant." Finn fake coughed the word into his hand.

Katie ignored that. She peered over the top of the page at Daniel. "It's day one. If you want to be stuck out here because you can't control your tongue, be my guest."

Finn sucked in his breath. "This won't be easy—excluding some of my favorite words." His hands shook, and he fumbled, then dropped his book. "Oh, sh—oops." A slight smile tugged one side of his mouth.

Shoops. Good one.

"See, you can do it," Katie chirped at Finn handing Daniel his book. "Please glance through your books to get a feel for what to expect."

It was quiet as the magnitude of the program's demands settled over them. There were sections on first aid, fire building, navigation, trapping and tracking, geology, making weapons and shelters—and then the behavior requirements. A bunch of hard stuff that would either bore her to death or kill her.

Jaq felt her heart sinking as the sun rose over the rock ridges. Finn stared at his book with glazed eyes, Daniel glared at his copy with unmasked hatred, and Russ flipped pages with eager interest. *What a dork.* Jaq tried to ignore the way his full lips pressed together in concentration. The early light accentuated his dark lashes. She forced herself to take interest in her book.

Over the next hour, Mick lectured from the curriculum book about the basics of living off the land. The limited resources of the badlands made it a special challenge that he seemed proud of, as if he'd designed the landscape just to test them. He distributed their limited supplies, which consisted of a large aluminum can with a wire handle he called a billycan, a length of rope, canteen, a bowie knife in a leather sheath, and a long canvas sack. At the bottom of the sack sat their rations: some zip lock baggies of flour, raisins, dried oats, lentils, powdered milk, a few beef bullions and three packets of mint tea. Altogether, it was about as much as you could eat in a couple of days, no problem.

Jaq's stomach growled loud enough that Mick noticed. "Guess you're pretty empty after last night. Don't worry, you can eat when we get to Number Two."

She glared at him, passing the new knife back and forth between her hands. The thought of waiting all day to eat again depressed her. But she couldn't wallow long. The first thing they had to get signed off in the book was learning to make a bedroll. There was a particular way to roll up the provisions inside the blanket and tie it up so it could be worn as a backpack. Jaq fought tears as the rope continued to slip when she attempted the series of knots needed to secure the bundle. *It's not like being a Boy Scout is useful in real life.* After several tries Jaq had a lumpy, crooked version of a bedroll tied to her back.

"You'll get it," Katie reassured her with a pat on her shoulder.

By now the sun had drifted up into the sky and Mick stomped like a restless mustang. He pulled a used pair of hiking boots from his framed pack and handed them to Jaq.

"These are from your dad. You'll need them."

Jaq looked down at her canvas slip on shoes and then at the boots Mick held out to her. They were the ones from the freaky shoe tree. *Gross.*

"That di—jerk." She caught herself and took the boots from Mick who looked at her with raised brows.

Jaq wrinkled her nose and tied the laces of the oversized boots to the outside of her bedroll.

"Let's move. While we hike today, I want you all to think about what you hope to get out of the experience. And pay attention to your surroundings—I'll quiz you on what kinds of plants and animals we come across," Mick bellowed over his shoulder, already on his way over the rocky earth.

They fell in line behind the large man, pausing at the stream. Mick dropped a tablet into each canteen and then motioned to the stream. "This will clean your water. After this, you'll be required to boil your water. Believe me, you don't want giardia—especially out here without toilet paper." He chuckled and shook his canteen cheerfully.

"Giardia?" Daniel scowled.

"Parasites that give you the runs." Mick took a swig of water.

As Jaq filled her canteen, she hoped she didn't get parasites from her drink the night before. She splashed her face with water, smoothed back her hair, and refastened her ponytail. She stood and ignored the obvious way the boys all looked away as if they hadn't been checking out her butt.

"Can't even drink the water. Great. This is heaven on earth." Daniel rubbed his stomach. The sun lit up his scattered blond hair as he bent to fill his canteen. Jaq noticed for the first time that he was cute. He had a strong profile and hazel eyes. Too bad he was such a jerk. He caught her looking at him and a glimmer of interest showed in his eyes as if he'd just noticed her for the first time too. She turned away from him. Yeah, she might look like the kind of girl on the cheerleading squad who would date him—but she wasn't that girl anymore.

Mick took the lead with Russ stepping quick and light close behind, followed by Daniel, Jaq, and an already dragging Finn being trailed by Katie.

There was too much to think about. Jaq rehashed everything that had happened the previous night. It didn't seem real. Her dad had really pulled one on her. Unexpected. It was difficult to imagine her dad paying for something like this. It didn't fit. She heard her mother in her head the day before she disappeared.

"Your dad is a tightwad. I can't live like this, knowing he cares more about money than my feelings." Her eyes welled with tears as she put on glossy pink lipstick and rubbed her lips together, staring into the mirror above her dresser.

"Mom, what are you saying?" Jaq froze, her eyes locked on her mother's reflection.

"Look. I did my best. But he never validates my feelings. He makes me feel guilty for wanting simple things! Is it a crime to want new clothes every now and then? Or to look good? I'm not out to pasture yet." She cinched up the straps on her bra with an approving look at herself.

"Those boobs weren't exactly cheap, Mom." Jaq felt bitter —she'd take her dad's side if it would make her mother stay.

Her mother had narrowed her eyes in a dangerous way. "Oh, I earned these. Having babies ruined my body." She looked into Jaq's eyes. "Someday you'll understand. All the times you wanted to do something with friends or needed something for school, I had to fight him for it! Fight to get what you needed. I love you and I've done everything I can for you. You're a big girl now—and I need to have my life back. Will you give it back to me?"

Jaq shook away the memory, kicking at the dirt under her feet, cussing in her head because she couldn't do it aloud.

The sun burned the sky up and sweat ran down Jaq's back. The smell of dirt and sage filled her lungs. Lizards skittered out of her path. Footsteps scuffed over rocky ground and the faint buzz of bugs played a disjointed melody. Hours passed, with occasional stops to rest and light, scattered conversation. It seemed everyone was thinking about why they were there. Jaq imagined confronting her dad over and over. Sometimes the fantasy ended with her punching him in the face.

Katie gulped water from the canteen that hung from a cord around her neck, then stood with hands on her hips. "We'll probably get to our next campsite in the next hour or so. It's a shorter hike today. Tonight, we want you all to get together and come up with a group name. So be thinking about that." She squinted up at the sun and wiped a trickle of sweat from her eye.

Finn sagged against a large rock looking queasy. He took a long drink from his canteen and gasped for breath. He tried to toss his bangs with a jerk of his head, but they stuck to his forehead. "Good thing it isn't a thousand degrees today." He gave a lopsided grin and Jaq smiled. He was kind of funny. For a loser.

Russ eyed Finn with careful interest. "You good?"

"Yeah, man. I'm as happy as a leprechaun with a jug of whiskey." Finn held up his canteen with a ridiculous wink.

"Dork," Daniel said just loud enough for Jaq to hear. He was doing that thing that popular kids always did. What he really meant with that one word was "He isn't cool like me and you, so we should stick together."

Jaq decided right then that Finn—loser or not—was her new BFF. She acted like she didn't hear Daniel. She laughed at Finn's joke. "You sort of look like one too. Are you Irish?"

Finn's eyes lit up, looking huge on his narrow face. "My dad is—my mom met him at a pub when she went over there as a tourist. I was born in California though." His grin was catching. "To be sure, at the end of the rainbow is a Golden Gate Bridge!" he lilted in a perfect Irish accent that made Jaq burst into a genuine laugh. It felt good. And she could see the effect of her laugh on Finn—he glowed.

She turned and saw Russ studying her with interest. When their eyes met he flicked his brows up and smiled on one side. Jaq's heart fluttered and she looked away as if she hadn't noticed him.

By the time they reached the clearing with the large canvas lean-to, it was the late afternoon. Everyone was exhausted.

"Okay, here's dinner. Enjoy it and save the can—including the lid." Mick pulled a bag from behind a rock that held a can of peaches for each of them.

There was a collective murmur of enthusiasm. Jaq couldn't believe how delicious the wet, sweet peaches tasted. As they slurped down their unusual dinner, Mick talked about the plants that grew in the area. Willows grew near water, bitterbrush and sage were good for making fires and twine could be made from the bark—they would all attempt that at some point.

"Did any of you notice any tracks?" Katie asked.

"Rabbit and wolf," Russ answered.

Mick looked surprised. "That's right. Very observant."

"I camp a lot. Used to hunt." Russ shrugged and kicked a rock.

Jaq frowned. Hunting was gross. Killing animals. Blood everywhere. She didn't understand how anyone could enjoy that.

"I need all of you to gather wood for the fire. We're going to make char-cloth tonight, which you'll use as a fire-starting technique throughout the trip. We'll go over that in the morning."

Later they all sat around the fire as the wind picked up and the temperature dropped. The sun was almost set. Jaq sat across from Russ pretending she didn't notice how he looked at her.

Mick showed them how to tear off strips of canvas from their supply bags, then fold the lid from their peach can like a taco and stuff the folded strips of fabric inside. The lids were pushed into the embers of the fire and left there until the canvas became black and delicate as tissue paper. After pulling the lids out of the fire pit they were instructed to let them cool overnight.

"In the morning you'll learn the magic of the char cloth." Katie grinned around the fire at them, the flames making her brown hair shine like a copper halo over her wholesome face. "So, did you decide on a name?" she asked.

Jaq hadn't really thought about it. The boys shrugged without interest, too tired and hungry to care.

Finn poked a stick into the fire. "I hate the stress I feel out here," he said in a trembling tenor voice, and his words seemed to speak for everyone. "We are the miserable ones. Les Miserables."

Everyone was silent, watching the fire.

"Les Miserables it is," Katie whispered. "Time to bed down."

CHAPTER 6

AFRAID TO EVEN THINK THE swear words, just in case Katie and Mick were mind readers, Jaq growled to herself instead. She shifted her knees in the rocky earth and blinked hard. No way would she cry over this. She gripped the flint stone in her hands and struck it again with the back of her knife. A spark bounced across the surface of the white rock and disappeared. She wanted to kill her father. Or someone.

Her fingers cramped and she forced her stiff hand open to drop the stone into the dust. With a groan Jaq sat back on her heels and glowered at her enemy, stretching her fingers and then making a fist.

A tinder bundle made of strips of sagebrush bark sat in front of her, inert as an abandoned nest, cradling the blackened square of charred cloth. Four freaking days and no fire! Mick made it look so easy. The boys had all figured it out within a day. Jaq hunched up her shoulders and gripped her knife. She had a strong impulse to viciously stab the stupid tinder bundle several times.

Her dad was such a jerk. Sending her to starve in this wilderness. All because he couldn't bother to be a parent.

Jaq hissed through her teeth and wiped the sweat away

from her forehead with the back of her arm. The sun went nova, shattering into rays on the edge of a cliff. The day was almost over. She squeezed her eyes shut to pretend she was someplace else.

Each night they had camped in a new spot after hiking all day. Funny how in just a week they'd all accepted their lot and this whole thing started to feel almost normal. But it wasn't.

Today they'd hiked only a few hours in the morning to the new camp, and then spent the day working out of the curriculum book. Site Number Eight was nothing more than a clearing of dirt beside a strange rock formation that pointed like a crooked red finger into the blazing blue sky.

Nothing was easy—the requirements were difficult to pass off, but even walking, sleeping, and eating suddenly required a lot more planning. And forget about having to pee or poo. Yuck. Rinsing off in the occasional stream was the height of luxury.

Jaq's stomach rumbled and she ignored the familiar sound, thinking she'd give anything to listen to music, watch a movie, or have a pillow—even a lumpy one. Or a chocolate bar of any kind. She sighed. Everything ached and her mind echoed like an empty cave. Bored. Tired. She looked down at her legs. Dirty.

"How's it coming, Crooked Pack?" Finn scuffed toward her through the brush. He had his plaid shirt tied around his waist and his IBSA t-shirt hung loose on his thin frame.

Jaq smirked. Sometimes they called her that after Mick dubbed her "Girl Who Walks with Crooked Pack" a few days before. Yeah, just another thing she hadn't gotten the hang of yet. Her bedroll was still a complete mess.

"It's not. I hate this." Jaq looked up at Finn and noticed his hands still shook a bit when he pushed his long red bangs out of his eyes. But he'd started to sleep better the last couple of nights.

His smile stretched wide and white, his brows peaked in sympathy. Jaq almost wanted to hug him and then marveled at how pathetic a little starvation and deprivation had made her.

"Aw. Yeah, not my favorite either." Finn squatted beside her and picked up her dropped flint-stone. He turned it in his hands and examined the stone as if it were to blame for her trouble. "Stupid thing must be busted."

Jaq took it from him and huffed. "Or needs new batteries."

Finn sat back on his haunches and sighed, his narrow chest rose and sunk, showing ribs through his shirt. "I was in a play once. *Waiting for Godot.* Sometimes this place makes me feel like that." He squinted blue eyes at the wavering horizon and rubbed a knuckle down his nose. "Waiting for something that might never come or never happen." He zoned out as he often did, unaware of Jaq. She wondered what he thought about when he did that.

He didn't blink for several moments. Jaq dipped her words in sarcasm. "You're a drama geek? I'm so surprised."

Finn jerked back into reality and blushed. "Oh, it gets worse than that. I'm a poem-writing, Shakespeare-Festival-loving, D&D-playing member of MENSA." He snorted and bent his head as if bowing before an audience.

Jaq had no idea what MENSA was, which meant he was probably a bigger geek than she'd thought. "Hm. I think I just got chills."

"I know. Sexy. Very sexy." Finn winked at her.

Jaq gave a short laugh. He reminded her of a mischievous elf with his sparkly eyes and narrow face. She wondered how Finn ended up a junky.

"What's so funny?" Daniel jumped down from a nearby rock, sending a cloud of dust up from the ground. Jaq sneezed and gave him a look that said, *Oh, it's you.*

"Finn is." Jaq struck the rock with her blade again with no effect.

Daniel put his hands on his hips with an unmasked look of competition on his cocky face. He'd been staring at Jaq for days and seemed frustrated that she didn't show that she noticed. But Jaq could tell he liked the challenge. Jock.

"He's funny, alright. Need help?" Daniel hovered over her as if waiting for her to look up. When she did, he shoved his hands into his pockets, flexing his triceps with a nonchalant expression.

"No. I got it." Jaq concentrated on her efforts, ignoring the two boys who seemed fascinated by what she was doing. With her audience, Jaq gave a determined go of it. To her surprise a single red spark bounced over the stone and landed on the target and stayed there: a red-hot point glowing on the black char-cloth.

"You got it! Okay, just pick it up and blow softly." Finn leaned forward and patted her shoulder.

"Whew, finally." Jaq took the tinder bundle in her hands and brought it to her lips. Her heart sped up eagerly. With gentle breaths, she made the spark pulse once, twice, and then expand. The red glow crept outward and then flared up into a tiny flame.

Jaq squeaked in delight and blew again. The tinder bundle crackled to life with several little feathers of fire. She set the nest down and quickly added the tiny wood chips and bits of dried grass that waited in a pile on the ground. The two boys whooped encouragement. In a few short minutes, she had a decent-size fire going with added sticks and small branches.

Jaq stared at her fire and a surge of joy rushed through her chest and down her arms. "Yes! I'm awesome!" She laughed and the boys joined her.

"She did it! Oh, great Fire Maker!" Finn called out, hopping around the fire in a dance.

Mick's and Katie's cheers echoed from wherever they were. Jaq warmed inside, irrationally fond of her little group of fellow castaways. So different, but they were all in the same place now. She grinned at the boys. "I'm starving."

"I've got an awesome idea for that." Russ's voice came up behind her. "To celebrate," he said when she turned to look at him. He shrugged one shoulder and ran a hand through his messy dark hair.

Jaq's heart jumped. He didn't speak often, but when he did it made her guts somersault. Especially when his dark gaze shone, like it did now. What was it about him? He was probably some kind of stoner. But his eyes… and that shy smile made her stomach tickle. Sean would totally kick his butt if he were here. Jaq looked away to hide the color of her cheeks.

Back at the group site, everyone was way too nice about Jaq's triumph. Mick's baritone voice boomed, "Crooked Pack, you have met with success! Let me sign that off."

She handed her orange curriculum book to the big man when he held out a broad, calloused hand. The book already looked dirty and a bit tattered. Mick skimmed the pages and scribbled his signature. Then he flipped the page and scanned. "Your First Aid test went well. And I noticed earlier that your Paiute deadfall traps are looking pretty good." He nodded with approval.

Those hadn't been easy either. Jaq forced away a goofy grin and cleared her throat. "Thanks." She shrugged and scraped underneath her fingernails with the tip of her knife.

"You should feel proud. And I know your dad would be." Mick's head shone with sweat, and his powerful, direct gaze seemed kind. Had it always been?

Jaq felt familiar anger at the mention of her father. But it would be worth seeing the crazy, hippy miser if it meant being back in civilization. Well, maybe not. But she did have an ache when she thought of home—especially her little sister. This place made her think a lot. There weren't any of the distractions of TV, music, or phones. No beer and boys. Mostly just nature, and her thoughts. She flexed her fingers and noticed several nicks and cuts on them. A few chips of dark blue nail polish remained, and she scraped them away with the blade.

The sun's reflected glow now lit the sky as if through sunglasses, and shadows moved toward the small group around the fire. The sagebrush rustled in a dry breeze and a hawk cried out from far away. The boys had built a large fire. Billycans full of water, bullion, and lentils were settled into the coals. As the contents boiled, a savory smell rose into the air.

Finn plopped down beside Jaq. "We apologize in advance for the lentils," he said with a cartoony look of guilt.

"Huh?" Jaq chewed on a mixture of dried oats and raisins for her dinner.

Finn let out a long flatulent sound between his lips.

Daniel coughed and laughed at that. "Dude!"

Katie put down the notebook that she was always writing in and grimaced. "Oh, it gets bad. Lentils are the great equalizer out here."

Mick nodded, eyes wide. "Don't sleep too close to the fire tonight, guys. You might combust." Everyone laughed.

Russ ducked his head, looking up through his lashes across the fire at Jaq, and smiled. She wondered what he'd been doing most of the afternoon. He went off alone a lot. He added some water to his baggy of flour and kneaded it, the veins in his hands popping out in the firelight.

"What're you making?" Jaq asked when he caught her staring.

"Ashcakes. Party." He held up a fist. "Cuz... you conquered the char-cloth challenge."

"Cool. Never had an ash cake. Sounds a little different." She tried to catch his eye but he focused on squishing the dough.

"Just wait." Russ grinned, stretching out the gooey blob before breaking off pieces. He rolled them into balls and then flattened them.

"Mmm, you guys will like these." Mick watched with approval. The glow of the fire lit up his rugged face and gleamed orange on his shaved head.

The ashcakes lay over the coals until dark brown bubbles erupted over their pasty surfaces. Jaq's mouth watered from the aroma, which reminded her of heating tortillas in a pan.

Russ handed out the cooked ashcakes, and they all sat around the fire nibbling their toasty treat making enthusiastic yummy noises. Simple pleasure.

"My dad used to make these on camping trips." Russ seemed to shape his words carefully. He gazed into the flames as if remembering something bittersweet.

"Cool, your dad camps with you?" Daniel chewed with smacking sounds, just adding to the grating effect of his bitter tone. His blond hair, heavy with dust and sweat, no longer stuck up. "My dad takes his new family to places like Disney World. Once he took them to Hawaii. His two new little brats and Diana." He sneered. "His wife is hot, though." He failed to sound off-handed. "She has this bright blue bikini..." Daniel sneered, a look of disgust in his eyes.

Jaq didn't like the uncomfortable skitter down her spine as he spoke. Anger lined Daniel's posture. A moment of tension silenced everyone.

"You do *not* want to see my mom in a bikini! Lord, she'd

scare a sumo wrestler." Finn piped up, shaking his head, eyes wide. Jaq giggled, grateful for the comic relief.

Russ and Mick snorted, but Katie eyed Daniel with concern. Jaq knew that look. The school counselor gave her that look all the time.

Once she'd been dragged into Mrs. Andersen's light green office with the fake plants lining the front of the large, dark-wood desk. A happy Andersen family picture mocked Jaq from the wall behind the counselor's head. Mom, Dad, and four chubby, grinning kids dressed like dolls sitting on a bale of hay in front of a fake farm backdrop. Gross.

Mrs. Andersen had given her that look. A mix of worry, frustration, and determination to do something. "Jaqueline. Why?"

"Why what?" Jaq slouched in her bus-yellow plastic chair.

Mrs. Andersen shifted and leaned forward over her desk. "You are an A student, a smart, cute girl. Why would you hang around someone like Sean Lafferty?"

Jaq snorted. "It's none of your business who I hang out with." Her voice came out casual, as if the question didn't send a rush of adrenaline flowing through her like lava.

The counselor ran a hand through her brown bob and adjusted her glasses. Her small, dark eyes blinked, and she breathed out slowly. "Whatever's going on at home—you can tell me."

Jaq shut her mouth tight. No way. There was a long silence with only the squeak of Jaq's chair as she bounced her knee in agitation.

Mrs. Andersen sighed. "Well, if you change your mind, you know where to find me. In the meantime, some advice: steer clear of Sean Lafferty. If he can get someone like you to cut school as often as you've been, over time he'll drag you down to his level. When he dropped out of school, he gave up on himself. On his future. Don't make the same mistake." Her voice scolded but her eyes seemed to plead.

Jaq had felt nothing but anger and hurt at the time. Now she had a nagging thought: to be honest, the frumpy school counselor had nailed it. Sean was trouble. The kind to help land her here. Pulling away from her thoughts, Jaq realized she'd been staring into the fire and not hearing anything around her.

Finn was telling some silly story about a man named Morris who thought he could fly and was always jumping off things and splattering on the ground. Jaq must have missed something crucial because everyone laughed as if it was the most hilarious thing they'd ever heard. Then she realized what it was. Every time the fictitious Morris hit the ground, there was a sound effect emitting from Finn's backside.

"So next, he spread his arms and leaped from the top of Elvis's towering bouffant." He flapped his arms as if falling and then squeezed his eyes shut. *Frrrmp.*

"Ew! That's disgusting!" Jaq choked through a laugh.

Finn hunched his shoulders and snickered, his face turning red. There was a collective groan punctuated by chuckles around the fire.

"Lentils." Daniel rubbed his stomach and grimaced.

"Sorry. I gotta. Who knew that IBSA stood for Irritable Bowel Syndrome Academy? Who knew?" Finn spoke from the side of his mouth in a comical impression of an Italian gangster.

He had a quick wit. Jaq scrunched her nose and pretended to be repulsed, but she couldn't stop smiling.

A feeling of sleepy contentment passed around the circle. As the laughter tapered off, a comfortable quiet settled on the group.

"Do you hear that?" Katie raised her brows and cupped a hand to her ear.

"Wasn't me this time!" Finn held up his hands in defense.

"No... it's the sound of the ice breaking," Katie announced with a gentle smile, eyes lit with satisfaction.

"Finally," Mick breathed with a gravelly voice.

Jaq glanced around the fire at the faces that danced with shadows and flame as they looked around too. Yeah, something felt different.

"In that case—let's play D&D! I call Dungeon Master!" Finn clapped his hands and everyone else groaned. "Oh, come on. You'll love my tales. And you can all have epic battles, which I will describe in detail with all of the blood and guts. Call me Legolas."

———

It was cold that night and Jaq had violent, fitful dreams. She woke halfway to the chattering of her own teeth. The scratchy wool blanket twisted around her bare legs. Long pants would be awesome right now. Her nose felt like an ice cube, so she ducked her face under the blanket, breathing in the smell of dirt and sweat coming from her shirt. Ick.

Shivering, she peeked out at the dark night. In the distance, coyotes yelped and howled, high and sad. Goosebumps rose on her arms, and she felt suddenly vulnerable and alone. Exhausted, she burrowed back under the blanket for comfort. The faint groans and occasional sounds of gas from the others sleeping nearby reassured her. A small giggle quivered in her throat, sounding a bit nuts, when another lentil-induced bubble erupted from someone.

Next thing she knew, a dream wrapped her in a dark hug. She stood in front of the open refrigerator at home, lusting over the food inside: Mountain Dew with water beading on the outside of the can, hotdogs, steak, cheese, everything needed to make an awesome hoagie sandwich, milk, fruit, a big chocolate cake with thick fudgy frosting. Her stomach rumbled and her mouth watered.

Chilled air from inside the fridge seeped into the skin on her face and arms and she pulled on a thick sweatshirt. She felt the warmth of it dragging up over her wrists and elbows, up to her shoulders. This sensation repeated over and over, even after she'd slid the sweatshirt on, down over her chest and belly. Strokes of heat that chased away the chill on her skin.

Jaq reached for a ripe peach that blushed with temptation on the shelf in front of her. She brought it to her mouth. It was cool and wet. Delicious. Her mouth worked over the soft surface of the fruit. The slight fuzz of it scratched against the skin under her nose. It warmed on her lips and grew steadily warmer. She hummed a yummy sound as the wet smacking of her enjoyment continued. Best peach ever. The sweatshirt still rippled over her skin, like hands. In fact, it felt heavier and rougher now, exactly like hands.

She slammed the refrigerator door and scrabbled with a panic at her arms to remove the undulating cloth. The peach vanished along with the crawling sweatshirt. Jaq toppled backwards for several moments and landed hard on her back in the dirt, thrashing her legs, waking in confusion to the sound of a retreating rustling. Her heart thumped hard inside her ribcage. She gulped a frigid breath. She opened her eyes to a charcoal sky that showed no stars. Everything was still and quiet except her own rough breathing.

The sensation of evaporating warmth tingled on the surface of her body and her mouth. The blanket wrapped around one leg and spread out in the dirt beside her where she must have kicked it. Grabbing it, she cocooned herself inside, chilled through with a creeping terror. She reached up to her mouth, finding it wet around her lips. Her tongue darted out, tasting a faint salty, savory flavor that was not her own.

Oh. Hell.

Jaq scrubbed her arms to erase the invisible hands that still seemed to eagerly skim them. A soft sob came out with her shallow gasps. Oh no, oh no. Was it real? And if it was, *who*? In the darkness, she imagined the perpetrator she could not see. Her stomach turned as she imagined the possibilities.

Trembling, she curled in on herself, not trying to sleep, only wanting to protect herself from the rising sense of vulnerability and confusion over what she knew deep down was not just a dream.

CHAPTER 7

IT WAS as if the sun never rose. A heavy, dark mass of clouds blocked the sky. Jaq found it difficult to shake off the events of the night before without the bright renewing of a sunny morning. The gloomy atmosphere was just an extension of the violating darkness. She shuddered and sat up to see that everyone else was already milling around the camp area. It was cold and she didn't want to surrender her blanket just yet.

"How did you sleep?" Finn asked, wadding his blanket up into a terrible parody of a bedroll.

Jaq frowned. Why would he ask that? Finn's face waited with innocent friendliness. He looked a little bit like a ginger cat with his sleepy eyes in slits and his red bangs sticking up. But did he look like a creepy pervert?

"Fine." Jaq didn't want whomever the secret freak was to think she was aware of what happened. It could have been any of the guys. Even Mick. Ew.

Katie walked by, her brown hair pulled back into a pony-tail, a bounce in her step as if living rugged and dirty was a trip to Disneyland. She gave Jaq a warm smile and tugged absently at a bra strap, readjusting her crumpled shirt.

What if it was her? Jaq shook the thought away and closed

her eyes. Once again, she found herself in the dark, not knowing what the people around her were capable of or what they might do to her. People sucked.

Mick stood over the beginnings of a morning fire, poking the smoldering branches with a stick and humming to himself. Daniel and Russ sat on rocks near the fire, crunching on something and spitting into the flames.

After Jaq tidied up her bedroll, she wandered closer to the warmth of the fire feeling bold—ready to challenge the boys. "Everyone sleep good?" she sneered.

Russ looked up, confused, and put another sunflower seed into his mouth.

Daniel let out a laugh and spit a shell into the fire. "Princess got up on the wrong side of the rock." His half grin was teasing and a little bit sexy.

Jaq glared at him, almost sure. "So, Daniel. Hear any coyotes rustling around in camp last night?" She rubbed her arms to warm them, then stopped. Someone else's hands had done the same thing to her last night as she slept.

Daniel cracked another seed open with his teeth and wrinkled his nose. "No. Mick, would they come into our camp?" His swagger faltered and he gave a nervous cough.

Mick's large hand grazed his bald head, and he watched Jaq with a wary expression. "What did you see?"

"Nothing. But I think I heard something." Jaq didn't want to say too much. She was vulnerable out here. The boys continued crunching their snack. Russ stared with exaggerated interest at the smoke rising from a charred piece of wood.

"Wait. Sunflower seeds? Seriously? What did you give the warden to get those?" Jaq reached her hand out to Daniel who had a pile of salty snacks hammocked in his t-shirt.

He pursed his full lips. "Mmm... ranch flavored. What will you give me?"

Jaq wondered with disgust if she'd already earned them. "What do you want?"

His eyes glimmered and he dropped several seeds into her hand. "One of your gorgeous smiles."

Scumbag. It had to be him. Jaq stretched a wicked grin across her face, thinking she'd love to shove Daniel into the fire. But she took the seeds and popped one into her mouth, savoring the burst of flavor. Ah. Crazy how tasty it was compared to the scarce, bland food they survived on.

Mick spoke up as if this exchange hadn't happened. "I don't think the coyotes would come in this close. Unless something specific attracted them. They're generally cowardly and rove in packs."

"I heard some howling last night." Russ spit another shell into the fire pit.

"So you didn't sleep last night?" Jaq searched Russ's face. His chocolate eyes and sensitive mouth made him look sweet and somehow darkly mysterious as if he understood something about pain.

"A little. I sat by the fire with my curriculum book for a while." He scratched his arm and crushed another seed between his front teeth.

Mick straightened his bulky frame until he towered over them. "Speaking of your books... Today is Layover. Which means we won't be moving camp or hiking today."

Jaq perked up, amazed and hopeful.

"About once a week, we'll stop over and have a day that we can recuperate and work on the curriculum." Mick's deep voice raised in order to reach everyone.

Daniel grumbled something low to himself and Mick flicked a hawk-like look at him before continuing.

"It beats hiking from dawn until dusk, and you all get to meet Patti," Mick said, scratching the scruff on his chin.

Jaq unconsciously raised a hand to her mouth remembering the feel of whiskers rubbing there. Mick's short, stubbly beard seemed like thick, rough wires. Maybe she could check him off the list of suspects. *Whew.* She eyed Russ and Daniel's jaws. Yep. They both had sprouting facial hair, much softer looking and sparser than Mick's.

Finn shuffled to the fire pit. "Whatever this Layover thingy is, I'm a fan! Who's Patti?" His narrow, boyish face had a pale fuzz growing around his mouth that was hardly noticeable. Jaq frowned and licked her lips, noticing a familiar salty taste. She startled and stared down at the seasoned seeds in her hand. Before she could really examine this freaky bit of info, someone brushed against her.

"She's our counselor." Katie answered, from beside Jaq. "And she's coming over right now." She pointed to the other side of a rocky formation about fifty feet away that resembled a crouching golden lion.

Two people picked their way over the uneven ground toward the group gathered around the fire. A woman in a white puffy coat with short, sandy curls that hugged her head walked beside a tall, skinny man with dark shoulder length hair. Jaq recognized him as they got closer. Craig, the other kidnapper.

Nobody said anything as they watched the approaching visitors. It felt alien somehow to see anyone from outside of the group. For a moment, Jaq imagined she could only communicate in grunts, and she pictured the group crouching around the fire picking fleas out of each other's hair.

The curly haired woman with round, rosy, Mrs. Claus cheeks greeted everyone with a cheerful wave. "Hello, Les Misérables!" She had a beaming smile that made her eyes sparkle. She looked so happy. Jaq swallowed. A strange resentment clawed away the warm feeling this woman awakened inside her.

"Hey, Patti. How are you?" Katie hugged the older woman and then stood back, grinning at her.

"Wonderful. Slept like a baby. It's a bit chilly though, huh?" Patti searched the circle of faces.

"Yeah. Starting to feel like our winter trek." Katie crossed her arms across her chest and shivered.

"Hi, Mick." Patti nodded to the large man.

His face wore a look of unmasked fondness. "Hey, woman." Then he raised his chin to Craig. "Hi."

Craig silently stood behind Patti, his shoulders hunched beneath a dark hooded sweatshirt. He gave Mick a stiff smile that showed off a crooked front tooth. Jaq observed his acne-scarred skin and stormy eyes, remembering how uncomfortable he'd been the night of her abduction.

A sudden desire to escape reawakened in Jaq as she recalled the desperation of the night she was taken. After the creepy incident of sexual assault, just seeing someone who was free to come and go made her eager to somehow slip out of this nightmare. She stared at Craig as if he was her door out.

His dark eyes caught her gaze. He cleared his throat and looked down. Something about him made Jaq think of an animal, fierce but nervous.

"Speaking of the cold weather," Patti piped up, continuing the thread of conversation, "we come with a heads up. The weather report says there's the possibility of a storm. Heavy rain, perhaps snow even, if the temperature continues to drop. So we brought help." She raised her brows at Craig, and he shrugged a large gray pack off of his back.

"Snow? You're kidding. Early for that." Mick narrowed his eyes at the sky, scratching his shaved head.

Each of them received a dark hoody like the one Craig wore. It had the same IBSA logo and eagle emblem on the back as their t-shirts. The heavy sweatshirt had a thick, fleecy lining.

Jaq eagerly slid into hers, shivering as it warmed her bare arms. Luxury. Then Patti handed each a set of thermal long underwear.

"Awesome." Finn hugged his new clothes to his thin frame. If anyone needed extra padding against the cold, he did.

Jaq settled around the fire with everyone else as Mick and Katie handed out their new provisions for the week that arrived with Craig and Patti. It was the same series of zip-locked bags that they'd been given for the first week. The boys whooped with enthusiasm over the meager amounts of oats, flour, raisins, and the rest.

Jaq snorted to herself. Pitiful to be so excited about food she wouldn't even blink at in the real world. She really had to get out of here. Two more weeks of being dirty, hungry, cold. Busting her rear hiking and learning skills she'd never need. Being molested as she slept. She wouldn't do it. As she chewed on oats and raisins, Jaq sneaked a peek at Craig again. He passed a handful of sunflower seeds back and forth between his hands and sat in a whispered conversation with Mick.

Jaq wanted to catch his eye. Maybe she could get him to sympathize somehow and break just one little rule for her—maybe pointing her in a direction where she could find civilization. He pushed his long hair away from his face and looked over at her as if he felt her watching him. He frowned and went back to talking quietly with Mick.

Patti had everyone introduce themselves and say where they were from as they sat around the fire that had blossomed into a hearty flame. Daniel came from Chicago, Russ from Maryland, and Finn from San Francisco.

"I was just there before I got brought here," Jaq said to Finn, who perked up. "I have some cousins in Martinez. But I'm from LA."

"Cool. I know Martinez—it's about a half hour from where

I live. Had some... friends there." Finn's face changed at the word "friends" like something in his mouth went sour. "LA, huh? Cool."

"Malibu Barbie. I knew it." Daniel eyed Jaq as if she wore a bikini. Her stomach turned. She looked away from Daniel and caught Russ giving the obnoxious jock a look of disgust.

Awkward moment. Again. The fire snapped. The air seemed to cool, tickling down Jaq's legs. She stared down at the scuffed and worn hiking boots on her feet. It had only taken one hike before she put the used shoes on. Good thing her dad was a scrounge. A brief homesickness assaulted Jaq before she could slap it away.

Patti let out a powerful sigh. "It is so nice to meet you all. Now that you're all cozier and maybe a little less hungry, let's talk." Her face brightened with another smile.

Daniel groaned. "Here we go. Shrink time." He sat back with a smirk and folded his arms.

"Shut up," Jaq muttered. Daniel was so annoying. He glared at her.

Patti's voice was warm and unperturbed. "I like to think of it as the opposite of shrinking. We're expanding our understanding of ourselves. Opening up—unfurling. Is anyone willing to share why they're here?"

A rumble of thunder sounded from far away and the wind stirred. Nobody said anything for a while. Daniel snorted. Jaq stared at the dirt and from the corner of her eye she noticed Russ pull out his knife to work on a wooden spoon he'd been carving. Then Finn hugged his knees to his chest band shuffled his feet in the dirt. He raised his head and scanned the circle, ending on Patti's friendly face.

"So, here's the deal. I'm here because I'm addicted to drugs. I was stealing from my family. Once I broke into my uncle's house and took his new flat screen TV and sold it—to those 'friends' in Martinez—to get what I needed." He puffed out his breath and tucked his chin to his chest and continued talking in a muffled voice. "Last month I OD'd and was hospitalized. They locked me up in the psych ward for a week, but I was able to get my hands on drugs there too—don't ask. My mom... ran out of ideas and sent me here." He looked up, his innocent, elfish face tight. "I'm terrified of myself. I hate who I am now. Which is hilarious in a way." Finn dragged his fingers through his long red bangs and bit his lip as if to stop his words.

"How is it hilarious?" Patti's voice floated across the fire pit.

Finn squinted over at her as smoke swirled into his face. "Because my whole reason for starting to use was because I thought it would help me feel less like me. Cooler. Happier. More grown up. Ha. 'Old me' is looking freaking good right now. At least then I could take pride in myself for being smart." He forced a smile and shrugged.

"So you feel like your recent choices have not been smart. Insightful. Thank you for sharing that. I'm looking forward to talking with you more, and watching you find the pieces of you that are still worth fighting for." Patti searched Finn's face and a silence followed as everyone shifted around the fire.

Jaq sat between Mick and Daniel feeling like a clenched fist. Her heart thumped through Finn's bout with TMI. She had no idea how he could just say that stuff. She felt herself shrinking away from some of the things he said. Was "old Jaq" better?

"Don't look at me." Daniel raised his hands defensively as Patti's eyes swept in his direction. "I just have issues with authority. And the people who try to run my life don't like that."

"Who's trying to run your life?" Patti asked.

"Duh. All of you. My parents. Teachers at school. Everyone."

"And they want to make you do things that you don't want to do?"

"Yeah. That's why I'm here."

"So you don't agree that you should stop getting into fights and shoplifting? And graduation is a bad idea?" Patti was hitting harder with Daniel. Jaq wondered if she had some file somewhere that told her everything already—and how each kid should be treated.

Daniel's face went red. He scowled and gripped the stick he'd been poking into the fire until his knuckles went white. "Whatever," he growled.

"We don't have to talk about it here. But I will listen if you'd like to talk later," Patti said evenly.

"There is nothing to talk about!" Daniel snapped, angrier than what seemed necessary. "What about her?" He jabbed a finger toward Jaq, his blond hair falling into his eyes. "She's got issues. She's always pissed—no matter how nice everyone tries to be."

Jaq cringed and her face heated. Why was he bringing her up? She curled up tighter, trying to disappear.

"Okay." Patti nodded. "She's angry at everyone—or just at you?"

"Okay, mostly me. She loooves Finn, the druggy. And Russ can do no wrong." Daniel stabbed his stick into the ground and stormed away from the fire pit, kicking sticks and rocks as he went.

Katie called out after him, "I heard that—you have to start your non-profanity day-count over."

In response, Daniel shouted a few choice words. He'd already blown it.

Jaq watched him go, his athletic build tight with fury. His hotness in no way made up for his personality.

"Whoa," Russ whispered. "He's intense."

"Yeah," Finn agreed, giving Jaq a sympathetic smile.

Patti sat straighter and gave Mick a look that sent him after the angry teen who could still be heard off in the brush swearing and stomping. Then she gave Jaq a long look.

"What? He's a jerk. Everyone else is fine, I guess." Jaq resented Daniel's attack. It only reconfirmed her suspicions that he was the desperate perv who got all over her while she slept. "He's just not used to rejection. I know his type."

"Rejection?" Patti leaned forward.

"Yeah, he's always flirting and trying to start something. He —" Jaq bit off her words, deciding against sharing the little detail that he might also be a molester.

Patti and Katie exchanged a concerned glance, but it was Russ who said something. "What? What did h-he do?" Russ coughed, his brow creased with concern. It struck Jaq how much his face could change—from shy and thoughtful to strong and older than his age.

"I don't want to—nothing." Jaq's ears burned. This had turned so awkward. Everyone stared at her, waiting to listen. She couldn't face Russ so she found herself locking eyes with Craig. He looked upset for her—like he had in the van. A glimmer of an idea scratched and sparked like a match in Jaq's mind. If she told anyone, it would be Craig. She would make him her confidante and then he would feel sorry for her—and maybe help her figure out how to get out of this wasteland.

When she refused to say more, the conversation moved on. Patti offered some platitudes and words of encouragement, letting them know that she would be available to talk alone. Finn took her up on it and wandered off with her in the direction she had come.

With Mick dealing with Daniel, and Patti with Finn, Jaq found herself at the fire pit with Katie, Russ, and Craig.

Katie stood and stretched. "Drama, huh?" She looked at

Russ and smiled. "Maybe you should try to talk to Finn. I think, since he was the only one who shared, he might feel kind of exposed. And I know he's afraid of being judged. And I think you—out of all of us—could make him feel understood."

Russ's face had a serious expression. "Yeah. I will."

Jaq noticed his strong jaw tighten. So he was a druggy too? That would explain why he was so good with Finn while he detoxed. Maybe withdrawal was something he was familiar with. He turned his warm brown eyes to her, and she got up, avoiding his gaze. Jaq was afraid he'd see the disappointment she felt. She'd somehow hoped he was better than the rest of them. It wasn't until that moment that she realized she even felt that way.

She threw a look like an invisible rope at Craig as she walked away, hoping he would read her signal. *Follow me.* Jaq found her bedroll and untied it, spreading it back out on the ground. She sat down and took a deep breath, closing her eyes.

Footsteps scuffed in the dirt, and she opened her eyes to see Craig standing nearby, fidgeting with the drawstrings on his hood. Of course, he came.

"So what's your story?" Jaq asked with some sarcasm.

Craig straightened and put on his adult face. "Story?"

"Yeah. Why are you here?"

His smile was stiff. "Here to help. I was a troubled teen, went through the program and..." He wrung his hands and paused.

"That couldn't have been too long ago—you look young. How old are you?" Jaq asked, sensing a possible inroad.

Craig cleared his throat. "I'm twenty-three." He smoothed on a mask of maturity.

"Your whole life ahead—how did you get stuck here?" Jaq watched his face react, like when a pebble is dropped into still water.

"Um. Well, things were messed up and R.J. sort of adopted me... and now I help." A hint of defensiveness crept into his voice.

Intriguing. "You a counselor?"

"Nah. More of a fetch-and-carry." He shrugged his pointy shoulder, looking young again.

"Yeah. I remember how you fetched and carried." Jaq narrowed her eyes as if angry, while making her voice sultry.

Craig rolled his eyes like he was above her remark, but he swallowed, and his hands froze, like he didn't know what to do with them. He shoved them into his pockets.

"I run things to and from the outposts and HQ." He raised one shoulder.

"Where's that?" Jaq ran a hand through her hair and blinked at him.

"Closer than you think," he said, as if proud that he knew and she didn't.

Jaq frowned. "Must be nice to come and go as you please. I'm stuck here. Wish I could take a nice, long, hot shower." Jaq sighed, reaching her arms into the air and arching her back in a stretch intended to give him something to look at.

Craig's cheekbones reddened. It was time for her to pounce.

"So, I didn't feel like I could tell everyone else—about Daniel. It's too embarrassing." Jaq picked up a stick and trailed it through the dirt, not sure how she wanted to continue.

"What?" Craig moved closer, his brows lowering.

"He totally attacked me, forced himself on me. I feel so violated." When tears stung Jaq's eyes, they were not entirely faked. It was true that she felt disgusting about the night before and saying it aloud triggered her emotions. She really, really wanted to get away from this situation. Jaq looked up and she knew Craig saw that her eyes were wet.

"Really? He... touched you?" Craig's head jerked back and forth a couple of times like he wasn't sure how to process what she had said. He came closer and sat down in the dirt across from her. A frown tugged down the edges of his mouth.

"A bit more than just touch. Listen, Craig." Jaq leaned forward, lowering her voice intimately. "I don't want you to tell anyone else. I know I can trust you. I just don't want everyone to ask questions and make me talk about it. You understand?"

Craig nodded, his mouth grim. "But I think you should. I think they could move him to another group or something."

That wouldn't help her at all. "I'd rather be moved. Out of here. I'm so unhappy." Jaq lowered her head and covered her face with her hands.

"I know. I remember what it was like. But it's good for you. Really. You should try to get something out of it." His voice was thin, like he needed more oxygen.

"No. I have to go," Jaq sobbed.

"Don't go." His voice hardened.

"I will. And then I'll probably get lost and hurt because I have no idea where I am. I have to get back to my little sister. She's with my dad—and he won't look after her. He's... abusive." Jaq cringed a little at her own lie.

Craig shook his head a few times. Jaq guiltily watched his reaction. For some reason she had influence over him. She could sense it—the same way she could tell he wasn't that bright.

"Will you help me? All you have to do is tell me which way to walk so I can find a house and make a phone call."

"I can't." He held up his hands in a helpless gesture.

"Why not? I don't belong here. I'm not a bad kid. My dad is just a control freak—and he wanted me broken so I wouldn't fight him anymore. Do you know what I mean?"

Craig stared at a spot in the air past her head, blinking slow, in deep thought.

"I heard you say once that you hate your job. So you're a prisoner here too. We can help each other." Jaq pushed, seeing Craig's hesitation and hoping she looked pitiful and pretty enough to persuade him. She cursed her lack of makeup—mascara and lip gloss would be priceless right now. For a brief moment she saw her mother's made-up face. Men were too easy.

Craig's eyes seemed to expand, and he let his gaze slip over her face and pop down to her body for just a nano second. He cleared his throat. "I can't do that, kid. No way." Suddenly he sounded like an adult again. He stood up and gathered his hair in one hand, pulling it back. "Look, this is good for you." He kicked at the dirt. "I'm sorry."

Jaq slumped over and leaned her forehead on her bent knees. She hadn't expected that reaction, which was suddenly humiliating. What was she thinking? That she could sit there looking completely pathetic, covered in dirt, flirt a little, and get one of the enemy to take her side?

"I understand. I just don't know how I can survive this. Especially if I have to see Daniel every day." Her voice came out strangled with disappointment and shame. She heard a soft groan come from Craig, but she couldn't look at him. She waited for him to leave, but through the lashes of her half-closed eyes noticed his hiking boots rooted to the earth in front of her. It was then that she heard rustling behind her. Katie came out of the bushes and walked past them. She threw a look at Craig. He hung his head and waited for her to move away, his hands curling into fists.

How long had she been back there? Jaq's stomach dropped.

Before Craig turned to go he said in a voice so low Jaq thought she imagined it, "It will be okay. I'll help you."

Astonished, Jaq watched the bony back of her new ally as he walked away. His wiry, muscled arms hung at his sides, hunching his shoulders against the cold, dark hair lank and long. It had worked—her flirting and sob story had done the trick. So, he was a man after all.

CHAPTER 8

LAYOVER WAS LESS restful than Jaq would have liked. It was all about learning stuff—how to make traps, first aid, orienteering—which Jaq paid special attention to in case she would be making a long walk on her own soon. The problem was, there was only one compass and it belonged to Mick.

They were also shown how to make coal beds for sleeping over in the cold and starting a bow-drill fire. Maybe those things would come in handy, too, if she ever escaped, but so far she sucked at bow-drill.

As explained by Mick, cordage made out of bitterbrush bark, when attached to both ends of a flexible stick, made the bow, a knife-sharpened stick made the spindle or drill, and a flat piece of notched wood served as a fireboard.

Jaq thought her arm would fall off, sawing the bow back and forth to make the spindle spin with enough friction to produce the hot powdery punk on the fireboard that would smoke and flame. After forty-five minutes, she gritted her teeth to stop the tears of exasperation and gave it up. Stupid freaking piece of useless wood.

Jaq kneaded her sore upper arm with one hand and looked around helplessly. Several feet away, Russ crouched over his bow-drill set, already blowing a flame to life in his waiting tinder bundle. He watched it flicker and snap through the small nest of twigs, unaware that Jaq watched, observing his amazing arm muscles and sensitive and attractive profile. She waited, knowing what came next. After days of spying on Russ, she had figured out a few things. Whenever he was alone, he would stare off into space for a little while, and then his lips would start moving as if he was having a conversation with an invisible person. Sometimes in the shadows of her mind, Jaq wondered if there was something really wrong with him.

Russ did space out, his mournful eyes absorbed in their own darkness. But instead of talking to himself, he suddenly turned his face toward Jaq. Busted. Her heart jumped and she felt like an idiot for being caught gazing at him. His face relaxed into a sideways grin.

"Any luck?" He lifted his chin toward her bow-drill set.

"None. I hate this," Jaq grumbled, her face still hot from embarrassment.

"Don't worry. You'll get it. It took me a long time."

"What? All of a half an hour?" Jaq hissed a noise through her teeth.

"I mean back when my dad taught me. It took days. I thought I'd... jam the drill into my eye. I was so f-frustrated." He grinned and turned his head away.

"I feel a little better knowing you've already done this. I feel like a total loser." Jaq slumped and pushed her blonde hair off her damp forehead.

"As long as you can have it mastered within a couple weeks, they'll let you go home. *No pressure.*" Russ's smile was beautiful. Jaq lost her breath for a second. She loved it on the rare occasion he smiled or spoke. His voice was so even and deliberate.

Then his words settled into her brain. "A couple weeks."

Jaq had no intention of being around that much longer. A twinge of regret pinched her chest. Why did Russ have to look at her like that?

Later that afternoon, Mick led the group around to do some tracking. There were plenty of mule deer, rabbit, and snake tracks. Desert mice left little scuffled tracks through the brush, and in one spot were signs of a coyote pack.

They made their way farther from camp. Jaq felt chilled as the sky continued to gather menacing clouds. Finn was quiet most of the day. He must have felt weird after telling everyone about his drug problem. Not that it was news to any of them. But it was brave.

Daniel watched Jaq like a hungry beast that both threatened to devour and pleaded for a scratch behind the ear. It was confusing to be repulsed and interested in somebody so annoying. Jaq avoided looking at him as much as possible.

Russ strode along, his body strong and energetic as he kept up with Mick. They were thick as thieves. Then they both bent their heads to the ground and Russ let out a low whistle. Mick knelt in the dirt and pointed out some indentations to the rest of the group when they caught up. The pawprint looked about the size of Jaq's hand.

"This looks like a *Canis lupis*—grey wolf, most likely. A large one. You can tell by the length of his stride while trotting" —he pointed to another set of prints a few paces away—"and the depth of the prints indicate he's a heavy guy, maybe 120 pounds. A sucker like this could drag a horse or turn over a moose carcass, no problem. They run around thirty-five miles per hour." He cocked his head to the side. "This one was hunting alone. But he more than likely has a mate and a nuclear family." Mick sat back on his haunches and rubbed his forehead. "Wow. This guy must be something to see."

"He got kinda close to camp. Who's spooning with me

tonight? I'm frightened and all alone." Finn grinned and gave Jaq a wink. It was almost not funny after last night—but Finn was okay, so Jaq smiled at him. Besides, she was glad to hear him joking again.

Daniel glowered at both of them. He was in such a mood. Jaq tried not to react—she didn't want to be accused of picking on him—but she couldn't help it. She stuck out her tongue.

"Tease. Don't stick it out unless you intend to use it," Daniel muttered.

"Daniel," Mick's voice warned.

Jaq shivered in the cold air. She'd taken off her sweatshirt earlier when they'd worked up a sweat orienteering, which involved running up and down the rocky rises looking for landmarks and racing to find a hidden apple. Jaq could kill for a piece of fresh fruit. She tried her best, but Russ won it, of course. He seemed to know a lot about everything.

Russ pointed under some nearby sagebrush. "He *wasn't* alone. His mate was with him. Look—those tracks are angled differently, and the width of the paw is narrower."

Mick scrutinized the tracks and flashed a proud smile at Russ. "Good eye, Russ."

Jaq squatted closer, curious despite herself. She'd been preoccupied all day by the thought that Craig had agreed to help her. And she didn't know how or when he planned to do so. Either way, she was out of here soon, but sometimes she actually forgot she hated everything about this place.

She shuddered and hugged herself when a cold gust of wind swept across the tops of the gray green sage, wafting a sharp smell like a blend of turpentine and camphor into the air. Without looking at her, Russ pulled off his sweatshirt and handed it to Jaq. She took it and mumbled a thank you before slipping it on over her head. It was still warm from his body and smelled like a guy. It didn't bother her.

The sun showed from behind the purple clouds, a faded white, circular stain like a water ring on old furniture. It had not rained yet, but the air was full of electricity and moisture. Jaq hoped the storm would miss them, or at least not have too much thunder. She hated storms. They headed back toward camp.

"I'm starved." Daniel chucked a rock through the air.

"If I had a rifle we could have some meat. And some fur." Russ rubbed his hands together briskly.

"Nasty, dude. You'd, like, cut it all up and use the pieces? Sounds messy." The pretty jock made a face.

"Yeah. Blood doesn't bother me." Russ shrugged.

Jaq shivered. The sight of blood made her nauseous. *No idea how anyone can just cut into anything that bleeds.*

———

To Jaq's horror, the thunder pounded its way closer, an angry drunk tracking down his hiding, frightened children. In the darkening night, the group huddled around the fire, making ash cakes, trying to find comfort. Then, like a door opening, light flashed bright into their faces—the thunder was in the room. Jaq actually felt it rattle her chest and teeth. That was close.

"Whoa!" Daniel shouted around a mouth full of ashcake.

Jaq had an overwhelming desire to cry. She ducked her head, shaking. It was strangely familiar, this feeling of shock and terror. Her skin crawled as a memory came back to her.

When she was five or six, Jaq awoke to a raging storm. Leaping out of bed, she ran down the dark hallway toward her parents' bedroom. Lightning flashed through the house like a strobe light and the door seemed to move away from her as she ran toward it. Before she reached it a dark figure stepped in front of her, and she bounced off her brother before she could stop.

"What are you doing, brat?" He sneered down at her, hands on his hips. His face lit up at the next flash, and his face turned white as a skull.

Jaq sat up, trying to look brave. He would be merciless if he knew she was afraid.

"I was just going to the bathroom."

"Liar. You passed the bathroom—and you look like you've seen a ghost. Well, have you? Huh?" Brian pushed down on her chest with one foot, pinning her on her back.

"Stop it, Brian. I'll tell." Jaq scrambled back like a crab and jumped to her feet.

"Tell who?" Brian acted confused.

"Mom and Dad, you jerk."

Brian held out his arms, blocking the hallway. "You can't go in there."

"Yes, I can! Move!" Jaq pushed against him, a panic rising in her chest.

Another clap of thunder shook the house, and the flash of light captured a still frame of her brother's angry face.

"Mom and Dad are dead, princess."

"No they aren't!" Jaq screamed, scratching and thrashing to get past the nightmare she called brother. "Where's Flower?" Jaq suddenly felt desperate to see her tiny blonde sister.

"She's with them. I killed them myself. I cut their throats while they were sleeping. There's blood all over their pillows." His voice took on a nasty, scratchy tone.

"No!" Jaq braced herself against the wall as dizziness swirled in her head. Her skin prickled and her fingers felt icy and stiff. What if he had killed them?

"Let me go. I don't believe you," she croaked.

Brian cackled like a cartoon villain and shoved her hard

onto the ground. She landed with a jarring pain in her backside.

"Believe me. What else would I be doing coming out of their room in the middle of the night?"

"You came out of your room! The storm scared you too! You were running to jump in bed with them yourself," Jaq growled, knowing she would pay for her remark.

Brian crouched down and grabbed her by the hair, pulling Jaq to her feet. "Me? Scared? I'll show you scared. C'mon. You're going to get a good look at the bodies."

Jaq howled in horror as another clap of thunder vibrated the windowpanes. All at once it seemed real. Her parents' white door had an eerie glow. She imagined their limp bodies in bedding soaked with blood, her little sister like a broken dolly lying between her mom and dad.

"No!" She dug her heels into the floor as Brian dragged her toward what had seemed like a safe haven just a few moments before. She reached up and clawed her fingernails into the fist that held a tangle of her hair.

"Ouch!" Brian let go.

Jaq darted back down the hall, her heart pounding so fast it hurt. She heard him in pursuit. She leaped into her room, throwing herself against the door and locking it. Out in the haunted hallway her brother "oooohhhhed" and moaned.

Shaking and weeping, Jaq cowered under the blankets on her bed as the storm battered the house. She hugged Flower's white stuffed bunny, named Popcorn, to her chest so hard her shoulders ached. Terrible images of gore and murder flashed in her mind. She dreaded the coming of the morning in a house still as death—alone with Brian.

An arm wrapped around Jaq's shoulders.

"Are you okay?" Russ leaned close to her and tightened his

grip as another crash of thunder caused Jaq to jump. Embarrassed, she realized she was shaking.

"I'm... fine. I don't like thunder." Jaq tried to sit taller, but another boom cracked the sky and she tucked herself under Russ' arm.

"Oh, brother." Daniel laughed cruelly. "Help me—the thunder is scary!" he squeaked in a girly voice.

"That's not cool. She's really scared," Finn said. "Some people have astraphobia—extreme fear of thunder and lightning. It's an actual thing, man."

Jaq smiled at Finn and noticed Craig standing outside the circle of light the fire created, his eyes aimed at Daniel, shining like a nocturnal predator's.

"She's ridiculous. All snarky and tough until she can get some free snuggling from Russ." He ran a hand through his scattered blond hair.

"What is wrong with you?" Jaq groaned and pulled away from the warmth and safety of Russ. She braced herself at the next clap of thunder. They were coming further apart now.

Daniel's fists pressed into his knees. He glared at her but there was more hurt in his eyes than his anger could disguise. "Screw you."

Mick spoke up. "Okay guys. Let's sing. Something loud and distracting." Clearing his throat, Mick boomed in a rich baritone to rival the storm. "Raindrops on roses and whiskers on kittens!"

Katie joined in with a harmonious alto on the next line of the song. Finn piped in with a hilarious falsetto soprano after her. Then, the three of them loudly sang the last lines of the song together, surprisingly on key.

"And then you don't feel so bad? What about me?" Daniel plugged his ears, scowling, while Russ rolled his eyes, looking amused.

Jaq burst into laughter when they'd finished. "Finn, why do you know that song?"

Finn batted his eyes. "I was a nun in a former life."

"Sister Finn," Daniel muttered.

"Actually, I was in a production of *The Sound of Music* at school a couple of years ago."

"Of course you were." Jaq grinned at him, ignoring Daniel altogether now.

The sky continued to rumble like Jaq's usually empty stomach, but the sound retreated as a light sprinkling of rain broke up the group around the fire.

"Get your bedrolls. There isn't much shelter, but over here against the rock will be better than out in the open." Mick wiped the sheen of rain from his forehead, turning to gather his things.

Where the fire pit blazed up against a rocky tower, a two-foot shelf several feet above formed a slight awning. Everyone settled their bedrolls tightly together against the rock under the shallow overhang, using the limited space that offered some protection. The rain came steadier, and Jaq knew it would be a damp night. Her bed lay against Katie's right, and at Finn's feet, who'd squished in next to Mick. Daniel and Russ shared a space below Jaq.

At least nobody could do anything to her tonight with everyone so close. Jaq wandered off to find a bush to relieve herself behind. The rain fell in bigger drops that splashed on her head and arms like little water balloons. By the time she returned to the fire, she was soaked. She boiled some water in her billycan to make some mint tea. It felt good and hot going down.

Mick, wielding his hatchet, threw more wood on the fire, making it leap high, casting demonic shadows onto the red and gold rock wall. Raindrops hissed on the stones that lined the fire pit. Steam rose from Jaq's damp clothes when she stood close to the heat.

Under her wool blanket, she slipped into the dry long underwear that Patti had brought. It felt so good to have her legs covered after enduring the chilly weather in shorts. Her t-shirt had dried by the fire enough that she put that on over the long-sleeved thermals, and over that she pulled on her new hoody, having left the wet one she'd borrowed from Russ by the fire.

Jaq started to relax. It felt good to get cozy, but she wondered where Craig and Patti had gone. The rain stopped. The boys came back from whatever pit stops they'd taken. Russ pulled off his wet t-shirt and held it out over the fire. Shadow outlined his muscles, smooth and tight. Finn and Daniel dried their sweatshirts, and the boys joked and quoted stupid movies together. The rain stopped and the murmur of their voices and the warm comfort of new clothes were almost enough to make Jaq's eyelids droop—if she hadn't locked her sights on Russ. He was just magnetic somehow, without trying.

Russ jabbed a long stick into the ground beside the blaze and hung his shirt on it. He turned around, all pecs and abs, to kneel on his blanket. Reaching around inside his bundle of provisions, he took out his knife and the prized apple he'd won earlier that day. Then he scooted over to where Jaq had cocooned herself.

"Feel better?" he asked as he carved off a large piece of the crisp, red fruit. He handed it to Jaq, his eyes partially hidden by dark eyelashes.

"Thank you—I'm fine now. I just hate loud storms. Childhood trauma or whatever." Jaq tried to ignore his chest and the flutter in her stomach. She bit into the apple and almost groaned aloud as the tart sweetness made her salivary glands contract with a painful pleasure. "Ah. This is amazing," she said, closing her eyes for a moment to chew and savor.

"I'm terrified of the horrible sounds of the... washing machine. Always have been," Russ confessed.

Jaq laughed. "You're kidding!"

Russ crunched the prize fruit and raised his hands in defense. "It's on the other side of the wall my bed is up against, and it makes noises!"

"Ooh, like, whirring sounds?" Jaq made her lips an "o" and waved her hands like something spooky.

"Nah, like thump-bump-chshhh..." Russ made a grim face.

Jaq almost choked on the bite of apple in her mouth. "You must have hated it on laundry day."

"Tried to wear my clothes as long as possible." He nodded gravely.

"Well, you're not wearing any now." Jaq froze realizing she'd patted his solid bicep and let her eyes linger on his chest. She giggled and popped the last bite of apple into her mouth while feeling her earlobes burn.

"Could you guys stop flirting?" Daniel groaned from under his blanket.

"We're totally not—" Jaq fumbled, embarrassed.

"Why? Jealous?" Russ asked, his shyness gone and the confident man version of him raising a brow.

"Shut up and put on a shirt," Daniel snapped.

Before things could get more blushy, Jaq yawned loudly and stood as if she had to stretch every inch of her body, wandering away from the fire as she did so. The smell of wet earth and brush sent her blood on a sprint through her veins. Behind her the boys murmured insults at one another, the low rumble of Russ's voice creating a tingle low in her stomach.

The shadows wrapped her in a soothing hug, her heated cheeks cooled in the crisp night air. Then one shadow broke away from the rest and fell in front of her. Her heart stuttered to a stop.

"Hey." Craig's dark eyes gleamed in the weak light of the moon behind shredding clouds.

"Crap, you scared me." Jaq slapped a hand over her heart.

"Sorry." The outline of his shoulder rose.

"I thought you were going to help me." She folded her arms across her chest.

"I will. I am."

"Which way is the real world?" Jaq hoped he would simply point in a direction and tell her how long to walk. Thanks to her new training, she could do it if she had a compass—and she knew where Mick kept one in his pack.

"I won't let you go alone. It's too dangerous." He took one step closer.

"Bull. How far?" Jaq raised her chin.

"Far on foot. We took the four-wheeler. But I have Patti with me and we're going back in the morning. Trust me... it isn't safe alone." Craig pushed his hands into his pockets. In the dark, his face was angular, dangerous, almost good looking. At least his pocked skin looked better.

"So you'll be back for me later? When?" Jaq leaned closer letting the air between them sandwich and fill with possibilities. He had to come back.

"I'll help as soon as I can. Go back to camp. Watch out for Mick."

Jaq wasn't sure what he meant by that, but it made her spine feel like icy water had been poured down it. Before she could say anything, Craig flicked back his hair and turned away, disappearing, stealthy as a starved, lone wolf.

———

Jaq tried to sleep as the sounds of howling drifted through the night air. The rain filtered down again, making *psst* noises on the coals of the fire. She squirmed under her covers, pretending she didn't notice that Russ slept at her feet.

"Awake?" Finn's voice rasped from above her, then a hand came lightly down and touched her head.

Startled, she opened her eyes. Finn hung over her, his red bangs dangling in her face. His smile gleamed in the charcoal shade of night.

"Yeah." She forced a casual expression on her face like it didn't weird her out to have him so close in the dark.

"Me too. My blanket's damp." Finn wrinkled his nose.

"Well, you aren't getting into mine." Jaq pulled her blanket up to her mouth. There would be no "dream groping" tonight.

He chuckled, lying back down. "Yeah. I figured. Actually, I had visions of Patti's tent. She and Craig are snug as bugs."

"She has a tent? Luxury."

"Yeah. Kinda makes you sick—like Bill Gates over there. Her own tent, made out of real canvas. Lucky beast. I mean, there are people starving in Africa." Finn talked around a yawn that made his jaw pop. "What am I saying... there're people starving right here," he muttered.

"Yeah. A tent and some Doritos would be nice." Jaq closed her eyes listening to another round of yelps and howls in the distance. "Goodnight, Finn."

"Sleep tight, Crooked Pack. Thanks... for not treating me like the freak that I am." His voice was sleepy and trailing off.

"Birds of a feather," she whispered.

A soft snort indicated he'd heard her and then his breathing slowed and deepened. Jaq followed his lead with the night sounds of the desert as her lullaby.

CHAPTER 9

THE SUN HAD BARELY PEEKED over the horizon, spilling a river of golden light over the flat expanse of scattered rocks that would be their new route. With a bedroll already on her back, Jaq waited through the morning lecture and moment of silence. When Mick finished talking, everyone else set to packing up their things.

"Hey, Crooked Pack, hear any coyotes last night?" Daniel walked toward her, tightening the rope on his bedroll. His handsome face was gaunt, like everyone else's from their survival diet.

"Yeah. They were noisy last night. But they kept their distance. Luckily." Jaq watched Russ over by the blackened fire pit. He searched the ground and his provision sack, as if something were missing.

"Lucky for them or lucky for you?" Daniel followed Jaq's gaze and smirked. She looked away and scratched her head.

"Lucky for the coyote." She hoped her voice sounded threatening.

Daniel laughed. "Hot."

Oh, he did not just body scan me, Jaq thought, turning red. "Give it up, Daniel. I know it was you." The words seemed to pop out on their own and Jaq felt the adrenaline buzz start. She hadn't meant to confront him about the night he felt her up while she slept.

Daniel cocked his head to the side, a slow smile growing on his face. "What was me? The man of your dreams?"

Jaq choked back her anger. That was practically an admission!

"Anyone see my knife?" Russ called, dropping a wad of his things onto the ground. Finn and Mick walked over to him, but Jaq couldn't hear what they were saying over the rush of blood in her ears.

"Pervert," she hissed.

"Yeah, duh. What about it?" Daniel's brows slanted in fake confusion, his bright eyes flicked back and forth as if to find the point she was trying to make.

Jaq's hand swung toward Daniel's head. He caught it just inches from his face, his fingers overlapping around her small wrist, gripping hard.

"What the hell?" His voice scraped, low enough to get away with cursing. "I know you're attracted to me. You just don't like me, so it pisses you off." His jaw tightened, his hazel stare trapping her.

Jaq's breath expanded in her chest, unable to escape. So what if he was a total babe? She hated his entitled, cocky, ill-tempered, objectifying, chauvinist attitude. Jerk. Sometimes he reminded her of... Brian. He was like her brother.

"Ouch." She yanked her wrist out of his grasp. "Never touch me again."

"What is your problem?" Daniel glared, his hands raised palm up.

"You are." Jaq jabbed a finger into his hard chest.

"What is going on over here?" Katie stepped between them. "Are you guys fighting?" Her wholesome face wrinkled in disapproval. "Knock it off. We have to get ready to leave camp. Have either of you seen Russ's knife?"

Jaq stepped back, breathing deep. Anger simmered in her stomach but she didn't want to make waves over this. She'd talk to Daniel later. "Last night he was cutting up his apple. That was the last time I saw it." She looked past Daniel, trying not to see him.

"Don't look at me. No idea." Daniel's shoulders slumped. For two seconds his face registered hurt before he plastered a mask of jock superiority back on.

"We're heading out soon. Patti wants to see everyone individually for five minutes first." Katie put her hand on Jaq's back and rubbed it in circles in a soothing motion as if she knew it was needed. "You first, Daniel."

"Great." Daniel glared but he marched away toward the rock formation where Patti had her camp.

Katie gave Jaq's back a quick pat, signaling the back rub was over. "Jaq. Can I talk to you for a sec?"

Shrugging, Jaq gave a nod. "What's up?"

Katie's eyes were soft and sincere. "I know it sucks out here. I also know that life sucked before you got here. Maybe people let you down. Maybe you let yourself down too. But you get to start over every day. Nobody writes your story but you. You know what I mean?"

Jaq felt a sudden emotion that made her uncomfortable. "Okay." She tried to sound casual.

"I see so much strength in you. So much good. But you can't yet, and change feels impossible. I'm telling you, all you have to do is *see it to be it*. See the good in you and you will be the good in you. Understand?"

Maybe it was cheesy. It could be the lamest advice she ever got, but it made Jaq's eyes sting. "Thanks," she said.

Katie smiled and gave Jaq's back one last pat of encouragement. "You got this. You're strong."

————

Waiting for her turn, Jaq found Mick with Russ and Finn telling gory tales of the Indian wars and wild Old West. "So, Wyatt Earp survived the shootout and lived to fight again. I mean, so much of it has been fictionalized. Criminals were epic and lawmen were legends." Mick rubbed his large hands together then flexed them into giant fists. "I would have thrived in the Wild West. A man could live off the land and back then justice was quick and lethal when it needed to be."

Jaq couldn't pay attention for long. She worried about what Patti would say to her and wondered if Craig would be there with a message. Something Russ was saying to Mick caught her attention.

"My dad used to be a cop. His stories aren't exciting like that. But I used to love to hear th-th-them." Russ cleared his throat and kicked the dirt.

Mick pressed his lips together and nodded, placing a hand on Russ's shoulder. Finn said something too soft for Jaq to hear. She wanted to know what they were talking about and wondered how she could get to know Russ better.

"Princess. She wants you next." Daniel came up behind Jaq, trailing a finger over one of her shoulder blades. She recoiled and elbowed him in the side.

"Oof. Geez. Why do you hate me?" He stepped away, rubbing his side with a grimace that showed his teeth.

"Why do you like someone who hates you?" Jaq shot back, surprised to see Daniel's face go thoughtful when she said it. He seemed to have a sudden interest in examining his shoes.

"Patti's waiting." All teasing and flirting had left his voice.

"I'm going." Jaq trudged away from the group toward the lion-like rock formation. It felt like a waste of time. Like the counselor, Mrs. Andersen, at school. There was nothing to talk about and not a thing the cheerful, curly haired woman could do for her.

The tent was an army-green canvas rectangle big enough for a few people to sleep in. Craig and the four-wheeler were nowhere in sight and Patti stood at the entrance, expectant and alert.

"Hello, Jaq. Come on in, huh?"

Two cots—each with an actual sleeping bag—on opposite sides of the tent provided seating. Jaq sank into one, unable to resist the not-on-the-filthy-hard-groundness of it. Things you take for granted. A couple of packs and a walking stick were the only other things inside.

The older woman settled herself, rubbing pink hands together to warm them and crossing her legs at the ankles. She had a lazy warmth about her like she had nothing better to do than bask in Jaq's presence.

"So?" Jaq twitched in her seat. She knew the drill. They acted like they cared about your feelings and then told you to straighten up. She waited.

Patti breathed in through her nose and then let it out, the hint of a smile on her lips. "The air out here is like odorless peppermint. Can you smell that? Snow coming?"

"I guess." Jaq smirked. If this was going to be a bunch of small talk, she was already bored.

Patti smiled. "So tell me about your siblings."

Jaq shifted on the cot. Nobody ever asked her about her siblings before.

"Big brother, Brian. Jerk." She made a face and stuck out her tongue as if it tasted horrible. Got that over with—she didn't want to dwell on him. "And my sister, Flower. She's a couple years younger than me. She's great." Jaq felt herself soften thinking of her little sister.

Patti nodded with a pleased look on her face.

"Flower and I are pretty close," Jaq continued. "She's probably the only person in the world who really knows me." She realized after saying it that it was true. None of her friends had a clue who she was. Her boyfriend didn't—that was for sure. Mostly because she totally played the role of bad girl when they were together. It was an escape. Her dad believed the act too. And her mom was too busy reinventing herself and being gone to notice. A bitter frown pulled down Jaq's mouth.

"And do you know Flower as well as she knows you?" Patti cocked her head to the side.

"Yeah. I guess." Jaq thought for a minute. Flower was just... Flower. She was sweet and kind of passive-aggressive sometimes.

"What is going on in Flower's life? Why isn't she here too?" Patti placed her hands on her knees, inclining her head.

Jaq sputtered in her head trying to think of how to answer that. How was Flower doing? She seemed... okay. Of course she had cried a few times over Mom leaving. But other than that, she was the same. "She's fine. I guess Dad likes her better because she doesn't give him any trouble. She's the golden child."

"Like you once were."

"I guess." *Go, team go,* Jaq sneered at her cheerleader self.

"Did you ever ask Flower how she's doing?"

"What do you mean? Not really. I could just tell." Jaq had a guilty tickle in her gut. Maybe she never bothered to ask because Flower was too busy listening to all of her big sister's rants.

"You could? Did you know your sister has been cutting herself?"

A cold jolt went through Jaq. "What? How do you know that?" It just wasn't true. Flower wasn't like that.

Patti pulled a folded paper out of her pocket. It crinkled as she opened it and scanned the page.

"She told me. She wanted you to know. And that your partying and personality change frightens her."

Jaq surged to her feet. "What? Is this some weird—" She didn't even know what to say. She felt angry and cornered. Just what did Flower think she was doing? It was bad enough that she was hurting herself—but the backstabbing was extra uncool.

"You aren't the only one who's suffering, Jaq. Sometimes we get too caught up in our own worlds to see what's happening to the most important people in our lives."

The words stung. Jaq had just been thinking those same bitter thoughts about her mother's behavior.

"I'm pretty sure this kind of therapy is unethical or unprofessional—or breaking some kind of rule." Jaq glowered.

Patti breathed out a sigh. "Think. Don't get carried away with your defensive emotions and just think." She glanced back down at the paper. "She wants me to read this part to you aloud." Patti cleared her throat.

"Jaqueline, this year has really sucked. Mom freaking out and leaving us being at the top of the list, and you getting abducted in front of me right up there with it. I'm not happy. I feel like I have to hold everyone together. Dad's stress over money and worrying about you isn't helping his personality. But he obviously thinks the world of you or he wouldn't be spending this kind of money to help you get your head straight. I found out that Mom drained his savings during her diva stage and then took almost everything in the divorce—including the equity in the house. He's been afraid of losing our home. So yeah, he's been

a jerk. His already frugal ways have been on blast because he's struggling to support us.

I know Brian has sort of traumatized you—he did things to me too. I'm glad he's gone. But I miss Mom. Even Diva Mom. I don't like taking her place. I can't do it alone."

A potent mix of shock and anger stiffened Jaq's spine and her face drained, making her lips feel paralyzed. She snorted as if everything she'd heard so far was a bunch of bull. But she felt sick from her sister's honesty. Patti paused and gave her a serious look before continuing.

"Please think about stuff while you're out there doing that survival thingy. I miss my sister. The real Jaqueline. She's an amazing person. And I still need her."

Jaq's heart ached. She tried to push her tears away with anger, but Patti wasn't done with the torture.

"I have never been as strong as you. That's why seeing you change and run away into a new personality has been so scary. Can anyone just keep it together? Are we all doomed to have a meltdown and become someone else just to cope? I never wanted to be one of those dramatic and depressed girls. I know I don't look like one—but I've started to become that in my mind. Sometimes everything feels so heavy and dark. I don't want to do what Mom did and forget who I am. I don't think anyone can find themselves by changing personalities and leaving the people who love them behind. So, I want to make a pact. I promise to be me and not escape my problems with unsafe behavior—if you do the same. We can do this together. I love you. Please come back soon. And dump Sean—he's so beneath you. And smoking? Really? You're too smart for that. Love, Flower."

Jaq sat rigidly on the cot, stunned. Tears burned tracks down her cheeks. She had no idea. It was like one of those movies where you see everything through one character's eyes and then all over again from a new point of view. Nothing seemed the same. A part of her mind cracked open and light streamed into it. A piercing and hot knowing throbbed in her chest.

Patti moved to sit beside Jaq and took her trembling hands. They sat like that for several minutes. Jaq's mind zig zagged as if to dodge the bullets of truth she really didn't want to know. Flower hurt herself. Jaq had failed her. Just like Mom. Dad really cared? Jaq felt like an idiot. A guilty, selfish, idiot.

"You have a lot to think about. I'll see you next Layover and we can talk. Aren't chances to heal and make things right the best thing in the world?" Patti's optimism and warmth wrapped around Jaq like a fleece blanket. The older woman softly thumped Jaq's back, then crossed the tent and reached into one of the bags pulling out an orange. She handed it to Jaq.

"Here. Eat this. Sweet and sour will wake up your dormant taste buds—and Vitamin C is good for you." She grinned at Jaq and matter-of-factly brushed her cheek to wipe away the traces of tears there.

Jaq cupped the round treasure in her hands, breathing in the tangy aroma. Everything would be alright somehow. But she had to get home. Soon. She had to fix things.

CHAPTER 10

JAQ DUG her fingers under the surface of the orange as she walked slowly away from Patti's tent, thinking. Fragrant oil sprayed up from the shiny peel where it tore. Her mouth watered.

"Hey." A dark form suddenly blocked her.

Jaq had an unexpected close-up of Craig's chest. She stumbled to keep from bumping up against him.

"Gah! You scared me to death." She stepped back, irritated that orange juice now ran through her fingers and down her arm. Jaq unclenched her hand. *Bleh.*

"Sorry." Craig squinted at her. "Crying." It wasn't a question. He frowned. "Patti can be brutal. She means well. But I remember it was rough." His dark eyes showed a glimmer of something, then went back to the flat stare she most often saw there.

"Yeah." Jaq rubbed the back of her hand across her eyes self-consciously. "She's harsh in a fluffy bunny sort of way."

Craig perfected the awkward pause. His neck convulsed in a dry swallow.

"Anyway." Jaq dragged out the word, waiting for him to say

something. She wiped her hand on her shirt. She just wanted to eat the orange.

He blinked and moved his lips as if trying to recall something rehearsed. Nodding, he spoke. "There's someone else coming out here to join your pack. R.J. might be around a lot watching the new student—Patti said there'll be trouble with this one."

"Oh." That made Jaq curious. Then she noticed how Craig seemed to shrink away from her. "So. What you're saying is...?"

"I'll try." His pointy shoulder rose.

"To help me, right? I have to get out of here. I already know the problem and now I gotta go fix it. I'm worried about my sister." Fresh tears blurred her view of his face—she could feel him trying to back out.

"I know." He glanced behind him. "Sorry. I want to help. I just don't know..."

He was giving up. Just like that. Craig was a coward. He reminded Jaq of an abused dog—skinny and skittish with those shuttered eyes that hid something. But he was her only chance at getting away from this wilderness weirdness and back to her family where she was needed.

She reached up and patted Craig's shoulder. White, dusty residue from her orange ended up on his dark sweatshirt. He flinched like she knew he would.

Jaq stepped closer, speaking low and soothing. "I trust you —you'll find a way to get me what I need. All I really need is a compass and a few coordinates. I can do the rest myself. Please?"

His breathing had quickened. Jaq blinked up at him, leaning closer.

"Mick has a compass." Craig's voice sounded hoarse. He pushed his fingers into his hairline.

"I know."

"Take his." He took a shaky breath and stepped away from her.

Jaq groaned and dropped her shoulders. Seduction was not on the menu today.

"That's it? Your way of helping is to tell me to get into Mick's heavily guarded pack and rifle around until I find his compass?" She glared, passing the orange back and forth between her hands. Frustration flared up under Jaq's skin. "Fine. I will. I don't need your help then. Whatever." She narrowed her eyes and started to turn away.

Craig frowned and caught one of her arms, making her face him. "If he catches you, he'll punish you. Might take away your blanket privilege or some of your rations. Or worse, extend your program." The warning came in his responsible adult voice.

"Thanks, Helpful." Jaq sneered and pulled out of his grip in disgust. He was useless. "I don't need you." She threw a look over her shoulder and saw him deflate in either relief that he was off the hook or failure.

Fan-freakin'-tastic. She was on her own. As always.

"Be careful."

Jaq heard him but kept walking, kicking rocks as she went.

———

It was probably near ten in the morning and they had already been hiking for a few hours. She was hungry again. The sweet, tangy orange had only seemed to heighten her appetite.

Mick marched ahead; his pack neatly tied to his back. Jaq wondered how to get into it and take his compass. Her mind spun, thinking about the hours of walking it would take. If she left early in the morning, she'd be in civilization before dark. Hopefully. But could she do it alone?

The unforgiving wilderness punished her with the uneven

ground and cold air. Jaq tripped over a rock and grabbed at the nearest thing to keep from falling on her face. Russ's pack slid off one shoulder in her grasp.

"Whoa. You okay?" His half smile made her cheeks warm.

"Sorry." Jaq helped him reposition his pack. "I'm not really in the zone." When she wasn't plotting how to get Mick's compass, each plan more ridiculous than the last, Flower's letter filled her thoughts. She had to go back and make things right. It felt futile with no outside help, but she had to try. She had to get into Mick's pack tonight.

"Thinking, huh? Patti's cool." He slowed his pace so that he walked beside Jaq.

"Yeah. I'm sort of mad and sad and freaked out over what she said. But it was good." Jaq wanted to be as honest as Flower's letter was. Funny how she'd tricked herself into thinking that she was no longer pretending now that she wasn't Happy Cheerleader Barbie. But her rebellion wasn't necessarily the true her either. She wasn't sure who she was.

Russ gave her a long look and a shy smile tugged up on one side. He turned his head quickly to hide it.

"What?" Jaq smacked at his arm. "What was that look for?"

Russ shook his head. "Nothing." A nervous chuckle in his throat gave him away.

"C'mon! What?"

He slanted a glance her way, not slowing his stride, then focused beyond her and lifted his brows. "Hey, a whole herd." He pointed behind Jaq.

Jaq turned to see several mule deer standing stock still, staring at them. Their grayish-brown coats blended into the landscape, making them appear like ghostly outlines. Large ears twitched as if picking up radio signals from the air, and then they ambled away from the two humans, seemingly unimpressed.

"They look delicious." Jaq breathed out, imagining roasted meat. "Is that wrong?"

"Right there with you," Russ said, his voice low and intense. "Wish I had my knife. I could eat just about anything at this point."

For some reason Jaq felt her stomach flop at his tone. He was so caveman sometimes. She blushed.

Russ didn't seem to notice. They continued to trudge along. "I'm setting up a Paiute deadfall trap when we get into camp. I've noticed tons of mouse tracks around."

"Weird... even that sounds like heaven right now." Jaq laughed, hoping to ease her awkwardness. By now, she couldn't deny that she was attracted to Russ.

Finn caught up to them, breathing hard. "I don't feel great."

"What's wrong?" Russ asked, his brows pushed together.

"I want a cheeseburger. Or... some medical marijuana. No—curly fries." Finn pushed the heels of his hands into his eyes with a groan.

Russ laughed. "Super nachos."

"Oreo milkshake and chicken fajitas," Jaq murmured.

Daniel hiked just ahead and must have heard them. He shouted over his shoulder. "Deep dish pizza. Chicago style. Tons of cheese and meat toppings with an icy Coke."

The group had clumped together by now. Mick and Katie smiled at one another as they listened.

"Steak, bleeding," Mick added firmly.

"Chocolate." Katie sighed.

Jaq's stomach growled. Thinking of food made her think of the real world. In just over a week, the intensity of the wilderness had erased the crisp edges of her reality. It seemed as if she'd been living in the dust and brush for months, with the quiet sounds of nature as her only soundtrack.

Jaq looked down at her filthy clothes. "A shower," she moaned.

Grunts of agreement sounded around her.

"Makeup," she added.

"Yes. Definitely." Finn nodded. "I feel naked without it."

"Great. I just pictured that," Daniel grumbled.

Russ shook his head and smiled over at Jaq.

She suddenly wanted him to say she didn't need makeup to be beautiful. "But seriously, I miss my makeup."

Russ opened his mouth as if he would say something, but he shut it again.

"I bet you do. You're probably one of those girls with fifty different profile pictures online, making kissy faces with globs of lip gloss or looking surprised at the camera—like 'Oops! You caught me being sexy!'" Daniel mocked with a breathy, high voice meant to sound like a girl. "I bet you have a bunch of pictures of you climbing all over your girlfriends and making faces. Am I right?"

"Shut up, Daniel." Jaq felt her face redden. He wasn't exactly wrong.

He laughed and nodded. "Got you pegged."

"Said Mr. Cliche Jock." Jaq snorted, giving Daniel a scowl. She turned away, determined to ignore the boy for the rest of the evening.

———

Getting to the new campsite, Number Nine, required climbing up a steep rocky ledge. The sun slanted low in the sky and Jaq's legs felt heavy. Her hands, stiff with cold, felt raw from grasping jagged rocks to keep her balance. It was hard to breathe. She leaned over, her legs planted wide for stability as she tried to catch her breath only a few steps from a fifteen-foot drop that yawned to one side. A sudden swooshing in her stomach made her dizzy. Her skin prickled and she felt lightheaded.

"You okay back there?" Mick called down to her.

"I think so," she answered, her words choked.

"Almost there, Princess." Daniel was somewhere behind her. Everyone else had gone ahead.

"I can't move." Jaq stared at the drop to the side of her, frozen. Nausea rose from her stomach.

Daniel made an impatient noise in his throat.

Jaq's vision blurred and closed in like the shutter of an old camera. A buzzing sound crescendoed in her ears. In slow motion, she slumped forward and stumbled, her feet losing their place on the rock.

Blackness. Then the sounds of shouting and a vague sense that she was emerging from a terrible dream. Something hurt. And everything had a muzzy muffled texture—sound and sight through a dense fog.

Daniel stared down at her, eyes wide. His hand clamped hard around one of her wrists. Jaq's knees were on fire. She realized with horror that she was dangling over the drop with only one knee on a ledge and Daniel's hand stopping her from falling. Craggy rocks gaped below her like teeth in open jaws. Her heart thrashed under her shirt.

"Hang on," Daniel growled, sweat rose on his forehead. "Hey! I need help!" he yelled, his light eyes intense and frantic.

A scrambling sound of heavy footfalls over rock and then Mick's and Russ's heads appeared above her, the same wild look in their eyes. Mick reached down and hooked Jaq under her other arm, his powerful chest heaving.

"Pull," he barked through his teeth.

Mick and Daniel grunted, Jaq's legs scrambled for footing.

She screamed when she felt herself slipping. "Help!" She dangled, heavy, with no strength of her own.

Daniel reached out with his other hand and yanked. Jaq's shoulders popped and ached, while the front of her body burned from being scraped over rocks. Then she was in Mick's large arms, shaking and crying.

"I don't know what happened. I was so..." Her teeth chattered too much to continue.

"I have you. It's okay," Mick's low voice soothed.

Jaq wiped her tears and pressed one cheek against Mick's thumping heartbeat. Her own heart beat so fast it was hard to take a breath. She felt sick in her stomach and dizzy. After a few moments, Jaq looked up. Her eyes met Daniel's, and he let out his breath in a burst. His hands shook. His face was red and wore a stiff frown. Daniel turned away and clamored up the rocks to where Finn and Katie stood watching, their faces masks of shock.

Jaq squeezed her eyes shut. That was almost very bad. Mick set her on a large rock, keeping one hand on her shoulder to steady her. He clapped a wide hand over his shaved head and blew through his mouth.

Russ watched, his fists clenched together, shoulders rising and falling with his lungs. "Y-y- you." He closed his mouth and swallowed before trying again. His face was lined with effort. He ran one hand over his mouth and breathed out his nose. "You... could have d-d-d—" He stopped abruptly, grimaced, and gave a short groan of frustration. He swallowed air and shook his head.

Jaq's shock was starting to wear off, and she realized with amazement that everyone was as shaken and freaked as her. Even Daniel. As Russ turned and hurried away over the rocks, as if he didn't want her to see him lose it, she knew this was the first time she'd seen him upset.

Katie rushed over and gave her a hug. "That was terrifying," she breathed and stepped back.

"Yeah." Jaq shivered, the adrenaline still surging through her veins. Everyone seemed to really give a crap, and it made her feel like crying hysterically. She took a deep breath and bit her lip.

Mick sighed. "You gave us a scare. You okay?"

"My knees hurt and I'm shaky." She rotated her shoulders. "Ow."

"I'll help you the rest of the way. We're almost there. Then you have to eat something." Mick rubbed his stubble, and the crinkles around his eyes deepened. "Let's go."

———

Within half an hour, Mick had Jaq up at the new campsite on the bluff. The rest of the group already sat on logs surrounding a fire pit lined with stones. Russ bent over the kindling, using the back of Finn's knife to strike sparks off a flint stone. His knife had never been found.

Jaq sank down onto the log. Blood showed through ragged tears in the knees of her long johns. She lifted her shirt to examine the scrapes on her belly. Her whole body felt sore and weak. Ugh. The smell of blood made her sick.

Russ made a hissing sound. "That looks painful."

Jaq dropped the shirt back down over her exposed skin. "It's not too bad."

Katie crouched beside Jaq and cleaned her wounds with an antiseptic wipe. It stung. She had bandages too. There was something very comforting about the clean, civilized first aid supplies she pulled from her bag.

"Didn't know you had that stuff. Thought I'd be tearing bits off my petticoat to bind my wounds." Jaq smiled to cover a wince.

Katie laughed and patted Jaq's leg. "There you go. The scrapes aren't deep. I'm so glad it wasn't worse. Told you you're strong."

Jaq took it easy while the boys got the fire going and set up their bed rolls before disappearing into the woods—probably setting traps or practicing other skills. Mick was nowhere in sight, and she assumed he was gathering more wood. She eyed his pack as she chewed and swallowed that last of the improvised trail mix of raw oats and raisins that Mick had given her. Heart beating hard, she glanced around and prepared to dart over to where the pack sat.

Then Russ was there, setting a billycan of lentils on the fire. He moved so quietly Jaq had not heard him approach. He lowered himself onto the log beside Jaq.

Jaq settled back down, disappointment and relief flooding her.

"You okay?" Russ clasped his tanned hands together, his elbows resting on his knees.

"Yeah. I don't know what happened back there. Fainting is a first." Jaq's embarrassment over being the center of attention was made worse by the fact that she hated to seem like a wimp.

Russ nodded. "Lack of food and sleep. You're exhausted." He took a deep breath and looked directly into her eyes. His cheekbones showed a rising redness.

"What about you? You seemed kinda freaked." Jaq prodded his ribs softly with a finger. She wanted him to tell her all the ways he cared.

"Yeah. I saw you go over. I th-thought—" He pressed his lips together and blinked slowly. "You... were g-going to fall all the way." Russ swallowed, took a breath, and then glanced at her, his eyes sharp. He hesitated before saying, "You may... have noticed. Sometimes I don't—I can't get my words out."

Jaq raised her brows in question. "What do you mean?" Russ examined the back of his hands self-consciously.

Russ spoke carefully. "When I was a kid, I st-stuttered pretty bad." He made a frustrated sound in his throat. "Super embarrassing. People think you're stupid if you can't speak normally." His head hung a little. "But I was determined. And after years of speech therapy—most people don't seem to notice."

"I never would have guessed." Jaq thought about how deliberately he spoke and had always assumed it was confidence. He wasn't really chatty and maybe this was why.

His face grew redder. "Yeah? N-never—" He coughed to cover the stammer and Jaq realized she's seen him do that before. "Never noticed?" Russ finished. A shy smile lifted one side of his face, and he peeked at her from under his dark lashes. Somehow he just got sweeter.

"No." She let her face soften.

He let out a deep breath. "It comes out sometimes." He shrugged as if to apologize. "If I'm really tired—or upset. Or nervous. But mostly I just don't say much if I feel it coming on."

"So the more emotional you are, the less you say. How did that work out with Patti?" Jaq tried to ease his discomfort by being matter-of-fact.

Russ laughed. "She's patient. I mostly just sat there staring at her—feeling like I was seven years old again in front of my class at school while everyone l-laughed because I couldn't for the life of me say George W-washington." He enunciated the name with care.

"Aw. That's sad." Jaq frowned, a little flutter in her chest. She pictured a little boy version of Russ, his dark eyes wide with embarrassment.

"Not fun. Never lived it down." Russ snorted a mirthless laugh.

Jaq gave a sympathetic grin. "I'm impressed that you overcame that."

"Mostly." He lifted a shoulder. "I felt kind of stupid when —I sort of lost it when you f-f—" Russ paused to clench his jaw, his Adam's apple bobbed. "Fell."

"Don't worry about it. I'm flattered that you were reduced to stuttering just for me."

Russ opened his mouth as if to say something but instead he gazed at her with his chocolaty eyes making Jaq's insides melt. She tucked her long blonde bangs behind her ear and stared back. Words were so overrated.

"Hey." Daniel approached the fire and looked down at Jaq, shifting his gaze to Russ with mild irritation.

"Hi." Jaq smiled at him. He had sort of saved her life. This was weird.

"You feeling okay?" The usually overconfident athlete looked uncomfortable, as if being nice was like speaking a foreign language.

Jaq nodded. "Thanks."

Daniel mussed his sandy blond hair and shrugged. "No big deal." He actually blushed. "Dang, you're heavy, girl. Good thing I have nuclear arms." He flexed a bicep and grinned, and Jaq was relieved that they could be insulting again.

"Well, normally I wouldn't let you touch me with a ten-foot pole, much less your hands." She wrinkled her nose in mock disgust.

Daniel's brows shot up and he gave a wicked grin. "Ten foot? I'm flattered."

Jaq groaned and laughed in spite of herself. "Oh my gosh. You're horrible."

"I know." Daniel winked and then his face sobered. "You're

welcome." He didn't seem to know what to do with his hands, so he folded his arms across his chest.

Russ stood and wandered off, as if to give them a moment.

Jaq eyed the boy who was both annoying and attractive. He had saved her from falling. Was he capable of what she had suspected him of?

"Was it you?" Jaq needed to know once and for all.

"What?"

"In my sleep... I woke up and someone was touching me. Someone was on top of me." She stared into his eyes, looking for the truth.

Daniel winced. A look of disgust crossed his face. "I wouldn't do that to someone." He said it with so much conviction Jaq's stomach flipped. "Ever." Abruptly, he stood and walked away.

Jaq wasn't sure why, but she believed Daniel. He was hiding something, like she'd suspected. But not for something he had done—for something that had been done to him. She just knew it.

The unexpected rumble of a four-wheeler sounded in the distance. Jaq's heart jumped. If Craig was coming, maybe she could talk him into helping her—with her injuries, he might take pity.

Coming from the opposite direction of the climb they had just made, a trail of dust rose up. Mick and Katie walked to meet the four-wheeler as it approached with the grayish wolf-like dog, Always, loping behind it, red tongue lolling out of its mouth.

R.J. sat astride the roaring machine, his dark peppered hair stiff and wayward, his icy eyes in slits. A tan duster coat hung across his rigid shoulders and billowed with wind. Only when he had dismounted like a cowboy after a long ride did Jaq notice the girl tucked behind him.

This must be the new kid that Craig had told her about. She was trouble? The girl was petite, on the scrawny side with scraggly, dyed green hair in a grown-out pixie cut. Freckles sprinkled her narrow face, and her eyes were large and cow-like.

After a murmured conversation R.J., Mick and Katie led the girl toward the rest of the group, which had gathered around the fire, watching with curious anticipation. R.J. put his hands on the frail girl's shoulders and propelled her in front of him, stopping when he reached them.

"This is Erica," R.J. rasped in his Clint Eastwood voice. "She's a part of your group now. Her own group graduated but she needed a little extra time to pass off the requirements."

"Hi." Finn smiled at Erica.

Her face, which had been expressionless up to that point, twisted into a sneer. Wordless, she lifted her middle finger at them. Jaq stared in disbelief.

"How long have you been out here? You look like crap," Daniel said with a defensive scowl of his own at her open hostility.

"She's been here for eight weeks," R.J. answered with a warning in his voice.

Lesson learned. That could be any of them. Failure to pass any of the requirements, or displeasing the trail leaders, could lead to an endless purgatory in the badlands. Jaq shuddered. The sooner she could escape, the better.

————

Later that night Jaq pretended to sleep. When all seemed quiet, she opened her eyes and stared into the crackling embers of what was left of the fire. She shifted her eyes to the sleeping forms rising and falling with breath in the darkness around her.

Nervous, she wondered if she could get to Mick's pack without waking anyone. She turned to where the large man had put his bedroll and her heart jumped. Mick was awake, sitting with his back toward her, silently staring out into the night. Jaq wasn't sure if it should make her feel safe or creeped out.

Turning onto her side, she sighed. A charred log in the fire pit popped, and she watched the sparks rise like fireflies. Getting that compass was not going to be easy. She'd have to wait for the right opportunity. She yawned, her eyelids heavy with fatigue. Maybe tomorrow.

CHAPTER 11

"SHUT UP! I hate you! Don't freakin' tell me what to do!" Erica screeched as she stomped away from Mick.

A shiver of irritation shot through Jaq. The girl had been arguing and whining all morning. She continued rolling up her things and shot a look over at Finn, who stared open mouthed at the spazzing, red-faced girl who gave a whole new meaning to the term crack-skinny.

"Stop," Mick barked. He had never shown any sharpness or temper before.

Erica looked like a homeless waif—short, faded green hair stuck up like wild grass with auburn roots, her torn jeans drooping away from her emaciated frame. Her filthy IBSA t-shirt was too large. Erica's body trembled, and she clenched and unclenched her fists in frustrated fury, sputtering obscenities in a low seething voice.

A gray sky pressed down on the group, the perfect setting for the mood. Everyone avoided each other's eyes. Erica had brought some seriously bad vibes with her. Jaq had rarely met someone who bugged her more.

"Come. Here. Now." Mick's powerful shoulders heaved

like a lid pulsing on top of a boiling, steaming pot. His face was hard cut and grim, color in his cheeks.

It was a little terrifying. Jaq looked away, wondering what was going to happen—she hated screaming fights. It reminded her of that month before her mother left. She focused on her hands as they tied the required knots on her bedroll.

"Holy hell," Finn breathed out, just loud enough for Jaq to hear. He leaned close to her, a frown on his usually pert face. "She is way scary."

"Seriously."

"No! Make me," Erica shouted, contorting her face into a scrunched-up sneer. She bent, grabbed a rock, and hucked it at Mick without hesitation.

The big man was quick, ducking out of the way, his eyes wide in amazement and then warning. "Do you ever want to go home?" he growled.

Erica ran.

"Really? What is she, twelve?" Daniel scowled, watching Erica as she darted over rocks and dirt away from them.

Mick let out a groan and took off after her.

"Yikes. It's like watching Wild Kingdom." He switched to a British accent. "The North American grizzly bear is unexpectedly fast for his enormous size..."

Russ let out a chuckle. "Wow."

Daniel plopped down on a log. "Crazy b—" Daniel noticed Katie and stopped to avoid restarting his no swearing day-count. "That chick is worse than Princess here."

"Thanks." Jaq's sarcastic tone made Daniel grin. "Please tell me I am nothing like that," she muttered.

"Not even close." Russ appeared, his pack already on, one hand shielding his eyes from the early morning sun that slanted in bright rays into his face. "Got her."

"The grizzly captures the scrawniest and weakest of the

pack and drags her back to his cave to feed his young ones..." Finn narrated.

Jaq glanced in the same direction in time to see Mick returning to the group with a kicking and squealing Erica over one shoulder.

"Shut up." Mick's voice boomed. Somehow the scrappy green-haired girl had cracked his calm strength, revealing a temper.

Katie trotted toward him and helped lower his prey to the ground. Erica thrashed and battered against his massive chest with her tiny fists.

"Okay. Okay. That's enough. It's okay. Erica. Erica." Katie's soothing voice rose over the wild girl's verbal assault.

Mick took the attack with an angry face that slowly melted into amusement. Exhausted, Erica let Katie pull her away from him. Erica snorted and spasmed into tears as Katie dragged her several feet away from Mick.

"I—hate that. I h-hate!" Erica hiccupped and savagely scrubbed away the evidence of her tears, hardening into fury again. "Never touch me." Venom seemed to drip from every word, her huge eyes squeezed into burning slits directed at Mick. She was like a cobra waiting to strike.

Mick heaved a sigh, calming. "I won't. If you never run. If you want to ever go home, you have to stop losing it like this. Just do what you're supposed to."

Erica looked away, staring out across the barren landscape. Katie patted her back.

"Okay, everyone, pack up." Katie waved toward camp.

Jaq stood up, brushed dirt from her legs, and swung the bedroll onto her back. Last night Erica had been so silent, going to bed almost immediately. Jaq had almost hoped she'd have a female ally, but there was nothing tolerable about the girl. She was wildly defiant... Maybe she'd be useful after all.

Reluctant, Jaq made her way over to Erica, where she stood staring and shaking with her back to the group.

"Hey. You seem ready to bolt," Jaq observed, trying to sound offhand.

Erica snorted. "Run, run as fast as you can..." Erica whispered in a broken and ragged voice.

"I want to run too."

"Just obey like a good little robot and you'll get home soon enough." Erica glanced at Jaq, her face like glass—hard and in danger of shattering any moment.

"Sooner would be better for me." Jaq wondered how she could get this girl to steal the compass for her, not wanting to risk getting caught herself.

Erica growled and turned away in dismissal.

"What about you?" Jaq hoped her voice sounded suitably commiserative. "You want to leave too, right? You've been out here forever."

The frail girl pushed a shaking fist against her mouth, a choking sound in her throat. Something between a chuckle and a sob escaped her lips. "Why the hell would I ever want to go home?"

That sent a cold jolt through Jaq's chest. Erica walked away, her small, rigid body radiating ferocious fragility. This was better than home? Jaq shivered. She didn't want to know.

The hike went by in a dreamlike repetition of so many other days. But it was colder. The sun, which had peeked out of gathering clouds in bright rays earlier, became smothered under mounds of dark gray by noon. Goosebumps prickled all over Jaq's body as an icy wind swirled around her in a gust.

Cold, tired, and thrown off balance by the new addition to

the group, nobody had been talkative. They trudged along, silent, stoically ignoring the misery because there was nothing they could do about any of it.

Another camp—rocks, dirt, fire pit. It didn't matter that it was a nondescript barren place; it was a reason to stop, which made it heaven. Mick instructed them to unpack, relax awhile and then later there would be a group meeting.

Jaq plopped down near Daniel, her feet aching. He smoothed his bedroll out on the ground and reached into his supply bag, stirring around and pulling things out.

"Might as well write my journal entry now. Get it over with," he muttered, pulling out his curriculum book.

Jaq nodded. Good idea. She'd been writing the minimum required paragraph each night, not saying much. But as she wrapped the wool blanket around her, she thought about Flower again—and how true her letter had been. She wanted to express herself like that. Nobody else had to read it.

"Whoa. Oops. This isn't mine." Daniel flipped through the pages of the orange spiral bound book, then he stopped and stared, a smile spreading across his face.

"Hey—don't read that. Whose is it?" Jaq leaned closer, curious.

Daniel didn't answer at first. He pointed a finger to the page to save his place and looked up at her, a wicked gleam in his hazel eyes. "I must have accidentally switched books with Russ." His gaze flicked back down to the book.

"That is so not cool!" Jaq looked around guiltily for Russ, wanting to read it herself. There was so much she didn't know about him—he was so quiet. The dark-eyed boy was nowhere in sight. Probably using a bush somewhere. But she didn't need to picture that.

"Oh, Princess. You gotta read this." Daniel snickered, pushing the book into Jaq's hands.

"No! I'm not going to—" Jaq caught sight of her name, scrawled in sloppy boy writing. *Okay, just a page, then.*

"*I want to say something to Jaq. But with my luck I would never get it out of my mouth. I could tell her without speaking. But maybe this isn't the time or place. I'm here for other reasons. Sometimes I forget the reason I'm here. I like forgetting. She makes me forget.*"

Jaq's heart was doing ridiculous things in her chest—pounding, jumping. She let out a breath and glanced at Daniel, who looked completely evil—he would never let Russ live this down. She blushed and frowned at herself for reading Russ's private thoughts and at Daniel for whatever he intended to do with this information.

"What a dork," Daniel whispered almost triumphantly, misinterpreting her frown. He continued to read over her shoulder, his face too close to hers. But Jaq didn't care—she was too eager to read more.

Jaq promised herself she would only finish the page.

"*I literally heard a song in my head today. It was like actually wearing earphones. I was watching Jaq as she messed around with her bow-drill set and laughing with Finn. He makes her smile. And a stupid song came in my head that I don't even like. Seriously, the entire song ran through my head, and all of the sudden the lyrics meant something to me. It was all about Jaq.*"

Jaq gasped in embarrassment and shut the book. Her stomach somersaulted and a red-hot blush spread up her neck and over her face.

Daniel's laugh was harsh and mocking. "Wow! That's hilarious. I bet the song is some totally lame stoner song."

"Hey. Stop it. Go give it back to him, Daniel," Jaq muttered, breathless. She got up and walked out into the brush, watching her feet scuff through the dirt, leaving Daniel to chuckle to himself at Russ's expense. Jaq couldn't get away from the uncomfortable banging in her chest. *Russ.* Just thinking about Russ, so quiet and steady, bursting with feelings like that sent a thrill through her whole body.

She couldn't face him while she felt like this. So, of course she ran right into him. Russ sat on a large rock, knees bent, staring out to the horizon. The cold breeze ruffled his dark hair and brought color to his face.

Jaq's heart flipped. She swallowed, wondering if she had time to back away—but his eyes caught hers.

"Hey. I was going to do some whittling, but I forgot that my knife is still missing." Russ shrugged, so casual and unaware of the party going on in Jaq's stomach.

"You can borrow mine," she blurted, pulling the knife out of the sheath at her waist. Keeping her eyes averted, she held the blade out to Russ.

"Thanks." His voice sounded a little questioning, as if he just realized she was acting weird.

They were quiet for a while as Russ tried out her knife. Jaq dared to look and saw his adorable mouth purse in concentration as he dragged the blade over a stick, peeling scraps of dark, papery bark from its surface. Her heart thumped. She wanted to kiss him; his mouth looked too good to resist. Russ looked up as if Jaq's stare touched his face.

"What?" He held the knife over his project, forgotten.

Why not go for it? Jaq smiled, slow and infused with meaning. There was no way he could mistake this for anything other than a direct flirt.

Russ swallowed and studied the knees of his jeans, a little smile playing around his mouth. Jaq sat beside him on the large rock.

"Nothing." Jaq felt bold. He had written about her, and she

knew how he felt. She leaned toward Russ until their shoulders touched. "What're you making?"

Russ seemed surprised that he had something in his hands. "Oh. Um. New drill. Bow-drill." He waved the knife a little and carved another chunk from the tip of the stick.

He was using as few words as possible. That meant Russ was afraid he'd stutter. He was nervous.

"Cool." Jaq turned so that her face was close to his. Sean, back home, had loved it when she was aggressive. "I want you to kiss me," she said.

Russ flinched. He glanced up through his dark lashes into her eyes for a short moment and set down his whittling. "Oh," Russ expressed in a soft gasp. He closed his eyes and leaned back onto the rock, keeping his knees bent. He covered his eyes with one hand.

Jaq's stomach dropped. *Oops.* Maybe the direct approach was a bad idea. Her face burned, and she cleared her throat. "Okay. Sorry. I totally embarrassed you. You don't have to—"

Russ let out a breathy, "Ha." His fingers parted so he could peek through them. "N-no, I'm j… just excited." He grinned and turned his head toward her.

Jaq laughed, relieved. "Aw." She leaned over him. "That's so cute. And honest."

Russ pushed up onto his elbow, his shy look settling into an actual smolder, dark gaze pulling on her insides like magnets. He raised one hand to the back of Jaq's head and slowly pressed her face closer to his own. Then he held Jaq there, locking eyes with her.

"Well, are you going to kiss me?" Jaq whispered, her voice shaky for some reason.

"P-probably." His lips curled up on one side. From this close, Jaq could feel the vibration of his heartbeat and see the caramel spokes in his chocolate eyes. *Yum.*

"Seriously?" Daniel's voice barked, shattering the moment.

Jaq jerked away from Russ. A very annoyed-looking jock stood with his hands on his hips, glaring at them from a few yards away.

"So all of that she-reminds-me-of-a-lame-song crap actually worked on you?" Daniel's look of disgust made Jaq's blood simmer.

She darted a look at Russ. He had a shocked look of dismay on his face. He sat up.

"What are you talking about?" he said to Daniel.

"Oh... sh-oops." Daniel laughed. "She read your journal, dude. It totally cracked us up."

Jaq picked up her knife as if in warning. "Shut up. Speak for yourself," she fumed, not daring to see Russ's reaction. It was horrifying. Like the time when Jaq thought she had to strip in front of the boys on that first night in the cabin. That night, Russ had rescued her from that embarrassment. But this time, he was the one who was the most exposed. She had done that.

Russ jumped down from the rock and stalked away before Jaq's apology could materialize in the fog of her distress.

"Great, Daniel." All she could do was focus her anger at her snooping accomplice.

"What?" He shrugged in pretended confusion.

"You are such a—"

"Watch your language!" Daniel wagged a finger, gloating.

"Jerk." Jaq sheathed her knife and shook her head. What was she going to say to Russ?

———

Russ avoided her completely. That night was so cold that Jaq could see her own breath in white puffs. It was as if the frigid air was a direct result of the cold shoulder Russ had given her.

The group surrounded the fire. Mick squinted into the dark, clouded sky. "Tonight, we initiate fire watch. The temperature is dropping, and we need to keep the fire going all night. Each of us will take two-hour shifts. Use my watch." He undid his wristwatch and handed it to Russ. "You have first watch. After two hours, wake up Jaq, and then she will get Daniel up. Daniel, you wake Erica." He scanned the group huddling around the fire with blankets. He shot a warning glare at Erica. "Do not allow the fire to die down."

They all agreed to the arrangement. Everyone found a spot to bed down. Erica remained silent, her eyes flicking around, nervous and accusing. Jaq pitied her.

Finn added some wood to the fire and settled down beside it with authority. "I am the fire keeper. Hear my tale." He swept a dramatic gaze around the group, holding up his hands for silence. "Long ago there were two mice named Tito and Ray. Little did they know that they were destined to be roasted and eaten by a group of starving survivors." He nodded in the direction of the area where Russ had set up several Paiute deadfall traps.

They listened with amusement as Finn spun a ridiculous story about the two doomed mice. Soon everyone except Erica was snuggled closer to the fire and laughing. Finn had a gift for humorous storytelling.

When he was finished, a peaceful quiet settled over the group. Coyotes yelped in the distance and the fire crackled in a soothing way. Katie sat close to Jaq and leaned against her shoulder.

"Everyone share one thing that has hurt them. Something that, even if long ago, still brings up emotions when you remember it."

A collective groan went around the fire circle.

Katie smiled. "Okay, I'll start." She trailed a line in the dirt with her finger. "When I was six years old, things were really hard because my mom was sick with cancer. I came home from school one day and my dad was in his pickup truck. There were boxes in the back. He said, 'I gotta go, kiddo. I'll see you on your birthday.'" Katie paused and her breath hitched. "I never saw him again. He left us. Just like that—when we needed him most."

Jaq looked over at Katie as she wiped a tear from her cheek. "That really sucks," she said. "What happened with your mom?"

"Well, she went into remission and we sorta survived without him. It wasn't easy."

Katie patted Jaq's knee. "Anyone else want to share something?" She looked around the group, the firelight glinting in her eyes. "C'mon."

Russ cleared his throat as if he might say something but then lowered his head. Daniel noticed. As if it were a competition, he spoke up with a smirk

on his face like he'd won something.

"My dad punched me once when I mouthed off at him. Still pisses me off," Daniel said.

Katie nodded. "Most people feel safest showing anger when they're hurt."

From the look on Daniel's face, he was about to say something brutal to the sweet college girl, so Jaq blurted, "My brother stole my stuffed animal."

"Wow, how did you ever survive?" Daniel fired at his new target.

"Hey, it was upsetting." She wouldn't go into the details of the way Brian terrorized her.

There was an uncomfortable pause.

"One time I got pantsed at school and everyone in the cafeteria saw my bum." Finn shuddered. "Sometimes when I slip into the abyss of my self-loathing I remember the look of horror on Becky Stanton's face." His dramatic words were followed by a mischievous grin.

Jake let out a chuckle. "We all have our crosses to *bare*—pun intended."

With that the mood shifted. There were laughs of exhaustion and then more silence as the sky darkened. The stars beamed like countless faraway flashlights. Jaq imagined angels on a mass search party for lost souls. *We're down here.*

After a while, Katie sang folksy songs in a gentle, lovely voice. It was comforting. Jaq's eyes grew heavy. She hoped Russ would let her explain—forgive her about the journal. She wanted to show him that she was not mocking him. He'd had enough of that in his life. As her mind drifted into sleep Katie's voice echoed as if from far away an old James Taylor song about good and bad times, loneliness and loss.

CHAPTER 12

WHATEVER JAQ'S DREAM WAS, it evaporated into the dark. It was so cold. Somebody gripped her arms, murmuring something she could not understand. The hands moved to her shoulders. *Not again!* Jaq sat up in alarm.

"Get off me, perv!" Jaq growled, pulling back to focus on the dark figure that loomed over her. The orange light from the fire lit half a face. *No.* "You?" Jaq's heart tried to stop.

"Me what? I think you were having a bad dream." Russ frowned down on her, shadows making his eyes look evil and hollowed out.

"Nice try. I'm pretty sure that I wasn't dreaming your hands all over me." Her surprise and disappointment to find Russ groping her as she slept turned into anger.

He stared. Russ rocked back from his knees onto his haunches. He held up his hands. "Geez, Jaq. I-I..."

When he didn't say anything else, Jaq rushed on before he could overcome his evident stutter attack to defend himself. "Just because I asked for a kiss doesn't mean you have an invitation to the whole party. And if I'd known you were my nighttime molester, I would never have even thought about kissing you! By the way, I totally take it back. I don't want you to kiss me. Perv." Although Jaq was upset, she kept her voice low and grating, not wanting to wake everyone.

"M-molester? S-somebody—who?" Russ gritted his teeth. "I've n-never. Never."

Jaq sat up, breathing shallow. "Russ. Did you kiss me or touch me while I was asleep?" She wanted to hear a straight confession. If Russ was some quiet weirdo who wrote about her and fantasized about her—and was too shy to approach her while she was awake—she needed to know.

Russ folded his arms across his chest. "Never. If I"—he swallowed, saying each word with force—"could get a w-word in! Your turn. For fire watch." He thrust Mick's wristwatch toward her. It glinted a reflection of the nearby flames.

Jaq's mind turned inside-out with an embarrassed realization. He'd been shaking her awake. She grabbed the watch, unable to say anything. Jaq let out a rough breath. So much for reconciling with him over her journal invasion. Wow. By now he must hate her. Was it too late to re-invite him to kiss her? Jaq cringed at herself.

Her eyes had adjusted better to the dark and Russ's face remained in a frown as he studied her. She waited for his anger.

Russ took a deep breath. His voice came out low and steady with no stutter. "Did someone really do that to you? Out here?"

Huh? It took Jaq a second to realize he wasn't about to tell her off.

"Yes. I thought it was Daniel. But I don't think so anymore. I don't know. I doubt I'm the best judge of character. I hardly know my own." Jaq ran a hand through her hair and scooted closer to the fire. "Two hours, right?"

"Yeah. Then wake Daniel for his turn." Russ' brow bunched. He was clearly bothered by what Jaq had said, but he didn't ask for details.

"Terrific. Me shaking him awake. He's going to like that way too much," Jaq snarled.

Russ covered his mouth and Jaq realized he stifled a chuckle.

"Who wouldn't?" Russ had a smile in his voice.

Jaq looked over at him. He pulled a blanket tight across his shoulders, sitting with his knees up, ankles crossed. She felt forgiven when he grinned at her.

Dang. He was cute.

"Aren't you tired?" Jaq wondered how much Russ had even slept before his turn came to watch the fire. His eyes were hooded with drowsiness.

"Nah." Russ turned his head to where Daniel softly snored in the shadows near Finn, who sprawled in the dust, making little sounds of discomfort now and then.

Ah. He wanted to keep an eye on Daniel. A little swoop in Jaq's stomach made her sigh. What made Russ so awesome? And so full of pain. What was it that he wanted so badly to forget like he mentioned in his journal?

"Why are you here?" Jaq faced Russ, watching his face pull into a tense mask. "Drugs? Like Finn?"

A tiny flinch of his eyes betrayed the strong feelings he held tight inside. "Drugs... in a way."

Jaq exhaled slowly. She wanted to hear about it. Maybe if she shared first.

"I'm here because I started making some really stupid decisions. Bad boyfriend, sliding grades, partying ... acting out and giving my dad—heck." She smirked at the euphemism and her confession. "My mom went Crazy Diva on us and left. My brother followed. But he was such a fantastic d-bag nobody cares. My little sister is falling apart and I was no help." Jaq sniffed her cold nose, feeling tears trying to come.

Russ nodded slowly as if to encourage her.

"I defaced a church," she blurted.

"Oh." Russ raised his brows.

"Yeah. Not proud of that now." Jaq stared into the fire that burned like her shame. "My bad choices. Hurting the people around me, and I only noticed that since talking with Patti." She let out an unamused laugh. "So, anyway, I guess I deserved it when Mick and Craig grabbed me and threw me into the back of a van and brought me here. Hijacked a life I was effectively destroying anyway." She grimaced. "I was so scared in that van. Priorities change when you're afraid. What was your kidnapping like?" Jaq rubbed her hands together to heat them, waiting for Russ to answer.

"I enlisted. Wasn't kidnapped." His solemn face showed no emotion.

"What? You're kidding, right?" Jaq thought she might stutter herself.

"No. I wanted to come." Russ set his jaw and lay back, settling down as if to sleep. *That was that?*

Jaq watched the fire flicker. She'd just shared with him. Maybe the only thing she'd accomplished was to add to his growing list of why he shouldn't like her. *Shoops.*

"I'm really sorry... about your journal. I swear I just saw a little part that Daniel showed me. And—I liked it," Jaq whispered, hoping he would understand that he didn't need to be embarrassed.

Russ's voice came through the darkness, soft and hesitant. "You did?"

"Yeah." Jaq was glad the darkness hid the blush she felt heating her cheeks.

After a long pause, Russ said, "It's okay."

Jaq let out her breath with relief. He evidently was not a guy who held grudges.

He spoke again, low and sweet. "Thank you—for talking. I

think... it's cool that you know you made mistakes with your family. And that you can say sorry. That always helps. Goodnight, Jaq."

"Goodnight, Russ." A warm swirl in her chest made Jaq smile. A compliment that had nothing to do with her looks felt good.

A distant howl in the darkness sounded. Otherwise, the crackling and popping of the wood in the fire was the only sound. No stars above. The smell of smoke and sagebrush filled the freezing air.

For two hours, Jaq could do nothing but zone out to her own thoughts, tossing sticks onto the fire every now and then. The anger she'd felt toward her dad felt more like anxiousness now. She wanted to understand him and let him understand her. And Flower. So much to fix there. Jaq needed to get home right away, but now part of her really didn't want to say goodbye to Russ. Weird. She had to know his story.

And she had to kiss him.

Russ breathed deep, nestled under his blanket. Jaq felt like a creep when she considered snuggling in next to him. It was cold. And he was so very adorable.

Jaq dozed, waking with a start. There was a low, vibrating growl and rustling in the sagebrush outside of the fire's dim glow. Her heart stopped when the eerie reflection of two silvery eyes glinted and blinked at her. Jaq yelped through a squeezed throat. She put a hand on the knife at her waist. Whatever it was darted away. She shook her head, straining her eyes. Had she really seen something? The dark outlines of bushes and rocks gave nothing away. A dream?

Jaq still had an uneasy feeling. She checked the watch, got up, and edged over to where Daniel slept. She nudged him in the side with her toe. He groaned and turned over in response.

"Hey. Daniel," Jaq rasped. She crouched beside him and

touched his shoulder. Nothing. She leaned closer to his ear. "Daniel. Get up."

His arms shot up in front of him protectively. "No. I don't want... Stop."

Jaq caught her breath at his pleading tone. She waited until his body relaxed back into sleep. His eyes still seemed squeezed, his mouth turned down at the edges.

"It's me, Jaq. It's your turn for fire watch." She placed her hands lightly on his upper arms.

"Fine." He reached up and pulled her body down against his chest. "Okay," his rough voice resigned.

It was so unexpected that at first Jaq just lay there, rising with his breathing. She struggled to get back to her knees. Daniel didn't fight her, but he sighed as if relieved as Jaq leaned away from him.

"Daniel." Jaq shivered as the warmth of his body disappeared from the surface of her skin.

"Diana." He groaned as if in exasperation or warning. Daniel's eyes flew open and he stared at Jaq, disoriented.

Jaq wasn't sure what to say. So, of course, the wrong thing came out of

her mouth. "Who's Diana?"

Daniel scowled, his face flushed. "What do you want?"

"Your turn." Jaq tossed the watch and it landed on Daniel's chest. He stared at it and pushed himself up onto his elbows.

"Yeah." He grabbed the watch and sat up. "Got it. Go get some sleep." He didn't want to chat or even look at her.

Jaq stood. "If you see anything in the bushes, scream."

"Don't worry. I will." Daniel scowled and turned away from Jaq, scooting closer to the fire.

———

Morning seemed to literally break. Sharp fragments of sunlight stabbed through the clouds like shattered ice. Jaq shook beneath her blanket while goosebumps prickled over her entire body. So cold. Again.

Mick growled, "You let the fire die."

"Uh-oh," Erica snapped with poisonous sarcasm.

Erica had had the final watch. Jaq turned over to see that nothing remained of the raging fire from the night before but charred black wood and some red coals.

She sat up, squinting against the cold. Russ and Finn had their curriculum books out, hunched sleepy eyed under blankets beside one another. Daniel wasn't in the circle.

"As a group, we count on each other. At these temperatures, fire is the only thing between us and a case of hypothermia." Mick's huge chest rose as he took a breath, his tone tight with forced patience.

"I care? Whatever, I fell asleep. Get over it, Bald Thor." Erica pushed her ragged green bangs out of her eyes. The color made her skin look sickly.

"Hey. You really don't want to lose your blanket privileges in weather like this," Mick warned.

"You wouldn't dare. Truth is, guys," she addressed the rest of them, "they have no power over you. What are they gonna do that wouldn't get them sued?"

"Try me," Mick bit out, his tall, muscular body rigid.

Jaq was sure that Mick was not used to being talked back to. His intimidating appearance was probably enough to demand cooperation. Not with Erica.

"Oh, I will." She spat on the ground and stepped toward Mick, her fingers curled as if she wanted to scratch his face off.

Katie put an arm around her. Erica's face scrunched in a ferocious snarl, and she shook off Katie's effort to calm her.

"Get off me," she hissed before stalking away into the sage. Katie trailed behind Erica at a distance.

Mick kept an eye on her back as she retreated. With a look that would burst most things into flame, Mick grabbed his hatchet and stomped off in the opposite direction.

Jaq wished Erica had never come. Somehow that girl put everyone on edge. And Mick totally lost his cool around her. Something Craig said prodded at her. He'd mentioned something about being careful about Mick. Jaq pushed aside the uneasy feeling that tickled in her empty belly.

Daniel appeared from over the rocky rise. He ambled back into camp and stood by where Jaq sat. "Man, it's cold. My pee practically froze on the way out."

Finn laughed. "Golden arches but sadly without the hamburgers. It's freezing. I'm half the man I was yesterday—if you know what I mean."

"Gross." Jaq didn't care to picture that.

"So, should we build up the fire? Or do you think Mick's going to move us out?" Russ poked a stick into the embers, stirring.

Daniel shrugged. "I guess we can snuggle to keep warm until he gets back." He plopped down beside Jaq and rubbed his shoulder against hers. She rolled her eyes but didn't move. The night before came back to her as Daniel's body warmth soaked into her skin. Jaq wondered what that whole Diana thing was about.

Jaq caught Russ staring at her with his beautiful brown eyes. He quickly lowered his gaze to the curriculum book in his lap and shuffled his feet in the dirt.

"I'm hungry. You'd think that by now I would be used to that," Jaq said to smooth over Russ's shyness and the tension that seemed to swirl with the smoke coming from the embers.

"Seriously, I could even eat a GMO, nonorganic, pink slime burger right now." Finn rubbed his stomach with a grimace.

"Whatever that means." Daniel shot Finn a look that clearly said *nerd*.

Jaq stood up. She had to empty her bladder now or totally embarrass herself. Pulling the blanket around her shoulders, she stalked away to find some privacy. Erica came from the opposite direction, walking toward camp with her head down. Jaq wondered how the scrappy little thing survived this long out here. She looked half starved. Jaq tugged up on her own loose shorts and patted her concave belly. The long johns might be the only thing holding her shorts up anymore.

Jaq noticed a high thatch of bitter brush and headed toward it. It would be an ideal place to be alone. As she got closer, voices came from behind it and she stopped.

"...sure? Oh, no. Look again." Katie sounded urgent.

"Again? Where would it be? I keep it in my pack. Always." Mick's voice boomed.

Jaq shrunk inside. Was he talking about the compass? Suddenly Jaq had the wild thought that Craig had done it. That because of her, he had sneaked into Mick's pack. A thrill went through her gut that felt a lot like fear.

"When did you use it last? Did you leave it at the last camp?"

"No. I used it to check in last night. I put it into my pack," Mick said with certainty.

"Do you think one of the kids...?" Katie's voice was strained.

There was no reply, but Jaq imagined that Mick nodded. He took a deep breath.

Katie made a small whine of distress. "This could be very bad."

"Well, if R.J. doesn't hear from us by tomorrow night, they'll check on us." Mick's calm voice sounded forced.

"We should confront the kids. One of them must have taken it," Katie said.

"They'd better not have." His voice thickened with menace.

Jaq darted away, heart pounding. She sensed something bad was coming, like a rising wave with something dark inside. It reminded Jaq of the days just before her mother left. And just like then, somehow it felt like her fault.

CHAPTER 13

BY THE TIME Jaq returned to camp after relieving herself, a small fire blazed in the pit and the group sat pinned under Mick's and Katie's glares.

"Sit." Mick poked a large finger in the direction of the other kids as Jaq approached.

Jaq hurried over to settle beside Finn. A nervous shiver ran down her spine. Seemingly on impulse, Finn leaned into Jaq and scrubbed his hand over her back in a brisk, helpful way, obviously thinking she trembled from the cold.

"Listen." Mick stood with his feet apart and his hands on his hips. His light eyes pierced like lasers from an intimidating height. "Someone has taken my walkie-talkie. I need it back. Now."

Jaq drew in her breath. She didn't even know Mick had one. But it made sense. So it wasn't the compass. Of course not. Craig had bailed.

"Why would anyone want it? So we could chat with R.J. and Patti back at HQ? Exciting." Erica sneered.

"I don't have it," Daniel announced.

Russ shrugged. "I haven't seen it anywhere."

Mick clenched his hands into fists and spoke through tight

lips. "Here's the deal. I communicate with HQ for safety purposes and to give them our coordinates every day. Until that thing shows up, we have to stay here. It's the last position I reported." He folded his bulging arms across his chest. "Thing is, we have a certain amount of miles to go before your stay is considered complete."

"Meaning?" Daniel sat up straighter.

"Meaning the days could pile up without us getting any closer to trail's end. Understand? I want that walkie-talkie back. Immediately," Mick's gruff voice commanded.

Everyone shifted and they all eyed each other. Nobody wanted to be stuck here any longer than they needed to be. Except maybe Erica. Jaq gave the other girl a narrow look. She had a smug expression on her face.

Jaq had the impulse to call Erica out right there—like how neighbors turned on one another just to survive when the Nazi's were ravaging Europe. Before she could say anything, Daniel stood up.

"Finn. Cough it up." The jock lifted his chest, as if to look threatening.

"What? Get real, meathead." Finn frowned.

"You're the klepto here. You admitted it yourself." Daniel's mouth twisted with disgust.

"Um. That's when I'm on drugs... so I can get more drugs." Finn's face reddened. He kept his eyes lowered in shame. Jaq felt sorry for him.

"Yeah, whatever. You took it. I know you did." Daniel watched with growing anger as Jaq placed a hand on Finn's arm.

"Did you see him take it?" Mick raised his chin at Daniel.

"No. But Russ's knife is missing. And this morning I couldn't find mine either. So unless it was one of the girls"—

Daniel snorted as if giving females any kind of credit was ridiculous—"it has to be him."

"That's so not fair." Jaq scowled at Daniel, beyond irritated at his chauvinism. "It could be Erica—or you. Remember how you somehow ended up with Russ's book in your bag? I'm beginning to wonder if that was an accident at all." Jaq pushed to her feet and gave Daniel an icy glare.

Russ cleared his throat. Jaq regretted mentioning the book. It must still be so embarrassing to him.

Daniel made a growling sound in his throat. "Women," he sneered. "Totally illogical, as always."

In a blur, Erica lurched toward the surprised jock with her claws out. Daniel flung up his arms and stumbled back as she threw her body against him.

Erica hissed. "Guys like you make me sick! Having a penis does not make you better than me!" she shrieked, pulling at his hair and trying to kick him in the crotch.

Mick stepped in, pulling Erica away by the scruff of her neck. Her arms and feet churned violently in the air while she screamed in protest.

"Whoa—anger management, b-word. Dang." Daniel glared, straightening his shirt.

"Enough. Shut. Up." Mick's voice seemed to shake the ground.

Erica reared back and her head made a cracking sound against Mick's face. He roared in pain, dropped her, and crumpled forward with a hand over his face. Blood fountained from his nose and ran down his chin and wrist. Erica's eyes went wide with fear. She scrambled back and clambered up a high rock for safety.

"Oh. Crap." Jaq froze. Mick's heaving chest and shoulders frightened her. She waited for some kind of fanged monster to tear its way out of the huge man and devour them all.

"Shoops," Finn whispered.

Katie dug something out of her pack and pulled Mick's hand away from his face. She unwrapped a thick maxi pad and pressed it to his nose. "You okay?" she asked in a motherly tone.

"I'm fine." Mick gripped the pad to his face with one hand and snatched up his hatchet out of a branch beside the fire with the other. "Katie, search their packs."

He pointed an angry finger up at Erica and turned away from the group. He didn't look at any of them. He disappeared over the small ridge, the sound of his stomping feet reminding Jaq of the dinosaurs in Jurassic Park. If she had a glass of water, it would be rippling right now.

Finn let out a long, "Whew."

"You have to appreciate the self-control that just happened." Russ shook his head.

Jaq silently agreed. That could have gotten so ugly. She'd half expected Mick to turn green and burst out of his clothes.

Erica slid down the rock onto the ground. She trembled as if cold, but Jaq thought it was probably fear.

"Maybe we should sing some jaunty sea shanties now," Finn suggested.

Jaq smiled and shook her head. "You've just been dying for the chance to suggest that, haven't you?"

"Guilty."

Daniel glared at Erica, who now huddled beside Katie, very still and quiet.

"What a screwup," Daniel muttered loud enough for her to hear.

Jaq heaved a sigh. Great. He was going to send Erica off into one of her tantrums again. But instead, the scraggly waif looked back with large, watery eyes.

"More than you know," she said in a broken, hoarse voice.

Then her eyes hardened. "Heroin, crystal meth, prostitution, and assault. That's me."

Erica wandered farther away and sat in the dirt. Katie sat with her and spoke in a low, soothing murmur. Jaq couldn't hear the words. Her mind, already spinning from what had happened with Mick, now seemed to pick up tempo with Erica's revelation.

What a mess.

Then Jaq heard the thunking sound. Everyone turned toward the noise of the violent crunching, like the sound of bones snapping followed by a heavy *chop, chop, chop.*

In the distance, by a cluster of small trees, Mick brought his hatchet down over and over, his powerful arms bulging and pumping. His red face was drawn into a furious mask, growling and grunting under his breath. A picture of wrath. An angry god forging lightning bolts.

Jaq stared, her mouth dropped open. Her eyes met Russ's briefly and he mirrored her astonishment. She looked around at the rest of the group.

Finn swore softly. "Look away."

"He's pissed." Daniel swallowed.

Erica flinched with every stroke of the hatchet, as if the blows were meant for her. Jaq had no doubt that, in a way, they were. Erica seemed to bring out a violent dislike in everyone in the group. Maybe she represented an exaggerated version of what was wrong with all of them. Jaq wondered how much her own family would think she had in common with the out-of-control, green-haired teen.

Katie forced a chuckle. "He's just working off steam. He'll be fine." She smoothed her ponytail and brushed dirt from her knees.

Finn clapped and stomped a foot in time with the ax. He sang in a pirate-like voice. "What will we do with a drunken sailor? What will we do with a drunken sailor? What will we do with a drunken sailor? Early in the morning! Way hay and up she rises,

way hay and up..." He trailed off as Daniel glared at him.

Nobody said anything else while the chopping continued. Katie went about searching through their packs, finding nothing. And nobody confessed to taking the walkie-talkie.

Jaq flipped through her curriculum book. Since they were stuck here, there was nothing else to do. She hadn't really mastered any of the skills, but she also had no intention of being stuck in the wilderness ever again. Although the clouds pressed down heavily, the day had warmed. It was a relief not to be shivering.

She combed over the section on first aid, then navigation by the stars. Jaq wondered if she could figure out how to get out of here that way. Of course, knowing where north was didn't help when she had no idea which direction brought her to civilization. She could easily head deeper into the badlands. A night trek was risky for several reasons. Had she really seen a coyote or wolf last night during fire watch?

"You really working in that thing?" Erica smirked, squatting beside Jaq.

"Um. Yeah." Jaq inched away without thinking.

Erica noticed. "I won't bite you. You're not my type."

Jaq tried to smile. "Okay."

"Hey. I know what you think of me. And you're totally right. I don't care what happens to me and I don't care what people think." Erica's face hardened. But the freckles that sprinkled her nose made her look like a child.

"Why not?" It was Jaq's experience that the people who insisted that they didn't care what people thought actually cared more than most.

Erica let out a blast of air through her lips letting them

vibrate like an ornery horse. "Why should I? Nobody cares about what *I* think."

Jaq stared back at her book. Why was Erica getting talky with her? She didn't know what to say to her—it was nerve-racking. It was a little like sitting beside a grenade with the pin already pulled.

The green-haired girl jabbed at the ground with a stick. Jaq noticed how small and bony Erica's hands were. She thought about what Erica had said about being a prostitute. It made her sick inside. No wonder she hated men.

"So you have, like, a real family, right?" Erica stared at the dirt.

"I guess. My mom took off, but whatever." Jaq shrugged. Her problems were almost embarrassing compared to Erica's life.

"It's weird. But, like, nobody loves me. You know?" Erica said casually.

Jaq felt irritated—as if saying things like that aloud was impolite. She couldn't really blame anyone for not loving Erica. But when she looked at the other girl's fragile profile, her heart squeezed. Erica's over-sized eyes made her look so vulnerable.

"Well, who do you love?" Jaq asked, thinking of Flower. Maybe Jaq would be just like Erica if she didn't love anyone.

"Nobody."

"I guess you and the world are even, then. Can't have something for nothing." Jaq realized that she wanted things she wasn't really willing to give either—trust, loyalty, compassion, forgiveness.

Erica looked at Jaq. "That kinda makes sense." She gave a slight nod. "But I still kinda want everyone to go to hell."

"I know what you mean." Jaq felt a genuine smile spring up on her face.

Erica smiled back. Her face morphed into something

darling and sweet. It only lasted a moment before her face tightened again.

"Anyway, I was just going to tell you... I'm leaving tomorrow. And since you're a girl too... well, I'd rather not go alone. Plus, I know you want to leave too." Erica kept her voice low. Her eyes darted around to make sure they were alone.

Jaq perked up. "You're really going?"

"Yeah. You wanna come?" Her pinched face said she didn't care.

Before Jaq could answer Finn approached them.

"Hey, girls." He didn't look at Erica.

"Finn." Jaq smiled.

"Can I borrow your knife?" Finn waved a stick at Jaq.

"What is the deal with the knives? Are you all just losing them?"

"No idea. I just wanted to make a new spindle for my bow-drill set and couldn't find mine." Finn's brows pushed together.

"Seriously? So all three of you guys. If I lend you mine, will I ever get it back?"

"I'll use it right here in front of you."

"Fine." Jaq pulled her knife out of the sheath at her hip and handed it to Finn.

He set to work shaving off layers of the stick in his hand. Erica gave Jaq a look that said she'd talk later. Jaq nodded, not sure if she wanted to run off with Erica. She noticed Russ bent near the fire making ash cakes. Maybe she didn't want to leave... at all. Then she thought of Flower again.

Erica walked away, leaving Finn and Jaq alone. Finn sagged in relief. "I can't deal with her."

"She's nuts. But... I don't know. Maybe she's okay."

Finn smiled. "You're so cool. I think you care about everyone."

"Me?" Jaq sat back, stunned. "Nah. I'm self-absorbed."

"But not heartless. Once you notice someone else, you care."

Jaq laughed. "Holy crap, Finn. Is that a compliment or not? I can't tell."

Finn's elfish face grinned. "Indubitably." When she made a face, he sighed and translated. "Most def a compliment. You're sweet."

Jaq blushed. And here she'd thought she was so hard-core. "I think you're exaggerating, but thanks."

"No. Thank you. It was way decent of you to stand up for me when Jockstrap was accusing me of stealing. You could have agreed with him, and I'd deserve it."

"Everyone deserves another chance. And I like you." Jaq shrugged.

Finn glowed. "See what I'm saying? Sweet."

"I'm telling you you're wrong. I'm a b-word. Mean, actually." Jaq smiled at Finn despite her effort to be tough.

"The lady doth protest too much, methinks." Finn raised a finger to his chin.

"What?"

"Shakespeare."

"You would." Jaq rolled her eyes.

"Indeed." Finn nodded with a kingly expression. "'Come, let's away to prison; We two alone will sing like birds in the cage.' That, oh bewildered one, was King Lear. Always in denial. I can relate. And you should too. Imprisoned by guilt, you won't ever see the reality of who you are."

Jaq made a face. "I keep forgetting you're a genius."

"Thank you? Hm. Perhaps I hide it all too well." A glint in his eyes revealed that he was having fun.

Something about Finn warmed Jaq from the inside. He didn't seem to be obsessed with her looks and she didn't feel like he wanted anything from her other than to be friends. She leaned over and hugged him.

A small sound of surprise escaped Finn, but he hugged her back. His slight, bony frame relaxed into her. Finn put his forehead on Jaq's shoulder, and he let out a sigh. It felt so good to hold someone that Jaq didn't want to let go.

"Yeah. You're as savage as a teddy bear," he murmured.

Jaq held tighter as they both trembled with laughter born of relief and need. She squeezed her eyes shut when she felt tears fill her eyes. She was becoming such an emotional wimp out here.

"Handing out your stuff again?" Daniel snapped. "So did I forget to take a number or what?" His hazel eyes flashed when Jaq looked up at him.

Finn pulled away from Jaq. "That didn't sound particularly respectful, sir."

"You are such a geek." Daniel huffed in disgust.

"Daniel. Don't you ever get sick of yourself?" Jaq groaned. She was tired of his constant pestering.

Daniel eyed her as if she were a scrambled puzzle. He kicked at the dirt and slapped his curriculum book against his thigh a few times.

"She let me borrow her knife. Guess mine is missing too." Finn picked up the knife where he'd dropped it during their hug and continued whittling.

"That explains everything." Daniel walked away, shaking his head.

———

Jaq sat on her bedroll not far from the fire as the sky darkened. The warm day had retreated, and a chill settled into Jaq's skin. Another mundane day had come and gone. Nothing new. But it felt different. Uneasy. Without hiking all day, everyone seemed to have pent up energy. They were all stuck there because somebody was stealing. If someone was collecting knives, they were all in danger.

Russ and Mick were out setting and checking deadfall traps. Finn and Katie were singing songs by the fire. Erica sat by herself against a large rock, arms wrapped around herself. She'd approached Jaq again about running away with her. Jaq had given her a maybe.

Jaq felt someone behind her. She turned to see Daniel, shoulders tensed, staring at her. He took a step closer and raised his brows.

"Sheesh. Freak me out." Jaq pressed a hand to her chest, instinctively lowering a hand to her knife.

"Walk with me." Daniel gave a half smile and held out his hand.

Jaq hesitated. Daniel could be the psycho thief. But Finn had just said that she was nice to everyone—and she'd told him that everyone deserved a second chance. She really wanted to be that person, the one who liked and understood everyone. Ultimately though, it was the I-dare-you showing in Daniel's eyes that made her grab his hand and let him tug Jaq to her feet. She dropped his hand immediately.

"What do you want?" Jaq hoped he couldn't tell that she really wanted to know.

Daniel's smile was confident and sexy. He strode away from camp without a word and Jaq followed. When she caught up with him, he looked over at her, still walking. It was light enough that she saw his face clearly. If he weren't such a jerk, she'd think he was hot.

"Look. Somehow we didn't hit it off. I can't see why not. We're the same kind of people. You're like me." Daniel jabbed a thumb at one of his pecs.

"Really. Is that how you see me? I guess I'm insulted."

Daniel laughed. "See? That's what I would have said."

"Whatever. You wish."

"I know you think I'm a big jerk. But since you're a psycho b—itch"—he whispered the rest of the word behind his hand, casting a glance over his shoulder—"we should get along perfectly."

"Gee, thanks—sounds like the winning combination. Like oil and water," Jaq grumbled.

"Nah, more like cinnamon and spice."

"Funny. Finn was just saying today how sweet I am."

Daniel snorted. "Right."

"And that brings us back to my original question of what do you want?" Jaq pursed her lips.

Daniel stopped and turned toward Jaq, his chin set and a gleam in his eyes.

"You know what I want." He raised a hand as if to touch the lock of hair that rested on Jaq's cheek, but she backed away a step.

Jaq swallowed. "Sorry. Fresh out of charity for today."

They had gotten far enough away from camp that Jaq could barely hear Finn and Katie harmonizing. She leaned against the wall of a large rock to feel support as a nervous feeling rushed through her.

"You just like to win, Jock. You like the conquest."

"Duh." He crossed his arms, causing the sleeves of his t-shirt to tighten over his defined biceps.

"Well, my legs are not goal posts. So throw your balls else-where," she said, hands on her hips. Jaq didn't want to like him at all, but there was something beneath his jerk veneer that made her feel sorry for him.

Daniel's eyes lit up and he laughed. "Wow. Just... wow." He

stepped forward, his face becoming serious. Jaq couldn't back up—the rock was behind her. Daniel leaned in, placing a hand on either side of Jaq's head on the wall. His face got closer and then he paused a few inches away. He smelled like sagebrush and sweat.

Jaq turned a cheek toward his face. "Stop it." She held up her hands to push against his chest, but he was as solid as the rock wall behind her.

"I have no idea what that means." Daniel's voice was low and scratchy.

Anger surged through Jaq. A panicked feeling of claustrophobia clawed inside, like when her big brother would trap her inside a sleeping bag. She brought her knee up hard.

Daniel was quick. He blocked her strike with his hip. "Ooh. That was close." He lowered his hands protectively to his crotch and stepped back, searching her face.

"You don't get it, huh? You can't see why anyone would reject you." Jaq smirked.

"No idea. I mean, it's what I'm good for—and you don't want it. I'm supposedly irresistible." Although his tone was sarcastic, Jaq knew his feeling of rejection was real. A movement, like something sinking in quicksand, gaped darkly in his eyes.

Realization lit her mind. "Everyone wants you. Even people who shouldn't?" Jaq remembered the way Daniel had reacted when she'd tried to wake him for fire watch. "Who is Diana?" The words dropped between them like something heavy and dangerous.

Daniel winced. "Shit."

Jaq waited, still looking at him. The deepening shadows of night seemed to cover his shame. He cleared his throat. "Is this the part where I spill my secrets and then you feel sorry for me?" Daniel grated.

"Yeah." Jaq put her hands back on her hips. "Think you can handle that?"

"No."

"Fine. I won't judge. Just thought it would be a good way for us to start over—without all this head gaming. But whatever. Did you at least tell Patti?"

"A little." Daniel raised his shoulders and then stood very still. "You really want to start over?" He took a step back as if he didn't trust her.

"Sure." She could be that person. The one who actually asked what other people were dealing with instead of focusing on herself. Like who she should have been for Flower. "But only if you respect the word stop and start treating me more like a human than a trinket."

He nodded. "Okay, that's fair. I've been a jerk. Sorry." Daniel shut his eyes and took a deep breath.

Jaq nodded. "It's not okay but I forgive you. This time."

He swallowed. "Got it. So you want to know my deal..." Daniel shrugged. "No big. My dad's new little wifey has a thing for me," he said in a flat voice.

"Oh." She remembered now—Diana of the blue bikini.

"My dad must know. I think that's partly why I'm here." Daniel stared at the ground.

"Oh." Jaq had no words.

"Yeah, disgusting, right? She's totally hot." He frowned and seemed to swallow something repulsive. "And out of her freaking mind." Daniel rubbed his hands down his shirt as if to clean them.

"How—when did she—?" Jaq couldn't continue—her heart was thumping fast and she felt ill.

"I was fourteen when my dad married her. She was like, twenty-five and my dad got her the same year he bought his red Maserati. She... noticed me right away."

"Oh my gosh. You were fourteen," Jaq whispered.

"Yeah." A bitter smile stretched his features into a mask of pain. "I'm quite the stud. All my friends think so. Guess I should be proud... but." He shook his head.

Funny how he seemed less like a jerk all of a sudden. The way he held his shoulders and the vulnerable look on his face made him look like a little boy. It made Jaq feel soft.

"What did she... do to you?"

Daniel swallowed. "Everything." He paused and looked away. "I... love my dad, you know?" His face crumpled for a brief moment and then he went poker-faced.

Her stomach dropped. Daniel looked so small and defenseless. "Come here." Jaq rolled her eyes, trying to be funny, and held out her arms. Daniel cocked his head in confusion. "Come. Here." She bounced her outstretched hands in emphasis.

Daniel ducked his head and stepped into her arms. Jaq hugged him, patting his back—like she would for Flower when she was little whenever she had nightmares. He shuddered.

"I know what it's like to feel like your looks are the only reason why people want you," Jaq said, the words coming to her like inspiration.

She almost expected a snarky remark at that, but Daniel heaved a sigh. His muscles tightened around her. He sniffed a little as if he might be getting emotional. "Do you ever wish you were ugly?" His deep voice rumbled in his chest against Jaq's.

"I wouldn't go that far." Jaq chuckled.

"I would." Daniel cleared his throat.

In the pause, Jaq's heart ached. This was getting too heavy. "Well, you're not. Deal. Don't worry—this doesn't mean I want you." Jaq pulled away and looked into Daniel's face. His eyes were wet.

He wiped a hand over his face. "Liar." He smirked.

Jaq pretended not to notice his tears. She smiled and punched him in the arm. "Jerk. You were milking that."

Daniel rubbed his arm. "Ouch. Duh," he croaked happily. "Friends?"

"Yeah. Just be cool, okay? No more acting all jealous and ragey."

"Deal." He looked at her thoughtfully. "You like Russ, huh?"

"I think so." She sighed.

He nodded. "Yeah. That's a good balance. His chill will balance your fire."

"Think so?" Her face warmed. It was strange to admit her feelings for Russ aloud.

"Absolutely. The lucky bastard." Daniel grinned.

On the way back to camp, Jaq felt good inside until she felt a prickle on her neck. Somehow she knew that somebody was watching them. Daniel walked in front of her, a swing in his step. She turned abruptly, searching, expecting to see the glow of silver eyes again. But she only saw the shapes of bushes and rocks in the dark. Sometimes the dark did that, especially out there in the vast nothing—it seemed like anything, or anyone could be there observing, stalking. Jaq shivered.

The others had bedded down when they returned to camp, except Mick who seemed to be on fire watch. He turned and stood as they approached. With his back to the fire, he was no more than a hulking figure outlined in orange. Holding his hatchet at his side he resembled something out of a horror film.

"Are we taking turns with the fire tonight?" Daniel asked.

"No. I'm keeping watch. Nobody is to leave their bedroll for any reason. You got that?" Mick bit out, sounding like a drill sergeant.

"Yes, sir," Jaq automatically answered. It was clear he didn't want anyone stealing anything else. She flopped onto her bedroll near the fire and curled up tight.

Daniel settled nearby. "Goodnight, Jaq. Thanks," he whispered.

"It's all good, Jock," Jaq answered. She didn't know how Daniel would ever be okay after what he'd been through—or what would happen when he went home. But she was glad they were cool now.

"Hey. Move your bedroll away from her," Mick commanded.

"Oh. Okay. Whatever," Daniel huffed, annoyed. "What do you think I'm going to do?"

"Just making sure." Mick folded his arms and watched while Daniel moved his bedroll further away than necessary—out in the bushes and away from the group.

"This good enough?" Daniel spat. Jaq knew that his defensive jerk side came out because he hated to be accused of anything. Too close to home. She knew she wasn't in any danger from him now.

"That works. Goodnight." Mick squatted by the fire, shoving another knobby log into the crackling flames.

Things were going to really clamp down until the stolen items showed up. Shivering under her blanket while coyotes yelped in the distance, she hoped it would be soon, so they could move on.

CHAPTER 14

IT WAS STILL dim outside when Jaq woke up with a start, her heart pounding, teeth chattering so hard her jaw hurt. Something weighed her blanket down, and it shifted and slid away as she sat up in alarm.

Snow.

Jaq reached out and touched the powdery white stuff in her lap. Her fingers ached in response. *No way.*

In surprise, she looked at the cocooned lumps of her fellow campers where they lay around her under a couple inches of creamy white. Mick's large body rose and fell with soft snores, hunched by the low fire with a blanket tented over his head.

"Jaq?" Russ sat up on the other side of the fire pit, his dark hair tangled from sleep. "Are you seeing this?"

"Totally. We are so screwed." Jaq trembled despite the long johns, hoody, and blanket.

Russ wrapped his arms around himself and let out a breath in a blast of white vapor.

With some grunting and stretching, Mick shook himself awake. "Ah. It snowed. Thought it might," he said, his morning voice deep and scratchy.

Katie's voice rose, shrill in the muffled stillness. "Erica?

Where's Erica?"

Jaq looked over to where the wild cat had been sleeping. Nothing there and no tracks in the snow. So, she had run after all—before the snow even fell.

"Damn it," Mick growled, jumping to his feet. Nobody dared point out the cuss word.

"This is bad. Very bad." Katie hugged herself, casting her eyes toward the barren land that faded into gray.

Finn thrashed and kicked, then sat up. "What the—am I awake?"

"Afraid so." Jaq crawled to the fire and put more sticks in it.

"Oh... shhh—oot," Finn whispered. "I dreamed I was on Hoth... looks like I am." He glanced around as if expecting to see stormtroopers.

Jaq waited for a remark from Daniel about Finn being a Star Wars geek but none came. She wouldn't mention that she caught Finn's reference. A fond memory surfaced of watching the movies with her dad on a sick day when she was a kid. They used to like each other. Funny how liking and disliking could change so much... She glanced in the direction of where Daniel had gone to sleep the night before. Still sleeping probably.

Russ and Finn pressed themselves beside Jaq and the fire. Jaq smiled at Russ and he put one arm around her shoulders. "For w-warmth," he murmured.

"We need supplies for this. It isn't supposed to be snowing right now," Finn said to Mick.

"I'm aware of that. But our walkie-talkie seems to have vanished and now I'm pretty sure who has it. We have to find Erica," Mick boomed, running a hand over his shaved head. The tip of his nose had gone red.

Katie was already circling the camp, as if trying to find a trail. But any tracks that might have been left were covered now.

The sun started to peek over the ridge and the grayness began the slow fade to orange. Body tense as if ready to spring into action, Mick squinted toward the horizon, the blade of his hand shading his eyes. Jaq felt sorry for Erica. She wouldn't want Mick coming after her like a pointer hound on steroids.

Then Katie screamed. The sound speared through the air with a terrifying

sharpness that raised every hair on Jaq's body. Everyone jumped to their feet and then

froze. Katie had wandered farther away and now sank to her knees beside something in

the bushes. Her voice rose over the sage and echoed toward camp.

"Oh god, oh god! Help!" Her frantic wail mobilized everyone at once.

The group moved as one, trampling over the uneven ground to reach Katie.

"What-what is it?" Finn choked out in terror as a body-sized lump came into view under a thin layer of snow.

Jaq's heart literally stopped. Everyone gasped as Katie brushed her hands over the form and the snow rolled away, reddened by the blood beneath it. There was blood all around the body, coming up through the snow. Oddly, it reminded Jaq of a snow cone, the way the red syrup was always darker at the bottom. Her stomach twisted and her brain short-circuited. This wasn't real.

"Daniel." Jaq stared. Daniel's face was swollen and battered, frozen blood clung to his eyelashes and in his blond hair. "No, no. Is he okay? Is he okay?" Her voice rose.

Mick shoved Katie's shaking hands away and placed his large, tanned fingers against the pale, bloody neck. He leaned close. "He's still alive."

"Christ have m-m-mercy," Russ breathed to himself, fingers

flicking the sign of the cross from his head to his shoulders. Jaq took his hand, squeezing tight. Hoping the prayer didn't end up in some cosmic, backlogged voicemail.

"What happened?" Finn placed a hand over his mouth and then turned away as he dry heaved. Jaq mechanically patted Finn's back with her free hand. She couldn't tear her eyes away from the gory mess that was her... friend.

Mick's hands traveled Daniel's body, searching for injuries. "Maybe a wolf." His baritone voice was grim.

Katie moaned, tears flowing down her face. She didn't seem to know what to do with her hands. "Oh crap," she said breathlessly, her eyes darting around in fear as if expecting an attack at any minute.

"Get me something for the bleeding. Look, his torso looks chewed up." Mick gently poked at the torn, bloody clothing.

Katie's face went blank with horror. She stood and hurried back to camp.

"What made them—c-come?" Russ stared at the still jock on the ground, his hand clammy and stiff in Jaq's grip.

"Maybe our traps? We'll have to see if we caught something... but I don't know. Sometimes a lone wolf will get crazy. You know—just get aggressive and... I don't know." Mick peeled back Daniel's t-shirt to reveal deep lacerations in his side and hip on one side. He cursed under his breath, wadding up a portion of the blanket still wrapped around Daniel's legs and pressing it into the wound.

"Looks like someone tried to chop him up." Finn swallowed back another gag.

Jaq listened and watched as if from a distance. Her head floated somewhere else as this scary movie about kids trapped in the wilderness with a predator played.

"The cold is working in his favor. Slowed the bleeding. But he's lost too much. This could have happened a couple hours ago—just before the snow fell. We need that walkie-talkie!" Mick pounded the ground with his giant fist. The sound reminded Jaq of the sound his hatchet had made the day before. *Thunk, thunk, thunk.*

Jaq gasped. What if Mick had chopped Daniel up? But why? Her body shook hard, and her mind frantically whirled with paranoid terror. Had Russ told him about Daniel attacking her in her sleep? None of that mattered or made sense. Mick wouldn't.

"Something... or someone dragged him further away from camp. And bashed his face in," Jaq blurted, remembering where he had set his bedroll the night before.

"Do wolves pound faces?" Finn asked low. His wide blue eyes caught Jaq's and she knew he thought it might be a person too.

"I guess... he could have gotten into a fight. Maybe he confronted Erica when she ran. She's unstable enough. And maybe... wolves did the rest while he was unconscious." Mick shook his head back and forth as if trying to think clearly but finding it hard to fight the panic. He didn't sound like himself.

"Or maybe the wolf got her too... and dragged her away." Russ stared into the bushes.

Katie returned with some first aid supplies. She and Mick started to clean and bandage Daniel. A few times a muscle ticked in Daniel's otherwise corpse-like face. He was barely there.

"Help me get him to the fire. We need to get him warm," Mick said when they had finished.

Russ and Finn helped lift Daniel and bring him back to camp beside the fire. He flopped in their grasp as if he had no bones. Mick worried aloud that moving him might be danger-ous. But he needed warmth. Now.

Nobody said much. Everyone was trying to deal with the

shock in their own way. Shivering, Finn busied himself collecting firewood while Russ went to check the traps and Katie sat beside Daniel holding his hand. An intense uneasiness had risen in the group. On top of the fear that Daniel was close to death was the shock that someone in the group may be responsible. Jaq wondered if Erica was involved... or was she just missing because something horrible had happened to her too? Suspicious glances flicked around the group.

Jaq kept busy making sure the fire blazed higher and hotter. She filled her billycan with snow and put it over the flames, making hot tea that she hoped she could get Daniel to drink... if he would ever wake up. She swallowed back a sob. Just last night he had been so... alive.

Katie tucked two blankets around Daniel's body. "I need to get some pain killer in him." Katie had calmed herself, but her lips were white.

When there was nothing left to do they gathered around Daniel and stared at him. It didn't seem real. Mick paced away and then back several times.

"I can't stay here. I have to go get help. I can't even be bothered to find Erica, assuming she's run off—I have to get to the closest outpost to get to a walkie-talkie and then we can get a chopper out here to pick him up. I gotta go." He grabbed his pack and slung it over his shoulders.

Katie stared up at him, her eyes wide. "You're leaving." She took in a sharp breath. "Yes. You have to. Okay. I'll stay here and watch these guys. Oh. God." It was more a prayer than a curse. It looked as if Katie might pass out. No matter how many college credits she was getting for this—it wasn't enough.

Jaq looked at Russ and Finn. They both had the same face: fear. Nobody wanted Mick to leave, but there was nothing else they could do.

"If I start now and go alone, I can be at the outpost and

alerting HQ by evening." He pulled out his compass and then stared back down at Daniel's pathetic condition. "If there was time to spare, I'd try to take him, but it's faster this way. And I'm not sure how I could carry him—or if he should be moved." He seemed to want to justify his decision to the group, but nobody argued. His fierce blue eyes snapped from one face to the next. "Keep him warm. You'll need to chop more wood—" Mick swung his head back and forth searching the area around the fire. "My hatchet. Where is it?" By now his voice had become almost hysterical. "What the hell?" He was furious. Jaq's chills increased.

"Oh man." Russ helped look for a few moments and then his shoulders slumped. "I'm thinking... it's gone."

Mick clenched his fists and took a huge breath. A look of determination set his jaw like stone. "We have a huge problem."

"So are we talking a murderer or a wolf?" Finn's voice squeaked.

Mick stared off into the distance again. His voice came out flat and deep. "If he wakes, see if you can get a little food in him. I know we're low—we were supposed to get more food in a couple of days. Hang in there, guys." There was nothing else to say. Mick peered at the compass in his hand and pointed the direction he would go. Jaq took note—toward the jagged rocks that looked like a freight train.

Mick moved away from them fast, jogging over the rocks and around bushes, his powerful body eating up the distance until he was a tiny dot that disappeared over a ridge.

"They won't even assume anything is wrong until tonight—we usually only checked in at the end of the day to tell R.J. where we stopped. So even if Mick doesn't make it there as soon as he guessed—they'll check on us tonight," Katie said, sounding more like she was trying to convince herself that everything would be fine.

"Maybe R.J. will show up. He sometimes trails us, right? To keep his eye on things?" Jaq remembered what Craig had said about R.J. hanging around to watch Erica.

"Maybe. I—I don't know." Katie shrugged and patted Daniel's shoulder softly. He twitched and Katie gasped. "He's going to be okay. I just know it."

"What about us?" Finn's narrow face had no color in it. His light frame trembled with cold and fear.

"Yeah. Are we supposed to relax when there's a rabid wolf nearby? Or worse, a maniac?" Chills moved through Jaq's body.

"Do you think it's Erica? Daniel didn't get along with her, and if he did catch her trying to run... and she had the hatchet..." Russ scratched the dark stubble on his chin and locked eyes with Jaq.

Katie coughed. "We don't know. It could have been a wolf." She didn't seem convinced herself.

"A wolf who knows how to box?" Jaq snapped. "Look at his face."

"Well, maybe it was one of you!" Katie stood and backed away a few steps. "You know, my dad actually warned me. He said if I was going to work with troubled teens I should be prepared. I thought I was." She let out a humorless laugh. "But honestly, any of you are capable of this, for all I know." Her eyes settled on Russ. "Sometimes pain and suffering can turn people into animals." Then she turned to Finn. "Not to mention what chemical abuse can do to the brain."

The ground seemed unsteady under Jaq's feet. They really didn't know each other very well. "Well, it wasn't me." She frowned.

"I know some things about you." Katie's sweet and calm personality had totally shattered.

"Like what?" Jaq glared at Katie, feeling her cheeks warming.

"Your boyfriend is a violent felon, for one. Birds of a feather..."

"Get real. What do we know about you?" Jaq slung back. "Maybe the pressure of being Little Miss Perfect was just too much and you snapped!"

Russ placed a hand on Jaq's arm. "Stop. We aren't doing this," he said in his adult voice. "We'll protect each other. Tonight, Mick will bring help. Right now, we have to k-keep Daniel alive."

Katie straightened and took a shaky breath. She nodded like a bobble-head doll. "You're right. You're right. Sorry. I-I didn't mean it. I'm just scared and I don't do well with blood." Katie pushed her brown hair away from her face. It had come out of the ponytail while she slept, and she looked younger and unsure. "Jaq, help me take care of him."

Jaq sat down beside Daniel. While Katie sang low, stroking Daniel's hair, Jaq took the tea off the fire. She let it cool a little. Russ offered a wooden spoon he had carved, and Jaq gently spooned some of the tea into Daniel's mouth. His swollen lips were tinged blue, but his Adam's apple bobbed convulsively as the warm liquid met the back of his throat.

"Good for you, Jock. Swallow." Jaq continued her efforts until he had downed several spoonfuls.

Katie crushed a few tablets and had Jaq mix it with some more of the tea. After Daniel had taken the medicine, there wasn't much more they could do. Just wait.

Jaq carefully ran her hands over her unconscious friend's arms, feeling his skin warm from her touch and the heat of the fire. Katie's soft crooning continued, comforting and calming.

Russ made ashcakes for everyone, and they quietly sat eating and watching Daniel. He didn't move at all.

In the afternoon Daniel's breathing deepened. Finn took a turn feeding Daniel some broth made with a bouillon cube. After a while, Daniel grunted and his eyelids fluttered.

"Hey. He's sort of reacting." Finn leaned close to Daniel. "Jock Strap. It's me, Geek. You okay?"

A weak moan vibrated in Daniel's neck.

"Can you hear us?" Russ squatted low and Katie peaked over his shoulder.

"Wake up, jerk. I miss you." Jaq felt her throat closing in on a sob. "Hey, I'm giving out kisses and your number finally came up." She gave a soft snort and lightly stroked his injured cheek.

Daniel's hazel eyes opened. His lids drooped heavily, and he didn't seem to be able to focus. He found Jaq's face and one side of his mouth twitched up.

"Knew... you wanted... me," he rasped in a voice so low and broken Jaq could barely make out the words.

Tears made him look fuzzy as Jaq sobbed out a gasp. "Yeah. I confess."

Katie sniffed and wiped her eyes. Russ chuckled. Finn leaned over and kissed Daniel on the forehead.

Daniel winced and narrowed his eyes at Finn and cussed.

"Aw. You have to start your five days over," Finn said with a mock scold.

"I didn't hear anything." Katie turned her head. "Move aside; let me check the patient." Katie kneeled beside Daniel, checking the pulse at his neck and feeling his forehead. Her brow wrinkled. "Your pulse is weak. No fever though. No infection yet." She shook her head, not bothering to hide that she worried. "I hope Mick gets here fast." Katie stood up and paced around, her fingers tapping on her thighs.

Russ bounced his knee in agitation. "What happened,

man? You remember?"

"I was asleep. Dark. Then... a lot of ouch," he wheezed.

"You didn't see who—what did this?" It sounded more like a statement than a question. Russ stared at Daniel, seeming to will the information from him.

Daniel's eyelids slid shut. He let out a breath that reminded Jaq of fraying cloth. Weak and ragged.

Someone had attacked him in his sleep. So maybe it wasn't Erica. Wouldn't she just slip away if nobody confronted her? Jaq wondered if Erica was crazy enough to take revenge on Daniel for his male chauvinism and obvious dislike of her—while he slept. But really, it could have been anyone. Jock got on everyone's bad side. Jaq hated that thought.

Jaq settled beside Daniel and peeled the blanket back. She stifled a gasp. Bright red blood had already seeped through the bandages. Jaq glanced up and caught Katie's attention with a wave of her hand.

Katie came closer, looked down with a grimace and then went to her backpack to dig around. Jaq waited to help with the fresh bandages, slowly stroking Daniel's arm. His eyes opened to hazel slits in his bruised and battered face.

"Hey," he whispered, trying to smile at Jaq.

"Hey." She squeezed his hand gently.

"So... am I ugly?" One brow rose a fraction.

"Yeah. Very." Jaq smiled, blinking back the stinging moisture in her eyes. Deep purple bruises and dried blood stood out from Daniel's pale skin like paint on a white canvas. Swelling hid his beautiful bone structure and deformed his full lips.

Daniel seemed to search her face a moment. "Good," he said with a weak grunt.

Jaq's heart felt as if somebody closed their fingers around it. "Oh, Jock," she murmured, with tears constricting her throat.

Daniel shut his eyes.

CHAPTER 15

NOBODY SLEPT MUCH THAT NIGHT. They waited, listening to the sound of coyotes and the occasional howl from a far-off wolf. It grew colder. Mick didn't come.

By the time any light pierced through the dark skies, Jaq, Katie, and the boys were huddled together over Daniel, clinging for warmth. The fire helped, but the fear didn't.

"I dozed. Did I miss Mick showing up to save the day?" Finn coughed and leaned into Jaq.

"He never came," Katie said. She stared out at the horizon, as if to conjure Mick into being. Her lips pressed together in a grim line and her wide, desperate eyes had dark circles beneath them.

Russ threw more wood onto the fire. "I'm going to check the traps. We need food." When he'd gone, Jaq considered how much food she had left. A couple handfuls at most. Even if Mick didn't get a message to R.J., they would deliver food soon. Within a couple of days. Daniel moaned softly; he didn't look any better. A couple of days would be too late for him.

"I don't know what I'm supposed to do." Katie's hands flapped. "I don't know what to do," she mumbled. She peered down at Daniel and frowned. "I can't save him."

Jaq swallowed back a scream. There was a psycho on the loose and the only adult here was useless. Mick had failed. Katie was failing too. She had to do something. Feeling helpless made her furious. Jaq clutched Daniel's hand, and a stark memory shot through her mind as she stared into the fire.

Jaqueline clenched her fists, her wrists bound behind her. She stared at the hideous, orange, papier-mâché mask her brother had made at school. It had a gaping mouth with tusk-like fangs and large soulless eyes painted red and black. A dozen candles surrounded the creepy thing where it was propped up on a small box. The flames flickered, and the mask seemed to change expressions. It was grotesque.

"Stop it, Brian," Flower begged. "I don't want to bow to it. It scares me." She lifted her small blonde head and scooted backwards on her knees across the worn wood floor. Her feet were tied together so she couldn't coordinate her legs to stand.

"You have to. If you don't, the spirits will be angry." Brian shoved his little sister's head down until her forehead knocked on the floor.

"Ouch! Jaqueline, help me—I don't want to bow to the monster!" Flower screeched.

"Stop it—you're scaring her." Jaqueline tried to free her hands.

"Kneel." Brian pointed to the ground, giving her a fierce scowl.

She was angry that he'd been able to overpower them and drag them into his lair. But he'd had Flower's toy—and she couldn't let her sister face him alone. Jaqueline backed away toward the door and flipped the light on with her shoulder. "No way. We're leaving."

"No. You. Aren't." He shoved her away from the door as she tried to fumble with the knob with her imprisoned hands at the small of her back. "Bow to it and chant the words," Brian growled.

Jaqueline stumbled against his bed. "Jerk."

Flower stuck out her tongue. "It's so ugly. I don't want to look at it."

"Close your eyes." Jaqueline hated that Brian was bigger and stronger. It was awful that she was too afraid of him to protect her sister.

The faint slam of the front door was followed by footsteps tapping in the hallway outside the door.

"Mom!" Jaqueline shouted, angry and scared.

A big sigh. "What is it?" her mother asked, her muffled voice came through the door annoyed.

"Brian is trying to freak us out and make us worship that gross mask he made," she yelled.

The door opened. Her mother leaned into the room, her brown hair frazzled, her shirt crumpled. Car keys dangled from one hand and an oversized purse was clutched in the other. Jaq's mom didn't really look at her daughters. She eyed the candles. "Brian, leave your sisters alone. And those are a fire hazard—put them out." She turned and left.

Jaq and Flower stared after her, frozen. "But—"

Brian held a finger to his lips and the words stopped on Jaqueline's tongue. Mom couldn't stop him; she'd only make him angrier.

Brian shut the door. "Tried to get me in trouble, huh?" He folded his arms across his chest and sneered. "Now it requires more than your worship. Now it needs a sacrifice." He pulled, Flower's stuffed bunny out from behind his pillow where he had smothered it. The bait that had gotten them in this whole mess hung limp in his hand.

"Popcorn!" Flower sobbed.

Jaqueline's heart dropped. They were at his mercy. There

was no point in yelling for her mother. She just hoped she could save Popcorn from the flames.

The fire crackled and spit, and Jaq scowled at the memory. She should have kicked Brian's butt. Jaq kinda wished he was here—and that by beating him up she could solve all their problems. But this time it wasn't Brian that threatened her and those she cared about. It was the badlands. And once again, there was no mommy to help her.

"Katie, what do you think happened to Mick?" Finn asked, obviously still under the desperate illusion that Katie was in charge and had answers.

"No idea. None. I can't even... Oh Lord." Katie shut her eyes. "I'm cold and hungry." She almost sounded like a child.

Finn nodded and gulped. "Yeah. Me too." His blue eyes gave Katie a bleak look. "It's okay. We'll be okay." He patted her back, his sharp jaw tightened in resolve.

"We've got this," Jaq said, hoping to reassure the young counselor who had always reassured everyone else.

Katie blinked and tried to smile. "We can't all be strong like you," she said softly.

Russ returned to camp holding a rabbit by the ears, it swayed lifeless in his hand. Finn let out a low whistle. "That must've been some trap."

"Mick set a big one." Russ held up the prize. The skull of the tan and gray jackrabbit had collapsed under the weight of the fall-stone and blood had dried on the furry face. "Anyone still have a knife?" He crunched across the hardened snow and set his kill on a stone beside the fire.

"Me—I sleep with it on my hip, and with my boots on. Ready for anything," Jaq said, partly as a warning in case anyone tried to kill her in her sleep. She held up her knife and Russ took it from her, a glint of admiration in his eyes.

Russ skinned and prepared the rabbit with a practiced

hand. He slid the skin and fur off in one piece and removed the slimy innards without a flinch.

Jaq grimaced in disgust and turned away. "Looks like you've done that before."

Russ glanced up from his bloody work. "Yeah. Used to hunt a lot with my dad." He cleared his throat and jabbed a sharpened stick through the gaping mouth of the rabbit, pushing down the length of the body until it came out through the lower stomach.

He lashed together a pair of crisscrossed sticks to serve as legs for the spit as Jaq watched. It was a small comfort to see his capable, tanned hands working. Jaq wished he'd hold her and pat her on the back with those hands. If he washed them first. They were slick with blood.

Russ glanced at her and she looked away. As if he'd read her thoughts, he poured water from the can that had been on the fire over his hands to wash them. It turned the snow below a slushy pink. They hadn't had any privacy or "moments" since a couple days before when they'd almost kissed. Daniel had interrupted that...

Jaq sat closer to the fading jock and put a hand on his chest. He was so still. Maybe if she tried to kiss Russ, Daniel would sit up to yell and complain. The thought made her want to laugh and cry at the same time.

Katie came back from her restless lookout walk and eyed the rabbit with a flicker of hope. Then she bent over Daniel's body. With a sigh she leaned closer.

"You still there?" She touched his shoulder and his eyelids quivered in response. His lips had turned a blue gray. Katie pulled back his blanket and checked the wounds. "Well, the bleeding has slowed. But I think it's because he's running out of blood." Her voice choked, she scrubbed her face with both hands, muffling a sob. "We...

can't go anywhere with him... like this. And if we... leave here..."

"Then they won't have any record of our location," Russ finished for her as she struggled to breathe. "If this is our last reported position, and we can't move him, we just have to keep him alive until our food drop-off tomorrow." He settled the rabbit into place over the fire, all business.

Katie shook her head and Finn joined her. "I'm not sure that's soon enough." Finn raked his long reddish bangs back over the top of his head, his blue eyes glued to Daniel's pale, battered face.

"I can't leave you guys here... and we can't carry him that far." Katie looked up at the sky. The sun was a bright spot behind dark clouds. "It might snow again." The college girl's hands trembled as she patted at Daniel's blanket again.

"Do you know where HQ is?" Finn squatted by the fire and poked at it with a stick. Sparks crackled in the air and scattered onto the dirt and the loose flap of Daniel's blanket.

"Not sure without a compass," Katie mumbled, watching Russ stomp on the sparks before they could light up their patient like a funeral pyre. Jaq worried at the dull look in Katie's eyes. "But I could find an outpost... I think."

"I hate how time keeps ticking by and we're just sitting here. Look at him." Finn frowned, pushing his hands into his pockets. The plaid shirt that had been around his waist for most of the trip was wrapped around his neck like a scarf. He tugged it off and spread it out over the top of Daniel's blanket.

"I know." Jaq swallowed. "Katie, do you think you could find help? You must know this place better than we do."

"Maybe. I—I might be able to." She grimaced and opened her mouth as if to say something else and then shut it.

"You're afraid to go alone," Russ said.

"Yes."

"I'll go too." Jaq heard herself say. Sure... she could go for help too. The whole trip would probably be cancelled now anyway. If she went back to find help, she could go home.

"I mean... I guess I was thinking maybe one of the guys." Katie looked at Russ and Jaq froze. She didn't want to be left out here without Russ.

Finn straightened. "I'll go with you. How far could it be? We'd be there before they got here with food, right?"

"I don't know." Katie shrugged. She looked to Russ as if he had the answers.

"If you go, you need to eat first. I can take care of things here. But if you think you would get lost, it would be better if you stayed. We have no idea what happened to Mick."

Jaq had tried not to think about the implications of Mick not returning. "I don't think they should go. But I'm afraid for... him." Daniel let out a small groan as if on cue.

"Let's get some more broth in him. Katie, do what you think is best." Russ turned his attention to the rabbit that sizzled and browned over the fire. The aroma of cooking meat was reassuring in a way. Maybe eating it would make things look better.

———

In the afternoon, Katie's mood changed. She fidgeted and paced, her eyes straying to the horizon as if to watch the sun slipping ever closer to it. "If he hasn't come back yet, he isn't coming." Swallowing, she stared off into the distance again. "Mick, what happened to you?"

Jaq curled onto her side beside Daniel so that her blanket covered them both. The rabbit sat solidly in her stomach. The smell of wool, dirt, and blood filled her nose as she burrowed closer to her fading friend. "What now?" she choked out.

Katie stomped her foot. "I'm going. Finn, come with me.

Russ, I need to rely on you to look after the other two. Can you do that?"

Russ, who had been hunched by the fire, straightened to a stand, his jaw set and a grim hardness in his dark eyes. "Yeah. I can do that."

A chill traveled over Jaq. It frightened her to no end that she and Russ would be alone out there. Daniel was dying. She reached her arm over Daniel's body as if to keep his spirit from leaking out to rise into the sky.

Finn flashed Jaq a look. He tried to smile, his blue eyes wide. He pushed his bangs away from his face. "Jaq."

"Yeah?"

His elfish face became somber. "Be careful. K? Don't leave Russ' side."

"I won't. You be careful, too." She turned her face back into Daniel's shoulder to hide her tears.

"We'll hike through the night by flashlight. If everything goes well, there should be someone here for you in the morning. If not..." Katie looked down at Daniel, who hadn't moved or showed any signs of life for hours other than shallow breathing that was almost imperceptible. "Head for those rocks and keep walking until you get to a place where two streams crisscross. Then turn west and try to stay in a straight line. You'll come to a small grove of trees. There is an outpost there. I think they're still using it." She pressed the heel of her hand into her eyes. "That's the problem—they could be stationed at any of four locations. Mick may have gone to the wrong one..."

Russ nodded as if memorizing everything she said. "All you can do is your best. We will follow you there when—if Daniel..." Russ stopped and rubbed his chest. Something ached there by the look on his face. "Yeah?"

Katie scuffed her boot in the thin layer of snow on the ground. "I guess that if help doesn't come by tomorrow night, you should try to find us." Nothing she said rang with confidence. It was clear she had no idea what advice to give. Katie was in panic mode, and they were on their own.

"We'll be fine. Go." Russ clapped Finn on the back. Finn grabbed the other boy and hugged him. "Don't let anything happen to Jaq," Finn mumbled.

"Don't worry. Be safe." Russ's voice dipped low and rough.

Finn crouched down to where Jaq lay beside Daniel. "Aa' lasser en lle coia orn n' omenta gurtha," he murmured.

Jaq wondered if that was Irish or something. She wrinkled her brow in question.

"May the leaves of your life-tree never turn brown. In Elvish." He quirked a brow.

Jaq couldn't suppress a small smile. "You really are a nerd," she said with affection. "Live long and prosper, Legolas."

Finn smiled at her, looking a lot like an elf. He placed a hand on her shoulder and leaned close, his face grew somber. "You're a good friend. I won't let anything stop me from getting you help."

Jaq couldn't speak, suddenly choked up. She sniffed and nodded her head.

Katie shouldered her pack, hugged Russ, patted Jaq's bent head and hiked away from camp with Finn following, his skinny legs swift, behind her.

———

When Jaq woke, the sun sat low enough to be obstructed by towering rocks in the west. She sat up with all her muscles aching and remembered their predicament. *Crap.* It didn't seem real. This must be how it felt to make history or get on the news. Stuff happened—the kind of stuff that only happened to other people or in movies. And your brain floats away from your body to remain an exception. These things didn't happen to you. She glanced down at her filthy costume and up at the movie set around her, then at the gruesome makeup job on her battered friend. She'd have to congratulate the director.

Her heart skipped when she realized Russ was not at the fire. "Russ?" Jaq sat up, turning her head in all directions. The badlands dimmed, shadows growing toward her, a mouth closing to swallow her whole. Her heart beat like a fist on a locked door. "Russ!"

"Jaq." He came from behind a rock, carrying something in his hands. "I'm here," he called out while jogging toward her.

She didn't feel the tears coming. They just seemed to appear in her eyes, squeezing her throat shut. Jaq covered her face with both dirty hands and hiccupped a sob.

The stomp of feet told her that Russ broke into a run. "Jaq." He was at her side, wrapping his arms around her, breathing deep. "A-a-are you ok? Is Jock...?"

Jaq rubbed her forehead back and forth on his shoulder. "I don't know. I'm scared."

Russ made a shushing sound and ran his hand up and down her back in a soothing rhythm. After a few moments he sat back and Jaq wiped her tears away, embarrassed by her weakness. When she could finally meet his eyes, a stillness came over her. Russ's dark gaze held a strength that seemed to prop her up. Obviously, this was not the first time he'd been someone's scaffolding. His determined eyes glinted with an imploring look, as if he willed her to lean on him and not give up.

"We can do this. You're strong. You with me?" His voice rumbled deep as he gripped both of her shoulders in strong hands. "You good?"

Jaq cleared her throat and rubbed her eyes. "Yes. I'm fine." Having him get all supportive and protective made her want to crumple in his arms like a baby. She wasn't used to someone being her cheerleader.

At the same time, they switched their attention to Daniel. No change. Jaq stroked his pale cheek and leaned down to his ear. "Daniel. Can you hear me?"

Daniel's swollen eyelids trembled. His lips parted.

"You can." Jaq let out a breath. "Daniel, they've gone for help."

Russ retrieved something from the ground he must have dropped when he came to her comfort. It was a dead mouse. Dinner.

CHAPTER 16

JAQ AND RUSS gathered a large pile of sticks for the fire. Russ said he didn't like the look of the sky. The thick, dark clouds made everything gray.

Before night fell, the snow did. It came soft at first, fluttering like cherry blossoms to the ground, but after a little while it came down like a heavy fog. Jaq couldn't see anything beyond the fire pit.

"We need to huddle." Russ added wood to the fire and squeezed in close to Jaq where she'd burrowed into Daniel's side. They tented one of the blankets over them, covering their heads.

The smell of wet wool and dirt was suffocating. Jaq shivered so hard she couldn't talk. She pressed her cheek into Daniel's neck. "God help us," she whispered.

"He will," Russ rumbled into her back. He draped one arm over Jaq's trembling body and rested his chin on her shoulder.

"Do you pray?" Jaq tried to soak in the heat coming from Russ at her back.

"All the time." His voice was low and matter-of-fact.

"Ever do any good?" Her teeth had started to chatter.

"Always." Russ pressed closer and tightened his arm around her.

"So, God rescues you and fixes your problems?" Jaq smirked. He was so warm.

Russ let out a soft chuckle. "That's not what it's about."

"Then what good is it?" Jaq didn't want to sound bitter—she really wanted to know.

"Well." Russ shifted so that his mouth was closer to Jaq's ear. His voice continued in a soft whisper, "I pray to stay centered. I tell God my problems and ask him to help me deal with them. It feels good when I pray. Problems don't just go away, but sometimes my strength to handle them goes away. That's why I pray to God to help me not give up."

For no reason that Jaq could understand, tears filled her eyes. "What if you want to give up?"

"It wouldn't be fair. To the people who count on me. Not an option."

Jaq thought about her mother—how she'd given up on the family. And then she thought about Flower. It must have been horrible for her to lose her mother and then have her big sister shrug off. "I want to be strong," Jaq rasped, clenching her hands.

"You are." Russ reached down and gently unfolded her fist with his thumb, then laced his fingers through hers. His hand was warm and hard. Jaq thought her own hand felt so small in his.

"Tell me your stuff. Russ, why are you so awesome?"

He snorted. "Me? Geez." His breath was hot on her jaw. He pulled back a little, turning his face up into the blanket that hung only an inch or two over them.

"I mean it. Why are you out here with the rest of us losers? You said it was kinda drugs, whatever that means."

He drummed the fingers of his free hand on his chest.

"My dad was a cop," Russ sighed, gearing up to tell her something hard. "He was pretty stressed all the time. Not home a ton. It was tough on my mom, you know. My older sister's married and out of the house, so my mom kinda relied on me a lot. But everything was cool until suddenly it wasn't." Russ paused.

When Jaq turned toward him, the sharpness of his sweat was reassuring. The smell of strength and life. She watched the side of Russ's face. Scraggly, dark stubble and dirt shadowed his cheek and chin. His eyes were closed.

Russ squeezed her hand. "My dad used to bust drug dealers a lot. So, he had access, you know? And I guess... all the stress and crap he dealt with got to him. And he caved."

Jaq swallowed as uneasiness clenched in her stomach.

"He just checked out." Russ's voice was flat.

Jaq knew what it was like to have a parent give up. "Is he an addict?"

Russ's jaw tightened and he nodded. "It started as his way to cope. Next thing you know—he's off the force. He was using a lot. I couldn't believe it at first. My dad—you know?" He covered his face with his hand. "It was like... m-m-my..." Russ's throat contracted. Jaq ran a soothing hand up and down his arm. She felt his emotions kick in—catching up with the words he'd been saying.

"I'm so sorry," Jaq breathed.

"M-my d-d-ad was gone." Russ turned his face away from Jaq, his chest rising with jagged breaths.

"And you took care of him." Jaq remembered how Russ had looked after Finn during his withdrawals at the beginning of the trip. "You tried to help him get off drugs."

He nodded. "B-b-ut he died. Over d-dosed." It came out in a groan as he tried to control his voice.

Jaq's heart ached. "How long ago?" She touched his cheek

and Russ turned to look at her. His dark eyes glistened with tears.

He took a deep breath. "A year." He gulped more air.

"And so, you weren't kidnapped. You came out here..."

"T-to... reconnect to who I am. With who my dad used to be. We used to camp together... he taught me how to survive in the wilderness. I guess surviving in civilization is a d-different story." He wiped a hand across his eyes. "The praying. It helps," he finished, speaking slow and deliberate—the way he did to stop his stutter.

Jaq thought about how everyone else's problems made her life look awesome. And it made her feel like a wimp. "So, prayer is how you've coped."

"Yeah. No side effects." He smiled on one side and let out a soft snort.

"Russ." Jaq didn't know what to do with the rush of affection that warmed her from head to toe.

"Yeah?"

"Thanks for telling me."

He nodded and wrapped both arms around her. Jaq's face nestled into his chest. The smell of sagebrush, wood smoke, and sweat was a comfort. His breathing was still rough with emotion but slowed as they lay there sharing their warmth. Jaq turned over again so that she faced Daniel, and Russ kept her tucked up against him.

Jaq reached out to touch Daniel's neck. Her fingers traced the soft *bump-bump* of his pulse. Daniel let out a breath and his eyes floated open a crack. Jaq's heart lifted.

"I'm still here." Jaq kissed his shoulder.

"You... missed," Daniel whispered so soft, barely moving his lips, but Jaq understood.

She gave him a small smile and reached up to place a soft kiss on his mouth. His lips were cold and dry as paper.

"Happy now?" Jaq blinked back tears.

A tiny twitch at the corners of Daniel's mouth suggested a smile and his hazel eyes seemed to sparkle for just a second into Jaq's before closing again. Jaq lay shivering between the two boys, her heart sinking slowly. Help had to come.

———

Jaq drifted to sleep without realizing it. She awoke to Russ scrambling out of the blanket with a shout. Deep growls and sharp yelping shot fear through her gut. She leaped up to the horrible site of three coyotes pacing back and forth in the snow less than ten feet away, ghostly in the early morning light. Their fierce eyes piercing, wild, their pointy snouts open, showing sharp teeth.

Russ grabbed a stick and Jaq fumbled for her knife. Russ didn't look at Jaq. He stood in a wide stance, his arms out, facing the prowling wild dogs.

In the semi darkness, their amber eyes gleamed and sandy yellow fur stuck out from their scrawny bodies. A low rumbling in their throats, like the earth coming apart, made Jaq tremble in terror.

One with a torn ear lunged forward only to immediately skitter back when Russ slashed his stick forward. Russ roared, loud and threatening. "Back! Go away!"

Jaq swallowed the dry lump in her throat. Adrenaline ran like lightning in her veins. "Go away!" She screamed until her throat hurt, hoping to scare them away.

The three coyotes tossed their heads, backing up and coming forward in a dance to find a weakness—an opening to leap through. Torn Ear lowered his head and crept forward, front legs bent close to the ground, while the other two circled slowly, one heading in each direction.

"You watch that one." Russ pointed at one coming around on Jaq's side, while turning to keep his eyes on the one moving around him. Behind them was the fire pit—and now they were flanked by two coyotes while the third one inched forward on its haunches toward Daniel's unconscious body.

"Oh. My. Gosh. Oh-my-gosh!" Jaq couldn't seem to breathe. She clutched her knife in a shaking hand. She glanced at the fire pit. Only embers. One long stick hung out of the fire; the side in the pit glowed red. Slowly Jaq squatted and gripped the stick, her eyes locked on the starved-looking coyote that stared back at her, its tongue hanging out. She waved the stick, causing the coyote to flinch and snarl. From behind her, Russ shouted, and a coyote growled and snapped.

Then the one in front of her tensed and sprang. Jaq jabbed forward with the stick, and it struck the coyote in the chest. It staggered to the side and lunged again. She dropped the stick, regained her balance, and swung her arm. Her knife hand connected to fur with a wet popping sound. The weight of the animal knocked Jaq sideways to the ground. Her face smashed into the snow. Flailing to a sitting position, Jaq held up her knife, startled to see blood all over her hand and running down her arm. She didn't feel hurt. Her heart pumped hard. The scrawny coyote backed away, leaving a trail of red in the white snow. Its eyes flashed, but it continued to retreat until it sagged to the side and crumpled, letting out a high whine. The fur on its chest was matted and soaked with blood. Jaq numbed out, feeling like nothing was real.

Russ screamed. Jaq turned to see him swing a large stick like a bat down onto the head of a coyote that had its jaws on his calf. Blood seeped through Russ' blue jeans. In shock, Jaq moved like a robot toward him. She had to help.

But something caught Jaq's eye, making her stop in horror. The third coyote, the one with the messed-up ear, had its dagger-like teeth sunk into Daniel's boot and had tugged him several feet. In a sick panic, Jaq flew wildly toward it, waving her knife. She didn't recognize the roar that came out of her mouth. The coyote backed away, dragging Daniel like a dead deer.

The thought of Daniel becoming dinner for wild dogs made Jaq frantic with hatred. She dove forward, her bloody hand gripping the knife, and the coyote released its prize, turning sharply to dart away. Jaq crouched on the ground as her enemy circled, snarling, baring its teeth at her. She glared back, knowing this game. Brian had taught her well.

A horrible thumping sound, punctuated by yelps and Russ's grunts, drew Jaq's attention. Behind her, Russ pounded a large rock into the coyote's head. It let go of Russ's leg and dropped to the ground, but Russ didn't stop. A grimace of loathing and fear distorted his features.

"Russ!" Jaq screamed. She needed him to look familiar—to come back from wherever his head had just gone.

Russ looked over with dangerous black eyes, his hands clutched the rock, his face and hands splattered with blood. He hurled the rock past Jaq and it bounced, landing at the last coyote's feet. It yelped and hopped back, shaking and growling. It swung its head back and forth, seeming to sum up who the winners were, then turned and loped away into the bushes, releasing a high howl as it disappeared.

Staring after the fleeing beast, Russ hung his hands at his sides. He limped over to Jaq dropping to his knees beside her. He pulled her into a crushing embrace. The metallic smell of blood made Jaq's stomach lurch, but she hugged him back.

"Are you okay?" he gasped, breathing rough.

"Yes. Yes. I'm okay." Jaq shook until her teeth chattered. A tremor ran over Russ's hard frame, and he tightened his grip as if to stop the shaking.

"You're okay," he repeated in Jaq's ear.

"Are you?" It seemed impossible they had survived. Jaq had the horrible urge to laugh hysterically, and she clenched her jaw, afraid that she'd never be able to stop.

"My leg. It hurts," Russ said through gritted teeth.

She pulled away and glanced where his jeans were torn open and bloody. "Katie left some supplies. Let's— "

"Not yet. Jock." Russ winced as he walked on his knees toward Daniel, using his hands to balance.

Jaq spun around—she'd almost forgotten about Daniel. She bent over his body and something inside stung.

"Is he gone?" Russ's voice was hollow.

Jaq held her breath. Daniel lay so still, half wrapped in blankets, his face so pale that even the bruising was faint now. His blond hair looked like tarnished bronze against the glowing white snow. Jaq stabbed her knife into the ground and reached for him.

"Daniel. Daniel." Jaq's hands fluttered over his chest and at his neck. She left bloody fingerprints on his white skin. He didn't move. "I don't feel a pulse. Don't feel a pulse!" Panic made her voice shrill.

Russ pushed her aside and turned his ear to Daniel's chest, his eyes squeezed shut. "C'mon," he muttered. "C'mon, buddy."

A few moments ticked by, and Jaq waited for Russ to say something. She clasped her hands together and thought about the last time Daniel had shown signs of life. He'd tried to smile for her. She just wanted him to open his eyes again—even if it meant giving him a hundred kisses.

But it was Russ who raised his head and covered Daniel's mouth with his own, breathing into him, causing Daniel's chest to rise. Russ repeated it two more times, then locked his hands together and pushed down on Daniel's chest. He continued doing this while Jaq watched, feeling like a block of ice worked its way down her throat and into her belly.

Russ listened at Daniel's chest again. He sat up and his dark eyes met Jaq's. All the breath left her lungs. She froze stiff when Russ put his arms around her.

"No," she whispered, shaking her head. "No. No. Nooo!" Her voice rose in a wail.

"He's gone, Jaq. He's gone. I tried. I tried. God. Oh, God," Russ choked.

Jaq sank to the frozen ground, feeling nothing as Russ held her.

CHAPTER 17

THE SHIVERING HAD STOPPED. Jaq huddled by the fire staring at the coals. They glowed red, snapping and hissing like snakes, devouring the sticks that Russ added. The hollowness inside of her muted her senses, and Jaq felt like she was asleep with her eyes open.

Russ let out another stifled sob. He was still capable of feeling. Jaq absently noted that this whole thing must bring up the ghost of his father. It was sad. But for some reason, she couldn't feel it.

After clearing his throat, Russ lowered himself beside Jaq. "W-we should try to follow K-Katie."

"What about his body." Jaq's voice sounded flat and distant, even to herself.

"I'm not sure we can c-carry him, especially with my l-leg" —he coughed—"the way it is."

"Oh." Jaq noticed how all the veins showed on the back of her hand like blue lightning. She clenched her fists and watched her skin move and tighten. Inside, her heart pulsed, slow and deep. She must still be alive. Even pale and numb, her body told her it was still doing its thing. Without wanting to, she turned to look over her shoulder. Daniel's body. It had stopped. When your body stopped, you went away. The person you are disappears just because your heart stops beating.

"Are you okay? The look on your face..." Russ leaned in and pressed his cheek to Jaq's. She could not feel his warmth or the roughness of his unshaven face.

"Russ." A crazy thought came to her. "Do dead people dream?"

"Jaq?"

"Because I think that I'm dead—dreaming I'm still alive," she murmured, wondering if her voice sounded just as strange to Russ as it did to her.

Russ held her tight. "No. Jaq, you're in shock."

"Oh." Jaq floated, watching herself by the fire with Russ.

"It will be okay." Russ ran a hand through her hair.

"I used to care about that—being okay. It's kind of weird what I used to care about. Seems silly now. Mad at my parents." Jaq listened as she rambled on like someone else was using her lips to speak. "Caring about what kids at school thought. I secretly wanted Sean to really like me. Even though I pretended to be a player too. And I was so bugged by Daniel, so I was rude to him." Her breath stopped. In the pause, something cracked the ice around her, and emotion trickled in like acid. "I was so horrible to him!" she choked out.

"No, no, shhh, shhh." Russ held her closer, one hand making circles on her back as he shushed and rocked her like she was a child. "You both gave each other a hard time, but he liked you. You looked after him and stayed by him when he was dying."

Dying. He really had been dying that whole time. Not waiting for help. He was actually gone. Jaq sobbed. Feeling returned in a painful burn, just like it did when a hand or foot went to sleep and life tingled back like needles. Everything was horrible. Daniel was dead. They were stuck in the middle of the badlands, and she just wanted to be home. "I wish I'd told him something nice—at the end."

"You were his last kiss," Russ whispered. "What a wonderful way to go."

Russ had noticed, of course. They had all been under that blanket together. She thanked God she kissed Daniel instead of making some snotty remark to him.

Jaq cried and cried into Russ's strong shoulder until her feelings clicked off again. While her body continued to shed tears and sob, she wondered why. Then the tears just stopped.

"Russ. We need to go." Jaq wiped her face with a sleeve.

"Yeah." He stroked her back once more and then stood. Clenching his jaw, he looked at Daniel's lifeless body. "I don't want those damn coyotes to have him." Russ limped over to the dead jock and knelt beside him. After touching Daniel's blond hair and cheek, he shook his head, his face a picture of disbelief and sadness. Then he picked up the red and white plaid shirt that Finn had draped over Daniel before he left and tossed it at Jaq. "We can't waste this—you need to get warm."

Jaq clutched the soft fabric to her chest. It still smelled like Finn and sagebrush. The cold flannel warmed in her hands. She slipped her arms inside it and brought the sides of the shirt together in front, slowly buttoning it up to the top over her IBSA hoody.

Russ peeled the two extra blankets away, leaving Daniel's stiff form tightly bound in one—like the victim of a giant spider. He shook out the stiff, charcoal-colored wool and then folded them in preparation for making bedrolls. Jaq wondered how Russ could still do anything. He busied himself gathering their few things and heating a billycan of water over the fire. Then he stopped to finally clean and attend to his injured leg. He used some of the hot water and the things Katie left, stuffing a maxi-pad under the bandage he'd wound around the ragged bite mark. His leg had continued to bleed, so he added another pad and wrapped his leg again.

"Are you okay?" She hated feeling dependent, but Jaq needed Russ to be fine. She didn't like the way he winced as he moved.

He nodded. "We'll eat. Then we'll go. I'll figure something out. I won't let you down." Russ's soft brown eyes were mournful and warm at the same time when he looked at Jaq.

"I'm fine. I don't need you to save me." Jaq closed her eyes so she wouldn't see his reaction to her lie and tried to pretend she was someplace else.

Russ walked over to one of the dead coyotes and prodded it with his foot before stooping down beside it. "There's a lot of good meat here."

"Ugh." Jaq made a face but the growling of her belly betrayed her.

Russ used her knife to sever one of the haunches from the dead wild dog. The sound of the blade moving through flesh and the gore it left on Russ's hands made him seem savage. His face, sprinkled with drying blood, had no expression.

Jaq watched, fascinated and with a growing uneasiness, as he prepared to cook the meat over the fire. An image plucked at the back of her mind of Russ, cutting into Daniel. Emotionless. Jaq shook her head, but the thought remained that Russ had his own reasons to hate the jock.

———

After eating the gamey meat, which she nearly gagged on, Jaq waited beside the fire while Russ gathered their supplies. She had withdrawn inside herself, following Russ with her eyes, wondering who he was, desolated by the fact that she had to question it at all. There was nothing keeping them from going—except their dead friend's body.

Jaq balled her fists and scowled at the ground. "Can we get out of here?"

Russ finished the last knot on his bedroll. "Yeah."

They put on their bedroll packs and stared down at Daniel. It didn't really look like him now. Waxy, pale, and distorted, his face frozen in a slight grimace. He emitted no warmth, no energy—a stone.

"Well. Do you want to see how long we can carry him?" Russ frowned.

"Okay. We could try," Jaq mumbled.

Russ hooked his hands under Daniel's armpits and Jaq took his feet. He was stiff and cumbersome to carry as they shuffled over the uneven and rocky ground. It was exhausting. They hadn't gotten very far when Russ lowered his half of the burden. He grasped his own leg, his face stamped with pain.

"You okay, Jaq? Do you need to rest?"

Jaq's arms ached but something unseen and hard seemed to wrap around her and she stood straighter. "I'm fine. Come on."

Russ's dark gaze was serious and intense. He nodded once, wiped the sweat from his forehead and lifted.

The next couple of hours were a blur of stumbling and grunting punctuated by stops to lower the body and breathe. Jaq's exhaustion had long since turned into a robotic determination. The burn in her arms and back belonged to another girl. She tried not to think about what they carried—until she was tempted to drop it and give up. Then she pictured Daniel—his handsome, cocky smile and the way his hazel eyes widened like a vulnerable child when he'd told her his darkest secret. Then the image of a mangy, feral dog with its teeth in Daniel's foot, dragging him off for a meal, made Jaq growl in her throat and reposition her hands. She would not leave him here.

The snow crunched in the morning but turned into slush by noon. The sun had burned away the clouds, causing the wet smell of mud and plants to rise like steam. Sweat rolled down Jaq's back, even though her face still felt the sting of a cool breeze.

Russ staggered and groaned. He collapsed to the ground, breathing so hard his whole body moved up and down.

"Please help," he whispered, gripping his leg.

Jaq knew he wasn't talking to her. She let go of Daniel's feet and sunk to the ground herself. Her hands shook and her mouth was so dry. As if in answer to her parched throat, Jaq heard the soft rush of water from somewhere not too distant.

"Katie said... to head for the rocks"—Jaq gulped for air—"and go until we get to the streams." She rubbed her biceps and moaned as raw pain seemed to bleed from her muscles. "Can you keep going? You don't look very good."

"Thanks." Russ softly snorted and shut his eyes, working to slow his breathing. "My leg is throbbing."

"Let's at least get to the water."

"Yeah." Russ ran a hand through his shaggy dark hair. It stayed back, plastered by sweat.

Neither one of them moved for several minutes. The vastness around them made Jaq feel like a tiny dot. Silence stretched in all directions except for the slight tinkle of water. It was the only thing anchoring her to the present. Jaq pushed herself to stand. Her whole body protested in a shudder.

Russ breathed in through his nose and stood too. He reached out one hand and touched Jaq's jaw. "Ready?

Jaq nodded. Shame flickered inside for the thoughts she'd

had earlier that day. Russ wouldn't hurt anyone. They gathered up their dead friend.

———

Strange how relief and depression sometimes settle in at the same time. Russ and Jaq lay beside the bushes and a few straggly trees that lined the banks of the water where it ran clear and shiny over rocks. Jaq was bone tired, and sadness was a heavy lead covering her body, pinning it down as the sky above and maybe God himself operated an X-ray into her soul. It revealed ugliness, as if a filthy, slobbering beast had rolled her around in its awful mouth. It had stained her and left internal damage. Jaq wanted to crawl into the water and wash away everything. She wanted to drink in its cool clarity and have it purify her from the inside. She felt dirty all the way through.

Neither of them seemed able to muster the energy to go to the water yet. Russ turned his head toward her from where he lay. Her face must have been doing something awful because he frowned and placed his hand on her arm.

"We got here," he rasped, grimacing with his own pain.

"Yeah. But we haven't gotten *there* yet."

"No. But here is closer to there." He smiled a little.

Jaq couldn't find her smile. "How are we ever going to have a normal life after this? Or feel happy again?" The sound of her own words surprised Jaq; she hadn't meant to say them aloud. The sun glared into her eyes so she shut them.

"I know what you mean." Russ sighed.

"You really do. Don't you?" Jaq watched his profile as he stared at the sky. His soft mouth, his straight nose, the black fringe of his long lashes. Patchy stubble on the bronzed skin of his cheeks and chin.

"Want to hear my favorite poem?" Russ rolled onto his

stomach and picked up a small stick. He dragged it, making shallow scratches in the wet, packed dirt.

"Yeah. Whatever." Jaq shrugged without enough hope inside to generate interest in much.

"I found it online... after my dad died." Russ spoke slowly, and Jaq knew he must feel emotional because he was controlling his stutter. "It's by an awesome poet named Ellen Bass. And it's called 'The Thing Is'." He recited it in a low, calm voice, pausing and clearing his throat now and then:

"to love life, to love it even
when you have no stomach for it
and everything you've held dear
crumbles like burnt paper in your hands,
your throat filled with the silt of it.
When grief sits with you, its tropical heat
thickening the air, heavy as water
more fit for gills than lungs;
when grief weights you down like your own flesh
only more of it, an obesity of grief.
You think,
How can a body withstand this?
Then you hold life like a face
between your palms, a plain face,
no charming smile, no violet eyes,
and you say, yes, I will take you
I will love you, again."

He stuttered the words on the last line and by the end of the poem Russ had tears running from the corners of his eyes, down his temples, and into his hair. Jaq let out a low sigh—he kept getting her to feel. It was a beautiful poem and Russ was so beautiful too. Her heart squeezed in a warm ache. She turned on her side and hovered over him.

Russ looked up at Jaq, unashamed as he blinked, clearing

the thick wetness from his deep chestnut eyes. "It will be okay," he breathed as if it was an oath, a promise that he would see to personally.

Jaq believed him. Somehow. "Thank you."

There was nothing for an electric minute but their locked gaze. Jaq's heart fluttered, a trapped moth struggling toward the light in his eyes.

Russ slid his hands into her hair and pulled her down until their lips touched. Once, twice, his soft lips pressed to hers, spreading a warm tingle where they brushed together. Jaq wanted to cry. Finally, something that felt good.

She kissed him back, but thoughtfully, focusing on Russ and not the kiss. He was so sweet. So steady despite his stitched-together heart. He had goodness inside him, and Jaq kissed him as if to draw some of it into herself. Then it was the kiss itself. Exciting, building in intensity as Jaq collapsed against Russ's chest. It was delicious and filling, like a favorite food that did more than just meet hunger and fill emptiness—it sparked the desire for more.

Russ broke the kiss and hugged Jaq against him so hard her back crackled. "It's you and me. I f-feel so..." He sighed and cleared his throat. "So light."

Jaq smiled into his neck, breathing in his musky scent. "I do too."

"Proof that there's life after pain. Right here in my arms." His voice rumbled against Jaq, deep and soothing, like a lullaby. She closed her eyes, the exhaustion of the hike returning as the relief of Russ' embrace invited her to relax, like coming home after a long journey. Jaq fell asleep.

———

She awoke to splashing sounds. Jaq sat up in a panic. Russ was gone. Jaq jumped to her feet, her heart punching her ribcage hard and fast.

"Russ?" Horrible visions of coyotes feasting on his legs flashed, hot and red in her mind.

"I'm here." Russ came out of the bushes. He was all wet, clothes dripping, his skin shiny and clean, his hair sticking up all over in soaked spears. He shivered, his lips a little blue. Jaq put a hand to her chest and took a deep breath. "Oh. Hi." The rush of relief made it impossible to say anything else.

He held up two ropes he had looped into bundles in each hand. "I found these. They were strung up across the water—I think they must have been there to hold on to when the water is higher and faster—to help people cross."

"Okay." Jaq noticed his bandages piled on the shore. "You should put those back on."

"I will. I needed to clean it out. Bled a lot on the hike." He scrunched his nose as if to say *Just a pesky little problem.*

"Yeah." Jaq frowned. Russ had to be careful. She didn't know what to do if he became incapacitated.

Russ seemed to sense her worrying. He raised his brows. "Try the water. It feels amazing. Way cold, but it's refreshing." Russ cocked his head at her, appraising. "You're gorgeous—even dipped in dirt."

Jaq felt a blush start in her cheeks. "Thanks." She walked over to Russ and smiled at him. He lowered his eyelids and dropped the rope. Then before Jaq could react, he gave her a little push with both hands and she stumbled backwards, falling into the stream with a splash.

The cold made Jaq's skin shrink and her head ache. She shrieked when her breath returned, and Russ chuckled. "Enjoy."

"Oh! You! How rude!" She smiled and shivered from head

to toe, and her teeth clicked together. Luckily, the day had warmed, and Jaq's hands and feet had grown accustomed to being constantly cold. After the initial shock passed, being in water was a little heavenly. She ran her hands through the current, staring at the sparkle of the water and the peaceful flow. It pulled on her and washed around her. She sunk to her knees and welcomed the numbing temperature as the water came up to her chest. She shivered without fighting it.

"See? Kinda amazing." Russ grinned at her for a moment, then his face became serious. "I figured out a way to keep Daniel safe and still get where we're going."

Jaq looked up. "You did?"

Russ held up the ropes. "When I used to go camping with my dad... we'd protect our food from bears... by tying it up in trees."

"Oh." Jaq swallowed, understanding. It made sense. But it was horrible too.

"It's our best chance." Russ lowered his voice, his face apologizing.

"You're right. Do you need help?" Jaq hugged herself, the fabric of her clothes clinging and wet on her skin.

"No. I just need to throw the rope over a high, strong branch and pull." He kicked the toe of his shoe into the dirt.

It seemed surreal to be having a discussion about this. Jaq realized that survival was a culture all its own. It broke all social rules about what was considered appropriate. She felt like a foreigner, trying to learn this new way of speaking and acting. Yes, tying her dead friend up in a tree to protect his remains from the beasts that would eat him—it made sense.

"Okay. Let's do it."

Russ inclined his head. "You wash up. I'll do this." He turned his back to Jaq and disappeared behind the bushes.

Jaq lay back in the water, shaking from the cold. She

scrubbed at her face and allowed water to seep into her mouth. The rushing in her ears muffled her thoughts and made her forget everything for a moment.

Jaq opened her eyes and saw Russ limping toward Daniel with the rope and realized something. She was focusing on her own pain again—like she had with her sister Flower. Russ was exhausted and injured. Why was he doing everything?

She stood up. "Wait. Let me help."

CHAPTER 18

JAQ GLANCED high into the branches. They had used both ropes so that Daniel hung horizontally but crooked, a rope around his chest and one around his knees. Wrapped in a wool blanket, dangling that way, their dead friend looked like the broken marionette of a mummy. It made Jaq's stomach turn over and she swallowed back the lump in her throat that threatened to gag her. Her body shook.

"You're freezing." Russ peeled off his own wet shirt and began to wring it out.

Jaq nodded and did the same with the plaid shirt she wore, watching the water as it fell onto the ground. Her soaked hoody, thermal top, and IBSA hoody clung to her body and she stripped them off too. She removed her shorts and thermal pants to squeeze them out too.

Russ turned away as she stood only in her bra and underwear. He cleared his throat and then looked back at her, a shy smile on his face. Jaq shrugged, self-conscious, and winked. He turned away again.

The t-shirt she'd come in was wadded up in her supply bag. It was dirty but dry so she put it on. She'd worn it that last night

—in the diner with Flower and her dad. Another life. Different problems.

She felt better in the dry shirt—even though her shorts and the thermal bottoms still felt cold and heavy. She continued to squeeze out the wet clothes as she wore them, shaking with cold while Russ knelt under the tree, his head bent.

Daniel's last rites. Russ clasped his hands in prayer and then touched his forehead and shoulders in the sign of the cross before opening his eyes. He gazed up into the tree.

"Rest in peace," he whispered.

When Russ stood and faced her, there were no more tears. His expression was grim. "Katie said that at the streams we should turn west and try to walk straight until we came to a grove of trees. The outpost should be there. We might cross paths with someone coming toward us, so stay alert."

Jaq nodded. She felt rested. And a little excited to be so close to possible help. In shame, she glanced up at the body, where it hovered like a huge, empty hornets' nest. Abandoning Daniel there felt wrong. And yet, it was a relief that they'd no longer be carrying the body. It made Jaq feel guilty and selfish.

As if Russ read her mind he said, "We did our best for him. Soon someone will be down here to get him—and his family will have his body back in one piece." Russ put his arm around Jaq. She knew he was right. Getting Daniel this far and putting him out of reach of predators hadn't been easy—and it was their gift to him.

"Yes. This is good." Jaq reassured him with a hand on his shoulder. Russ smiled sadly and kissed Jaq's cheek, leaving a warm spot on her cold face. She wanted to burrow into his arms, but he turned away.

Russ and Jaq gathered their things and filled their canteens at the stream. They had a handful of dry oats—almost out of food now.

"Let's go." Jaq paused, looking above at her lost friend. "Goodbye, Daniel. Nothing and nobody can hurt you now." She choked back her emotions. "You'll never have to worry about that again. Your body is safe." From the coyotes and the predators back home... Jaq's hands curled into fists. Poor Daniel. She knew she had so many more tears—but later.

Russ gave her a curious look, seeming to sense there was an unseen layer to what she'd said. But he didn't pry.

"Goodbye, Jock," Russ whispered.

———

Russ had all the skills in the curriculum book memorized. He navigated through rocky ravines and brush, glancing at the sun to keep his bearings. His limp and occasional groan of pain made Jaq bite her lip. They had been hiking for a couple of hours since their break at the stream and the sun was high.

The temperature had risen to warm. A few wispy clouds spread like torn cotton high in the sky. The clothes dried stiff on their bodies. Only small ridges of loose snow clumped in shadows remained. It was as if the freaky premature snow hadn't happened—except for the mud. It sucked at Jaq's shoes and made the going slippery. Ahead, Russ staggered and landed on his knees with a bark of pain.

Jaq stumbled, sliding and waving her arms for balance to get to his side. "Russ. You okay?" she gasped.

His head bent down, breathing ragged. "Jaq. I'm sorry. I just d-don't know if I can keep g-going right now." He leaned down on his arms, his hands pushing into the ground, mud rising between his fingers.

Jaq squatted beside him and ducked her head low, trying to see his face. His sweaty hair hung in the way in stringy dark waves.

"How much farther?" She was so tired and felt as if she walked a tightrope over a gorge of grief.

"Don't know. Katie said go s-straight," he rasped.

"To the grove of trees. Yeah. We could be miles away." Jaq squinted into the distance, a long, uneven expanse, unmarked by anything green. Rocks, scant yellow grasses, and silvery sage forever, broken up by layered ridges. Overwhelming. "It's okay. We've been hiking all day. We can rest for a while. Okay, Russ?"

Russ looked up then. His face shiny with sweat, and redder than it should be. His eyes looked bright and dazed then rolled as if he couldn't focus properly.

"Russ, oh no." Jaq grabbed his shoulder and forced him to lie down against a flat, slanting rock embedded in the earth. She placed her palm over his forehead. Hot.

Russ panted and let out a low moan.

"Fever. A fever. You're burning up. Oh, oh no," Jaq muttered, her hands flapping ineffectually, glancing around as if to find help. Her inner balance wavered, like she was on the brink of falling.

"I'm. Okay. Just need to rest. Just a little." Russ closed his eyes. The sun fell over his face causing shadows in the hollows of his cheeks and eye sockets. A chill ran through Jaq. Her next step on the tightrope missed. Her stomach seemed to gape like a fathomless depth. And she plummeted.

"No. Wait. You can't—can't close your eyes! Don't!" Jaq's panic rose inside with no rational thought—she just had to see him open his eyes.

Russ stared at her, an alarmed expression on his face. "Jaq." He reached up and gripped her hand, caking it with mud. "Oh." His brows tilted in understanding. "I'm not dying, Jaq."

Jaq sobbed, her lungs convulsing. "I-I kissed him. And he died." Her words came out broken and raw. "Please don't close your eyes!" She was falling apart, and a blurry part of her brain felt like an idiot—weeping and grasping his hand in both of hers, holding it to her chest. Jaq didn't recognize herself. Pathetic and needy, utterly lost.

"Please. Please." She pressed her lips into the back of his hand, tasting the mineral and earth—the flavor of her desolation. Out here in the badlands with nobody to help her but Russ. "I need you," she whispered so low, hoping he didn't hear.

Russ struggled to sit, a grunt in his throat. "We're almost there. I'm ready. Let's keep going." He forced the words out steady and strong, but his neck trembled with a pounding pulse and his breathing hissed. "I just need a drink of w-water." Russ licked his lips and swallowed.

He was trying so hard. Jaq's heart turned over. In shame, she tried to calm herself, clamping down on the tears and forcing the sobs back into her tight chest. She let go of his hand and shook her head. "No. I don't want you to push so hard. I just... it's stupid. Of course, you should rest." Jaq fumbled with her canteen so that she wouldn't have to look at Russ. He didn't argue, just took in a scraping breath.

She dug through her things to find the last two pain pills out of the small kit that Katie had left with them for Daniel. When she found them, she offered them to Russ. Jaq held the water to his mouth, and he drank with eager gulps.

When she lowered the canteen, Russ met her gaze with determination, blinking back his delirium. He sat forward as if to get up. Jaq crawled around to his back and leaned against the rock, pulling Russ down so that the back of his head rested on her shoulder, his body cradled by hers. Wrapping her arms around his shoulders she whispered into his ear, "Rest like this. I feel better if I'm holding you."

Russ let out a sigh, the weight of his body relaxing against her. "Works for me. Guaranteed I'm not going anywhere. Wouldn't miss this for anything," he murmured.

Jaq smiled into his hair, absorbing his heat and the way he smelled, masculine and like the outdoors. If this were back home, she'd have said he stunk. But now it didn't bother her at all. She let her head fall back, telling herself that they would be fine. That Katie and Finn had gotten help and it was on the way right now. An ugly word pushed through the smoke screen of her thoughts. Rabies. Jaq scowled—she didn't even know what it was, just that it came from animal bites and usually killed.

No. Not going to think about that.

A soft breeze passed over Jaq's face. She imagined the beach. It was only twenty minutes from her home. Drifting clouds, waves on the shore, sun on her skin, a cold soda... a hammock swaying. Hammock. Daniel, hanging in the trees.

Stop thinking!

Jaq flattened her hands on Russ's chest, concentrating on the reassuring rise and fall there. She sent a small prayer to heaven with his name on it.

Please.

They both dozed for a while before Jaq noticed his breathing change. He was in pain. Jaq was weak and over-heated. She loosened her grip on Russ so he could reposition himself. Cool air rushed between them when he leaned forward. He resettled, shoulders tense.

"Tell me," Russ said, quietly.

"Hm?"

"Everything. About you." He slid his injured leg back and forth as if to move away from the pain.

"Me?" She swallowed, uncomfortable. Jaq hated talking about herself. Nobody wanted to hear about her pathetic crap.

"Distract me." Russ turned so that his face was in her neck. His breath was hot.

He needed her. Jaq breathed in deep, kissed the top of Russ' head, and started talking—all about growing up in Southern California. Her sister Flower, jerk brother Brian, who now, with the perspective of true horror she had experienced, seemed like nothing more than a powerless bully. She spoke about her weird dad and her crazy mom. But they didn't seem so bad anymore either. She spilled out all her insecurities and all the stupid decisions she'd been making—her shame at not being there for her sister and regrets over her unfair view of her dad. She had been a coward—hiding in some rebel persona, using her boyfriend, Sean, like a prop in her act.

"I guess I've always done that with guys. I've never really liked any of the guys I've been with—not for who they were. When I was a cheerleader I just ended up with football players, and then when I freaked out, I found bad boys. I started to wonder if I really could fall in love. I just couldn't open up and feel it. You know?"

Russ had listened through everything she'd said, responding with few words and nods. But this time he turned so that they were chest to chest, arms braced on the ground to either side of Jaq, their faces just inches apart.

"What about now?" It was Russ's man-voice again, his brown eyes searched hers, so warm and intense.

Inside, Jaq felt a zinging encircle her heart and pool in her stomach. She didn't want to be vulnerable but was so done with being a chicken. She went for honesty. "Well, this might be the trauma bond talking... but I do feel for you." Jaq let out a shaky breath.

"Because I fit into your new thing as a survivor girl?" He raised his brows, as if he was teasing. But Jaq saw that he was serious.

"No. I don't have a role for you—you're just you. And I feel —I mean I *really feel*... stuff for you." Jaq felt her blush happen and Russ followed it with his eyes, the corners of his mouth drawing up.

"Stuff?" His voice dropped huskily and his arms tunneled under her back.

"I really like you," Jaq whispered, avoiding his gaze, feeling dizzy.

"I like you too," he said, dropping his head and smiling into her neck.

It seemed a little weird to be talking about this in the middle of all the craziness. And she didn't want to force Russ into saying anything he wasn't ready to say. "I know we have bigger things to worry about right now—"

Russ cut her off. "This is the biggest thing that's ever happened to me." He pulled back to give her a stunning smile, made all the more poignant by the dust and perspiration on his face, and then he kissed her. Jaq forgot everything while his mouth explored hers, soft, and hot from fever. His unshaven face rasped against her skin. Sensations shot like stars through her whole body, as the heat, dirt, and sweat blossomed into sweet, soft fire.

———

The sun had sunk low before they finally saw the cluster of trees as they trudged up out of a ravine. Russ didn't look like he felt very good. Jaq linked her arm through his and felt him trembling. "You made it. We're here."

"Finally." Russ limped, leaning on Jaq.

Birds darted through the trees letting out high trills as they entered the grove. A small wood cabin sat in the middle, with one window and a door facing them. Jaq's insides rushed. They made it—there was help here. As they drew nearer, Russ slowed, looking around with a troubled expression. Jaq's instincts shivered. Beyond the now-cold temperature, there was something odd here.

Weeds and brush grew along the log siding. It felt vacant and still. A light wind stroked Jaq's skin and glided around the cabin. Goosebumps prickled on her arms.

"Russ. I don't think anyone's here." She spoke in a hushed voice without knowing why.

"No. They must be at one of the other sites. Maybe there's a map inside, or some supplies—a walkie-talkie." A howl rose up in the trees in the distance. "And it'll be safer if we spend the night inside." Russ took Jaq's hand and led her to the door.

The warped wood door opened with a high squeak. The dim interior of the cabin made Jaq blink, waiting for her eyes to adjust. Fireplace, table and chairs, bean bag, a door to another room. It smelled like mold, ashes, and pine. And something stale.

"Hello?" Russ called, causing Jaq to jump a little. The door swung shut with a clunk. Russ ambled over to the fireplace. There was already a stack of wood inside and more logs and sticks in a crate on the hearth. "I'll make a fire. You see if you can find anything useful."

"Okay." Jaq's shoulders drooped with exhaustion. It felt strange to be inside a building of any kind. Pushing open the other door, she found a room with a small counter with four cabinets beneath. An electric lantern sat on top of the counter, and two large cots with sleeping bags were pushed against opposite walls. Jaq couldn't wait to sleep on a cot.

In the cabinets, she found a few cans of peaches, first aid kit, two protein bars, matches, a jug of water, a binder, a small zipper bag with travel-sized toiletries inside, and a red flashlight. Jaq clicked it on and then off—it worked. Feeling ridiculously excited, hope resurged through her tired limbs. They were going to be okay.

———

Jaq sat with Russ by the fire, eating peaches and half a protein bar each. It was heaven to be warm, fed, and not walking. They'd redressed Russ's wound, using a generous amount of disinfectant and antibiotic cream. The coyote bite had punctured deep and torn a bit but at least hadn't taken a chunk out of his leg. Fresh bandages glowed white on Russ' calf. There had even been Tylenol in the kit, and it already had taken effect. Russ looked better.

"I can't wait to sleep on a cot," Jaq said dreamily, licking peach juice from her lips.

"Yeah. This is amazing. I don't believe it—it's snowing again." Russ pulled his gaze from the window and settled on Jaq. He swallowed what he'd been chewing.

"But we're cozy and dry inside," she said.

"Feeling kinda spoiled. I think I saw an actual outhouse." Russ grinned.

"Luxury!" Jaq laughed.

"I think I'll put it to use." He stood and Jaq tossed him the flashlight and he walked to the door.

Jaq followed him outside. She'd taken off her shoes but she didn't care. She stood outside in the snow, watching Russ disappear around the cabin in the dark, the beam of the flashlight waving in front of him.

Jaq stared up at the sky. The snow was already an inch deep. It came down soft like feathers. A distant howl made Jaq shiver. But she raised her chin, brave with the cabin at her back. Her eyes felt keener, her ears more attuned. After living outside for so long, Jaq felt a heightened connection to her surroundings. She imagined that the original inhabitants of the land may have felt like this. She had learned to track, navigate, build fires from almost nothing—and she'd survived a wild animal attack. Her chest puffed up and Jaq raised her face to the sky, letting out a long howl of her own that soared up through the snow into the quilted sky.

Jaq stopped when she heard a shout of horror coming from where Russ had disappeared. The flashlight beam bounced up and down as Russ ran toward her. For a moment she was startled—then she laughed. "Russ, it was just me!" She wanted to tease him for freaking out, until she saw his face.

His eyes were wide with terror and his face had gone pale. So pale. It reminded Jaq of Daniel. She bit off her laugh as all air left her lungs.

"Russ! What is it?" she gasped.

He stumbled into her, grabbing her arm with iron fingers. Then he folded over and vomited with a gurgling groan.

Jaq stared when he lifted his head, wiping his mouth. "Russ, are you sick?"

His body shook so hard Jaq became alarmed. She patted Russ's back and tried to murmur reassuring things. He swung his head back and forth as if to deny something. Russ opened his mouth several times with no words. He grimaced and forced his voice to work, closing his eyes as he did.

"K-K-Katie. I f-found her. S-stabbed d-dead—a knife in h-her chest—in the out-h-h-house."

Russ hyperventilated as Jaq turned to ice. More howls sounded, spooky and haunting—mocking and echoing Jaq's howl of triumph just moments before.

"No, that's not funny. I don't believe you." Jaq's voice fell flat and lifeless from her lips. But she knew Russ didn't lie.

CHAPTER 19

RUSS BARRICADED the cabin door with the table and chairs as Jaq stood staring, unable to move. He turned to her, still no color in his face. "Jaq—do you unders-stand w-what's going on? It's someb-*body* not some-*thing*."

The obvious truth leaked in past the padded fortress around her mind, coursing through her veins like quicksilver. "What're we gonna do?" she whispered.

Russ shook his head, hands on his hips. "Not sure." He forced his breath in and out, long and steady, as if he'd just run a marathon.

The dim room flickered with the fire's blaze. "I'm scared." Jaq teetered on her feet.

Russ was by her side in three long strides. He took her into his arms and pressed her close, his hand on the back of her head, guiding it to his shoulder. "It'll be okay." He patted her back gently, his hand trembling. "Gotta think."

He was using few words again. Jaq knew he was freaked out. She couldn't let him feel alone in this. Like it was up to him to make everything okay. He'd had enough of that burden in his life. She straightened, pushing down the panic in her chest.

"Okay. Whoever did this is probably not hanging around here. Maybe we should try to get to the next outpost—to find help."

Russ swallowed. "Where?"

Jaq pulled back. "Not sure... let me check something." She went into the next room—opening the door slowly, as if expecting someone to jump out from behind it. She clicked on the electric lantern, relieved by how well it lit the room. In the cabinet, she found the binder she'd seen.

Russ squatted beside her. "What's that?"

"Not sure... I just thought maybe..." Jaq flipped it open. It was an IBSA manual. Regulations, instructions, walkie-talkie etiquette and use... and a map.

"There." Russ jabbed a finger at the photocopied, hand-drawn map. Amid the squiggled lines and symbols were four stars, spread out in four quadrants. "Outposts," he said.

"Yeah. You're right. We're... here." Jaq pointed to the star surrounded by a crude representation of trees that looked more like lollipops.

"Yep." Russ scanned the map, placing his fingers against the key that showed the scale of the map, inches to miles. He moved his spread fingers across the map. "About eight miles to this one." He pointed south to an outpost beside what looked like it might be a pond or small lake. "It's the closest one. We'll head there in the morning." His stutter was gone again.

"Okay—as long as we get away from here. A lot of rises and hills to climb." Jaq bit her lip in thought, worried about Russ's leg. She remembered a lot of climbing they'd all done as a group. Before.

"Yeah. It's also downstream"—he traced the blue wavy line down the map—"and should take us closer to people."

"Russ. What happened to Finn?" Jaq put a hand to her forehead.

He shook his head slowly. "Don't know. He was with Katie."

"So... he's either dead or he ran somewhere. He could be all alone and totally freaked out." Jaq pictured Finn, his elfish face and wide blue eyes, and her heart hurt.

"Or..." Russ stopped and the look in his eyes said the rest.

"No way." Jaq liked Finn. He couldn't be a killer—probably. She couldn't imagine it. "Why would he do something like this?"

"Why does any maniac kill? He didn't particularly like Daniel."

Jaq shivered. The night before Daniel had been attacked, she'd gone on that walk with the jock. They'd had a moment, hugged... and there was that tingle up her spine as if she knew somebody watched them. She shook her head. "Then why kill Katie too?"

"Maybe... she saw something. Maybe he just wanted to be able to get away—with nobody to follow him. I've seen how desperate a user can be when they can't get to their fix. If I wanted to escape this place, I'd try to break up the group too. Daniel's attacked, Erica disappears, then Mick leaves for help because the walkie-talkie was conveniently missing. Mick never returns, so someone else has to go... S-scattered." Russ was shaken, talking in a rush.

Jaq had an uncomfortable feeling about this theory. She might be a little bit of a narcissist, but it kind of looked like everyone was being peeled away from *her*. Only Russ was left. "No, Finn is a nice guy."

"So was Ted Bundy. Jaq, it could be anyone."

"How do I know it isn't you?" Jaq said it flippantly, but now she froze. Alone with Russ, the hunter, who handled a knife with ease. She pictured him again, his hands covered with blood, cutting into flesh.

Russ's eyes darkened. "Why would I kill Jock?"

Jealousy. "I don't know." Jaq shrugged nonchalantly but her heart hammered. Daniel had humiliated Russ with the journal incident and constantly flirted with Jaq.

"And Katie?" He folded his arms across his chest.

"You found her... body." Jaq cringed. "How do I know you didn't do it?"

"I found her using the outhouse and stabbed her?" Russ looked ill at the thought.

Jaq's frown turned into a weird giggle. "I have no idea." She felt shaky and unsafe—suddenly nothing made sense. "I mean, who knows, right? The only two for sure who didn't do it are Daniel and Katie."

"Unless Katie got Daniel—and then someone else killed her." Russ's face was weary and sick. He rubbed his face. "This is nuts."

Jaq's head spun. "Mick, Erica, Finn, you, me." The paranoia spun her mind around and it made her ill.

"Yep. That's the list of suspects. Oh, and if we want to get really creative, R.J., Patti, and that other guy."

"Craig? I don't think it's any of them. I mean, they run this thingy. If they were psycho, wouldn't there be a history of missing kids on this program?" Even as she said it Jaq had doubts. Craig was a weird guy.

"Maybe there is." Russ gave a dismissive shrug, seeming to tire of the subject.

"No. They'd be shut down if people knew that."

"Yeah." Russ took a deep breath. "Jaq. We just don't know. Maybe it's some other random person—a poacher or hillbilly. The point is, it isn't you and it isn't me."

Jaq searched his eyes. Warm chocolate, sad, exhausted... mysterious. "It better not be you." She poked him in the chest.

He gave a weak smile. "Even if it was, I wouldn't kill you.

You're such a good kisser." His effort to joke touched Jaq, calming her for the moment.

She hugged him, grasping for anything to keep from free falling. This was a nightmare. The feeling of being pursued and terrorized was familiar—but never this real. This made the crap her brother used to do look like family bonding. This was beyond awful.

———

In the darkness, the sleeping bag was warm and the cot soft, but Jaq's heart hadn't really stopped pounding since Russ had come running toward her with the news of his horrific find. She had wept quietly until her mind started to create distracting visions of terror. The wind blew outside, haunting. Maybe it was really Katie, trying to get in. Jaq clenched her teeth, jittery and paranoid. Trying so hard not to picture what Russ had seen in the outhouse.

"Russ?" she whispered. "You sleeping?"

"No," he croaked.

"Was the knife one of the missing ones?" She kept her voice low.

"Yeah. Think so. Same handle." He sniffed and cleared his throat.

It sounded like he'd been crying. He'd shoved his cot to block the door into their room and Jaq could only see the outline of his body, like the silhouette of one of the ridges in the badlands.

"Oh." Her mind continued to whir. Jaq's body ached. The exhaustion was enough to make her whimper and beg for sleep. But the fear stalked her. Relentless.

Russ sniffed again and turned over on his cot. Jaq wondered if he needed more Tylenol. "You hurting?"

"A little." He shifted.

"Want me to get you another pill?"

"Or three," he mumbled.

Jaq reached for the flashlight beside her cot, clicked it on and rustled through her sack where it sagged in a pile on the floor. She'd packed the first aid kit to take with them. Tapping three pills out of the bottle sounded loud in the quiet room. Jaq crawled out of her cot with the pills and canteen in her hands. The temperature in the room was chilly and the wood floor was ragged. She walked carefully to prevent splinters.

Sitting on the edge of Russ's cot, Jaq waited while he sat up. He took the pills and canteen. In the dark, their hands touched and it grounded her.

When he'd swallowed the pills, he set the canteen on the floor. "Thanks."

A high, mournful howl sounded outside. The wind whipped it around the cabin and threw it into the sky. Jaq shivered. "Russ, I can't sleep."

"I know."

Jaq blushed, but her hands shook and her fear won out over embarrassment. "Can I sleep with you?"

There was a breathless moment as Russ hesitated. Then he raised one arm and held his sleeping bag open.

Jaq slid her legs in, burrowing down into the warmth. Goosebumps rushed across her skin. There was an awkward few seconds while they both moved around, trying to find a comfortable position. At first Russ scooted away until his back was at the wall, then he flopped onto his back. He didn't seem to know what to do with his arms. Jaq tucked her head into the crook of his shoulder and draped one arm across his chest. His hand slid down to rest at the small of her back.

With the front of her body pressed into his side and his arm at her back, Jaq felt surrounded and safe. Warm. The throbbing of Russ's heart in her ear was comforting. His breath hitched and he let out a sigh.

Jaq reached up, placing a hand on his cheek. It was wet with tears. He grunted and turned his face away as if ashamed.

"Russ. It's okay. I'm here with you."

A soft snort answered. His arm tightened around her. Russ kissed the top of her head. "Sleep," he said.

Jaq rubbed her hand back and forth across his chest, hoping to soothe him, but his heart sped up, thumping against the side of her face.

She stopped. "Goodnight, Russ."

"Goodnight, Jaq," he whispered, his voice thick and low.

Jaq glanced up at his face and saw the sheen of his eyes. They were wide open, aimed at the ceiling. She breathed in his smell, warm, reassuring. Her mind drifted in the dark room. She wondered if Russ was praying right now. *Thump-bump, thump-bump, thump-bump...* the lullaby slowed and slowed. Her eyes drifted shut and the heaviness in her body dragged her down like a stone into the black waters of sleep.

———

Jaq crawled out of the sleeping bag and stepped off the cot, surprised to see that it had been moved away from where it had blocked the door. She'd slept right through that. Her feet patted on the rough wood floor, and as she entered the next room she stopped and stretched until her back popped. Russ looked up from where he knelt poking at the fire, and he gave her a shy grin.

"How'd you sleep?" He set down the stick he'd been holding.

"It's weird, but—better than I have in weeks."

Russ nodded as if to agree, his cheekbones coloring. "I

opened another can of peaches," he said, tilting his head in the direction of the food.

Jaq's mouth watered. The can of peaches sat on the table and beside it was her knife. Her hand automatically went to her hip where her leather sheath hung empty.

Russ stood and came to her, still limping a little. He took her hand and led her to the table. "Good morning." He gave her a small kiss. "I packed everything already. Taking most of what we found here. I'm taking one of the sleeping bags. I used my blanket..."

He'd wrapped Daniel in it. "Good. Okay." Jaq looked into his face. He still looked tired, with dark shadows under his eyes. She wondered if he'd slept or spent the night staring at the ceiling, trying to stay alert. Afraid. Guarding her. She re-sheathed her knife.

Jaq ate in silence while Russ dozed by the fire. The light of day came in through the small dirty window—things seemed less menacing. But they were still in the craziest predicament. It was unreal. A scary movie.

After she'd eaten, she washed with some of the water from the jug. Among the things in the small bag of toiletries was a little deodorant and a toothpaste tube. Jaq used her finger to clean her teeth. The sharp minty flavor cooled her mouth and made it feel fresher than it had in a long time. She was determined to use the small shampoo and soap at some point—when they reached the pond or lake.

Part of Jaq didn't want to go back out into the open. It would be so nice to stay here and just survive like old homesteaders until people came to help. If this were frontier times, she and Russ would probably even be married at this age. They'd live in a place like this and carve out a life together in the unforgiving wilderness. Russ would trap and hunt. She would... what? Make soap, candles, and butter? Jaq snorted and rolled her eyes at herself. *Oh, please.*

Back to reality. There was a dead person in the outhouse. Katie. Jaq felt sick at the thought. Poor Katie. She was a sweet girl. It was terrible—she'd come out here to help messed up kids and ended up dead. Yeah, the sooner they got out of here the better.

Bedrolls packed on their backs, Jaq and Russ started out into a wet morning after relieving themselves behind some trees. The air was misty and the sun softly glowed through it, diffused. The light snow that had fallen the night before hadn't stuck. The ground was muddy; the squelching and scraping of their boots broke the deadly quiet. They traipsed through the trees, pushing branches out of the way as they went.

From the corner of her eye, Jaq noticed the small, bleached wood outhouse, like an upended coffin, obscured by gangly branches. The mist swirled around it, a vaporous specter. She stopped and stared, unable to look away. Icy fingers wrapped around her heart as she struggled against the grip of terror. The low honking of a grouse came muted from the brush, startling her.

Russ stepped to her side and grabbed her hand firmly. She gripped back with a fierce gratitude for his touch.

"C'mon," he whispered. He pulled Jaq behind him and her legs obeyed. She controlled the urge to keep looking back over her shoulder as if something were there, stalking. Like death could follow her because she'd passed it.

Soon they had cleared the trees and they faced south, with tan and red hills and ridges to climb. Russ had taken the map out of the binder. He held it up and examined it. "That rock formation—the one that looks like a crooked tower—that's this." He pointed to a drawing on the map. "We head toward it."

Jaq looked at the strange rocky tower. It reminded her of the drip castles she used to make at the beach with Flower. If you let really soupy sand drip through your fist, it formed a dribbly, layered tower that tapered all the way up. Like melting candles, puddling on one other.

"I miss the beach," Jaq said.

Russ gave her a funny look. "Oh."

"Just can't wait to get back..." She squeezed his hand and they trudged forward, together.

———

By midday the mist had burned away. It grew warm and Jaq needed a rest. They sat together on a flat rock, eying the tower which loomed closer. They ate another half of a protein bar each and drank some water.

"We're getting close. A few more hours, maybe." Russ sat forward, his arms on his knees.

"Hours?" Jaq deflated. It was a rough hike. A lot of ups and downs and stumbling over rocks and mud. "I don't care what we find when we get there—I'm staying until someone finds us," Jaq moaned.

Russ gave her a long look and then smiled. "You're doing great."

Jaq rolled her eyes. "Said the guy with the injured leg who is still kicking my butt."

"If it makes you feel any better, I don't think I can last much longer. I think the pain killers have gotten me this far." He laid a hand gently over his bandaged leg. "C'mere." Russ reached for Jaq, and she scooted closer.

Jaq nestled into his arms, her place of comfort. "Thanks."

"Hm?" Russ played with her hair, running his fingers down the length of her blond ponytail.

"For being here for me. For being mine." Jaq tilted up her head and kissed his chin.

Russ gazed at her, his beautiful brown eyes full of adoration. "I *am* yours. Totally. Are you mine?" He brushed his lips over her forehead.

"Yes," she breathed. "Definitely."

They hugged one another close. Jaq looked out over Russ's shoulder, her eyes catching something obscured by rocks and brush. A shape in the bushes—some kind of machine? A wheel. "What's that?" Jaq sat back and pointed.

Russ squinted in that direction and cocked his head, his brows scrunched down. "I don't know. Let's go look."

They hopped down from where they'd perched and stomped through the sage and bitterbrush. The low branches rasped against their legs, and they kicked rocks as they went. Russ, being in front and taller than Jaq, saw it first.

"Oh, it's a... turned over four-wheeler!" His voice rose in surprise.

Jaq peeked around him and saw the vehicle, one side in the air among the bushes. "I wonder who—"

"Jaq, stop." Russ threw his arms out, blocking her from getting closer. She tried to step around him, craning her neck to see what the deal was, and Russ spun around. Both his hands came up to her shoulders. "Jaq. No. Don't look." His eyes were wide and urgent.

A horrible sinking feeling dragged down Jaq's innards. "Who?" she squeaked, her heart jumping.

Russ's face crumpled and he squeezed his eyes shut. "P-Patti. It's Patti."

CHAPTER 20

JAQ CLOSED her eyes and froze. Russ released her shoulders and his footsteps thumped toward the four-wheeler. He made little noises of distress in his throat and let out a groan.

"Christ have mercy. Who would d-do this?" The crunching sound of his boots got closer and then he was holding Jaq in his arms.

She leaned back her head and opened her eyes, focusing only on his face. Russ looked back, serious, grave. But this time he wasn't pale, and a look of defeat made his eyes mournful. No shock, no surprise, just a horrible acceptance.

"Don't look like that, Russ," Jaq begged.

"Like what?" he whispered with no expression.

"Like we're gonna die too."

Russ swallowed. "No. We won't"

"Say it like you mean it." Jaq felt herself go rigid in his arms.

"We won't die. But I might barf." Russ closed his eyes and grimaced. Jaq had the strong urge to pound his chest with her fists, but she just clenched her teeth.

"I liked Patti. She was a good person." Jaq felt the surprising serum of anger pump into her blood. It felt amazing

—a shot of strength and energy. She pulled away from Russ and felt her body being pulled toward the four-wheeler. Russ held up a hand but didn't stop her.

A few feet from the overturned vehicle, Patti lay her side, curly hair coated with dirt and blood, open eyes staring without sight into a bush. Her gray face was still as marble. Jaq gasped when she saw the knife. The wood handle protruded from the side of Patti's neck. The blood, darkened to almost black, spread all over her shoulders, chest, and the ground beneath her. Jaq screamed.

She needed to run. All anger drained in a sudden swish to be replaced by a roaring nausea. Jaq spun away from the horrific scene, gulping back the gagging in her throat. Her stomach twisted violently and won the fight. She fell to her knees and heaved into the bushes, digging her fingers into the muddy earth as another wave hit her.

Shaking and spitting, she stayed on her hands and knees, trying to breathe. Patti. Patti was so sparkly and good. *Who. Did. This.*

With her face so close to the ground Jaq's eyes focused on something scattered and almost camouflaged in the dirt and mud. Sunflower seeds—the broken shells. Jaq kneeled up in shock. The killer left those. Whoever stabbed Patti stood here, spitting seeds—while waiting for her? Or afterward, examining the crime scene, calmly cracking seeds in their teeth, satisfied with the results. Jaq shuddered.

"Russ." Her voice came out raw. The sour, foul taste in her mouth made Jaq shiver in disgust.

"I'm here."

She realized he stood right beside her. Jaq held out her hand and Russ took it, pulling her to her feet. He had a canteen in his hand and he gave it to Jaq.

"Jaq. I didn't want you to see. Are you okay?" He patted her back, looking dazed.

"No. I'm not. But see that?" Jaq pointed at the ground. "Sunflower seeds. Salty and delicious." The sting of bitterness in her own voice matched the flavor of her vomit. "I need water." Jaq took a drink while Russ crouched down, picking up one of the seeds and staring at it in his palm.

"Man." Russ shook his head.

Jaq lowered the canteen, her hand trembling. "Russ, who gave all you guys sunflower seeds that day?"

"Oh. It was the morning we first met P-Patti." He frowned and glanced over at the dead counselor. "Mick did." Russ scrunched up his brow in thought.

"Mick?" Jaq's mind snapped to an image of Mick chopping wood in a rage. It stopped her breath.

"You think that Mick...?" Russ seemed to short-circuit. Jaq knew he admired Mick a lot. He'd probably bonded with the big man more than any of the rest of them had. Russ shook his head. "No way."

"And the time I woke up after being molested in my sleep—that flavor was on my lips." Jaq grazed her lips with her fingertips. "The salty ranch or whatever—from the seeds!" If it had been Mick and Daniel knew somehow...

Russ opened and shut his mouth, outrage flashed in his eyes. "Oh, man."

"Think about the rest of it. He never came back, Russ. He went for help and didn't return. It was his hatchet that took Daniel out. His word that the walkie-talkie was gone. Erica went missing; Mick hated her! It would be easy for him to track anyone—and who could fight him off? He's huge!"

"But why? Why would he?"

"I don't know. Maybe I wasn't the first student he perved on—I bet Katie and Patti found out. Maybe that's why they're dead too." Jaq's whole body shook. It all fit. Even the salty flavor.

"But. But—maybe Mick..." Russ trailed off and let his hands fall to his sides. The wind rustled through the fragrant sage and grouse honked nearby. "I just don't know."

"It's a theory. But it makes sense." Jaq pressed a hand to her concaved belly. She felt ill. "I can't look at her again."

"Don't." Russ took a deep breath and limped to the four-wheeler. A short bungy cord fastened to the back held a sleeping bag and another bundle. Russ pulled the sleeping bag loose and unrolled it. He turned and looked at Jaq, his face gaunt and strained. "We can't do much for her. And I'm not sure she should end up too far from the scene... These are murders."

"You want to put her in the sleeping bag?" Jaq said, hugging herself.

"Yeah. Then I could drag her up into that rock crevice—it might help." He raised his chin to where a deep gash divided the big flat rock they'd been resting on.

Hide Patti from the predators. It was too late to hide her from the biggest one. Mick. Jaq could see that Russ didn't find the task any more appealing than she did. She wouldn't make him do it alone.

"I'll help." Jaq clenched her fists.

"You sure?" The hopeful tone in his voice made Jaq's heart squeeze.

"Yeah. She was good to me."

Jaq forced her mind to a numb place, pretending she lifted the legs of a sleeping person. Then she held the sleeping bag taut while Russ raised Patti's body and pushed her in. He zipped up, zzzzzz, over the chest and arms that had hugged Jaq in compassion, zzzzz, past shoulder and neck that once pulsed with life, and then, zzzzzz, over that face that had been so cheerful and those bright eyes that had sparkled with intelligence and kindness. Finally, the curly mop of sandy hair that had once smelled of vanilla, now filthy with dirt and blood disappeared with a *zzzzip*. Patti was gone, and only a drab cocoon lay at their feet. Jaq pictured Patti emerging as a winged angel and floating into the blue sky.

Russ bowed his head, muttering a prayer and making the sign of the cross. Jaq shut her own eyes and thought about Patti and the kind of person she was. She thanked anything that listened that she'd met her and sent a hope for her spirit to have rest. There were tears on Jaq's face, but a weird calm steeled her—the familiar numbness of shock.

They carried her, like they had with Daniel, between them. It took some hefting and grunting effort to get the body up into the cool interior of the rock. They settled her there and then worked to pile stones at the entrance: a wall and a monument.

Jaq rubbed her hands on her knees. They were so dirty. They would never be clean again. Russ hobbled to the four-wheeler. "Jaq, help me with this."

Jaq followed him, understanding. "Do you think it still works?"

"Maybe."

Together they pushed and pulled. A metal groan, the slosh of liquid, and thud—it rested on all four tires, shocks creaking and the body of the vehicle jiggling. Jaq had half expected to see the engine chopped up or something. It looked fine.

She wiped away the sweat on her forehead. The sun burned bright now, and Jaq held her breath, hoping they would be able to ride the rest of the way. The heat was not going to be good for the bodies. Daniel. Katie. Patti. Hiking just wasn't fast enough. Jaq wanted to be as far away as possible, as fast as possible.

Russ circled the dusty black vehicle, running his hand over it. He unscrewed the gas tank and peeked inside. He nodded to himself and replaced the lid. As he stooped over to examine the controls, Jaq went to gather their stuff. She'd slipped her pack on when the growl of the engine broke the silent air. Her heart leaped. The sound could alert the killer, but it was also their only way out of this nightmare.

Jaq skidded down the side of the rock and jogged through the brush to get to where Russ sat astride the four-wheeler, his back to her.

"Russ!" she called out, a spike of excitement shooting through her.

He looked back over his shoulder. He didn't smile but he seemed triumphant. "Get on, girl," he shouted, looking like he meant business.

Jaq hopped up and sat behind him. The vibration of the machine and the smell of gas spelled e-s-c-a-p-e. She wrapped her arms around Russ's waist, his bedroll sandwiched between them.

Russ gunned the engine, and they lurched forward. Jaq held tight as he navigated around bushes and rocks, picking up speed. The tires bounced and the four-wheeler moved in jolts and dives across the rough terrain. It felt like the thing wanted to tip over, and Jaq hid her face in Russ's back. The jarring ride hurt her spine and made her grit her teeth, but the ground passed beneath them at a speed that made up for it.

With her mind on the ride, Jaq was able to evade the thoughts of blood and loss that darted after her like mosquitoes determined to feed on her sanity. She wondered what Russ was thinking about. She rested her head on his back. *Thank you for*

Russ, she prayed. Any tiny doubts disappeared. Russ couldn't be the killer. She had been with him when he discovered Patti.

Jaq wondered if Finn had survived. Poor Finn. She squeezed her eyes shut and zoned out to the roar of the engine.

After a long, rough ride, they passed under the long shadow of the rock tower. Jaq looked up at the staggering formation that pierced the sky. Weeds and desert plants grew out of the cracks, determined, surviving.

The engine growled on. Russ's dark hair ruffled as they sped up on a decline. The ground became smoother, and the plant life became taller. Jaq peeked over his shoulder and saw the blue shine of the lake. Russ steered along the line of the water. A breeze off it felt cool and soothing on Jaq's face and arms. Tiny ripples on the surface of the lake caught the light of the lowering sun, making the lake look like crumpled aluminum foil in motion.

Jaq squinted across the small lake and spotted the cabin. Within minutes, they'd pulled up to it, and Russ killed the engine. The silence buzzed in Jaq's ears.

Stiff and shaky, Jaq dismounted. Russ brought one leg over and slid his feet to the ground. "Ahhh." He rubbed his back. "That was amazing. We'd still be walking right now."

"True." Jaq took in the wood cabin with no windows. "Here we are." Jaq dropped her pack to the ground and stretched.

"Yeah." Russ took her hand and gave Jaq a small smile.

"How's your leg?" Jaq looked down at the bandage.

"Sore, but better than if we'd hiked the whole way."

"Middle of nowhere," she whispered, looking out over the surrounding wilderness. She wondered if they were better off here.

"Together," Russ said. He kissed Jaq's cheek and pressed

his forehead to hers for a moment. "Stay here. I'll make sure we're alone."

Jaq watched, nervous as Russ approached the cabin, mounted the steps, and slowly opened the door. He waited a moment, listening before he peeked inside and scanned the room. He looked back at Jaq and gave her a thumbs up.

She sighed with relief.

Russ walked toward her. "Someone was here recently. Some embers in the fireplace, but they've been gone at least since this morning." He nodded toward the lake. "C'mon. We're coated with dirt."

Jaq grabbed the small bottle of shampoo from her pack and Russ led her down to the water where it lapped softly at the shore, clear and cool. Slimy green rocks peeked through the surface. The air was still warm enough that Jaq eagerly took off her shoes and waded into the water beside Russ. The cold water felt wonderful after the hot day full of dust and mud.

Russ peeled off his shirt and threw it onto the shore. He backed into deeper water, lowering his body under the surface quicker than Jaq would have liked. Splashing his face, Russ moved farther out, then held up a hand to Jaq. "Come out here."

Jaq pulled her shirt off. "I don't want to get my clothes wet."

Russ raised his brows and nodded. She peeled off her shorts and the long johns. She tossed her clothes onto the shore and turned back to Russ. He watched her with his chocolate eyes, a half-smile on his face. She felt self-conscious in her bra and underwear, even if they covered more than some bikinis.

Jaq dragged her feet through the water, trying to brace herself against the cold, but it made her legs ache. When it got to her waist, she dove under, the wavy glowing shape of Russ ahead. Gliding over the mossy rocks, where tiny fish darted, she felt peaceful, safe. Her hands reached out, and ripples of light striped her arms, white and strange, corpse-like. *Patti.*

Jaq resurfaced with a gasp in front of Russ. "Wow—that's cold." The muscles in her calves cramped and her toes and fingers burned. She pushed her long bangs back over her head.

She let down her ponytail and spread out her hair, letting it hang down into the water. The shampoo oozed into her hand, pink and fragrant. The best smell ever. Jaq worked it through her hair, enjoying the white lather, the perfume of it. Then she plugged her nose and dunked under for a rinse. Her scalp tightened in the frigid water. "I feel so clean!" Jaq sighed when she came back up, her teeth clacking together.

"You missed a spot." Russ cupped his hands squirting a stream of water into her face. Jaq squealed, rubbing her eyes and cheeks. "What is it with you and water? It turns you into a bully!"

He chuckled and slid his arms around Jaq's waist, but she pushed against his bare chest. "Ha! Hands off!" She tried to hide her smile and failed. His arms tightened, and her hands slipped over his smooth skin to his muscled shoulders, still clutching the small bottle of shampoo in one hand.

Trapped by Russ's solid body and the electric look in his eyes, Jaq trembled in the cold. "I'm turning to ice."

The heat of his mouth on hers came as an answer. Warmth spread through Jaq's whole body as his hands trailed up her back and into her hair. Russ tilted his head slowly, changing the angle, his soft lips thorough and aggressive, running his tongue lightly over her lower lip. Jaq tasted him in return, loving the tingle that radiated everywhere he touched. He made an encouraging noise in his throat, and she did it again.

Jaq marveled at how amazing it felt to make out, even after everything. Her mind went somewhere dark, and she paused. When he broke the kiss, Russ smiled, water dripped down his face and clung to his long dark lashes. He cupped her cheek with his palm and bent in close. Against Jaq's ear, he whispered, "But seriously, I'm freezing my butt off."

Jaq laughed. It was just what she needed. He always seemed to know. "Shampoo first, scruffy. I'll help."

Russ leaned back and gave her a flirty look, raising one brow. "Sounds fun."

———

They entered the cabin dripping wet, Russ leading, his dry shirt in one fist. Jaq stared at his beautiful back muscles and how they moved. The light from outside flooded the dusty room. There were a few chairs, a tall cabinet with double doors and a homemade bunk bed made of logs against one wall. Jaq glanced at the faint glow of embers in the fireplace and the protein bar wrappers on the table, feeling more nervous than she had in the bright outdoors.

"Who do you think it was?" Jaq didn't know if she should be elated or scared.

"Not sure," Russ said, rubbing his forehead, causing his bicep and pecs to flex. He held her hand tighter and pulled her back outside. His dark eyes searched the lake and rocky shore. "Hopefully R.J. or someone else who works for the program."

"But not Mick." Jaq felt a chill. "Will the person staying here help us?"

"We can't be sure." Russ pulled his dry shirt back on over his head and grabbed his bedroll off the seat of the four-wheeler. He undid the bungee holding the other bundle to the back. "I guess we wait here to find out. I need to re-bandage my leg."

"Okay." But neither of them made a move to enter the

cabin again. They sat on the plank porch in front of the cabin, alert. The sun hadn't set, and it sent warm rays toward them.

"What's in that?" Jaq waved a hand at the bundle Russ had tucked under his arms.

"Let's see." Russ unrolled the canvas fabric. Inside were several ziplock bags full of their normal provisions. Flour, raisins, oats, dry milk, bullion, lentils, tea bags... and a half-empty package of ranch flavored sunflower seeds.

"Hey." Jaq took the package. "Patti had some."

Russ scratched his head. "Maybe they all did. Privilege of being one of the leaders—Mick was just cool enough to share his with us," Russ said, his voice gathering energy. "R.J. and Craig had them too."

"This doesn't take away all the other facts, Russ." Jaq put her hand on his knee of his wet jeans. She could see that Russ wanted to make Mick innocent.

"No, but it gives me reasonable doubt." His jaw clenched.

Jaq wished she felt safe, sitting there with Russ. But goosebumps ran down her arms knowing they were not alone. Whoever else was there might be exactly who they ran away from. She clutched the handle of her knife and leaned into Russ.

AT SUNSET, low-lying clouds glowed red in streaks, like claw marks in the belly of the sky. As shadows crawled toward the cabin, Jaq had the prickling feeling at her neck that eyes in the rocks and trees watched her.

"Russ, let's go in. We can block the door." Without the sun to warm her skin, the wet underclothes had chilled, and she shivered.

Russ squinted out into the growing darkness, scanning the sky. He sat forward and then stood. "Do you see that?"

Jaq strained her eyes in the direction that Russ pointed. "Smoke."

Across the water a small trail of smoke wisped and curled into the sky.

"A campfire." Russ put his hands on his hips.

"Someone's camping over there?" Jaq felt uneasy.

"Looks like it. Maybe we've found help."

"Or we found the psycho—who didn't want to come back to the cabin when he saw us here." Jaq frowned.

"Nah. If he was hiding, he'd be smarter and not send smoke signal greetings."

"Unless he's drawing us out."

Russ gave Jaq an amused look. "You think like a cynical cop —like my dad." His teasing smile faded, and he reached up to move a stray blond wave away from Jaq's face. "He would've liked you so much," he said in a softer voice.

Jaq looked up through her lashes—one of her old flirt tricks. Then she realized that she'd never really had to use them on Russ. She could totally be herself with him.

"I'm sure your dad was awesome. Like you."

His smile was sad. "He really used to be." Russ turned away from her and faced the oncoming night. "I'm going out there to see if it's someone who can help us. But I want you to stay here—with the door blocked." He straightened his shoulders.

"You are not leaving me!" Jaq grabbed his arm, her heart flipping out.

"Jaq, it'll be fine. I'll sneak up, take a peek, figure out if it's safe to approach. You can be here getting warm by the fire—out of danger." Russ used his man voice when he said it. Which meant he wouldn't change his mind. And she didn't want to seem like a coward.

"I'll go with you," Jaq announced, raising her chin.

"No." Russ steered her by the shoulders into the cabin. "You'll wait here for me. And I'll hurry back to help warm you up."

He grinned but Jaq pouted her lip at him.

"I'm sure that it's safe." He pressed her into one of the chairs.

Jaq sat and folded her arms, frustrated. "Bossy. I'm not going to—"

Russ dipped his head and planted a kiss on her protesting mouth. Jaq kissed him back, wrapping her arms around his neck.

"Trust me," he whispered between kisses. "It'll be fine."

"Be careful," Jaq begged, knowing she'd lost the argument.

He stood tall. "I'm always careful. Use the table to block the door and anything else you can drag. Stay here. I'll be back soon." He looked at her with his intense brown eyes for a long moment before going out the door.

Jaq hopped up and leaned against the jam, watching Russ slip into the twilight, weaving quietly through the rocks and bushes. He grabbed a large stick, holding it in his fist like a sword. Jaq's heart beat hard. He had to come back.

When he was out of sight, Jaq built up the fire by the light of the lowering sun, then shut the door, slid the small latch, and shoved the table and chairs against it. There wasn't a window, so only the orangey fire lit the room. Jaq stripped her damp clothes off and laid them by the fire to dry along with her wet underclothing. Then she pulled on her IBSA t-shirt, which had dried wrinkly and stiff from her dip in the stream the day before. Over that she buttoned Finn's plaid shirt. It hung to her mid-thigh.

Jaq held up her teal underwear with the lace and rolled her eyes. She almost couldn't remember the girl who picked them out. What she wouldn't do for a pair of comfy, cotton, granny underwear right now—or boxer briefs. Well, at least they were sorta clean from two swims. She draped them over a stick she found in the small pile of wood on the hearth. Dangling from the stick over the fire, they dried pretty quick. They were still warm when she put them on.

Russ had only been gone about ten minutes. Jaq let out a loud breath. She had to find something to do, or she'd go crazy waiting. She walked to the double doors of the tall wood cabinet. The hinges creaked. Inside was an electric lantern like the one at the other outpost, a couple large cans of beef stew, another first aid kit, some bottled water and a couple wool blankets. *Jackpot.*

Excited, Jaq grabbed one of the cans of soup. She opened it with her knife and pried the lid up before nestling it in the coals away from the full blaze of the fire. Russ would come home to a hot meal. She smiled to herself. Ashcakes. Yeah. That would be good with stew.

For several minutes Jaq occupied herself by finding the flour, adding water, making dough balls, and patting them into flat cakes. She made several, stacking them on the hearth as they came off the ashes, bubbled and darkened. They smelled delicious mixed with the aroma of the beef stew. She moved the can to the side when it started to boil. Jaq's mouth watered.

She undid her bedroll and wrapped up in her blanket beside the fire. Jaq dozed, until her head snapped up at the sound of a long howl. She scrambled to her feet, wondering how long she'd slept. The fire had burned low. She bent to touch the ashcakes—they were cold.

The cabin was dark now and she reached for the lantern and turned it on. The room lit up enough to see that she was alone.

Nervous flutters started in her stomach "Where are you, Russ?" she said aloud, pacing the floor.

As if in answer, she heard a shout echoing from far away. Jaq sprang to the door, pulled away the table, and threw the chairs to the floor. She opened the cabin door and stepped outside. The cool night air rushed up the plaid shirt, reminding her that her legs were naked. She hugged herself, shaking, and scanned as far as she could see under a large full moon. It was an indigo night under a cloudless sky. She could see the shining lake, rocks, and trees better than usual.

Jaq strained her ears. After a minute she thought she heard something reverberating off the water. A thud? A cry? She ran back into the cabin, pulled on her stiff shorts, reattaching her sheath and knife. Jaq pulled out the red flashlight and ran back out onto the porch. If something was happening to Russ, she was afraid, but she was also angry. It hummed in her veins. If anyone hurt him, she'd go feral on them. The badlands had changed her—she felt a little wild. *Girl who kills coyote.*

She wouldn't be stupid about it, wouldn't be the air-head blonde in a horror film, loudly calling "Is someone there?" Jaq knew someone was there—and she was the one doing the stalking. She gripped the handle of her knife and knew she could use it. She had killed that coyote. Shadow to shadow, she crept from the cabin, her heart thumping in her throat.

Barefooted, she stalked through the brush, alert, cautious, holding the turned off flashlight. There was no wind or sound, just a heavy silence and her own breathing. Her feet gripped the earth, quiet and steady, moving forward across the uneven ground. The stab of rocks and cool air were just background sensations. Everything in her focused on finding Russ.

Then the sound of running feet, stomping the ground, broke through the stillness. Jaq ducked behind a large boulder and waited, her lungs frozen. The crunching and snapping of bushes and then a figure appeared, stumbling, breathing like a chainsaw. She couldn't see his face as his arms waved for balance, one hand gripping the handle of a hatchet. He stopped, looking back and forth wildly.

Oh. Shoops.

Jaq unsheathed her knife, fear shooting through her body and out her fingertips and toes. She hunched, waiting for her cue, trying not to blank out. It was like having horrible stage fright—knowing she was about to go on and do her part, but not remembering her lines or what to do.

He turned, long bangs flopping forward. *Finn.* Jaq jumped up, confused, angry, and excited. She clicked on her flashlight and pointed the beam into his face.

He shouted and staggered backwards, arms blocking his face.

"Finn!" Jaq stepped out from behind her rock. "Put down the ax," she ordered while holding up her knife.

Finn straightened up and lowered his arms. His eyes glinted in the flashlight, crazed.

"Jaq?" He wobbled on his feet, his hands covered in blood, a streak of red running down the side of his face. Russ's blood?

Jaq gasped, afraid of the madness stamped on his face.

Finn froze, blinking into the beam.

Her heart sputtered. "Finn. Oh, Lord. What did you do? Put it down." She heard the hysteria in her own voice. Her mind raced to make sense of anything.

Finn's chest heaved, he gulped for air. "No." He raised the hatchet, narrowing his eyes. "What did I do?" He paused, disoriented. "I always liked you, Jaq. Why did you—"

"Get away from her!" a masculine voice shouted.

Jaq swung the beam toward the voice. Craig stood there, his long dark hair in a tangle, fists clenched, glaring at Finn.

"Craig! Everyone is going nuts!" Jaq babbled. "All the leaders are gone. Finn has an ax!"

Craig nodded, coming closer to Jaq. "Finn. Where did you get that ax?" His voice was low, calm, but he sneered.

Finn had not moved. His eyes swung from Craig to Jaq. He grimaced and a sob came out of his throat. His mouth stayed open, as a long, creaking *ahhhhh* escaped. "I pulled it out of Erica's face!" he roared, shaking the bloodied hatchet at Craig.

Jaq flinched. Erica's blood. She swallowed a gag, sickened by her relief—not Russ's blood. "Oh, Finn..."

"Jaq, are you with Craig?" Finn demanded, dragging his fist over his mouth. His eyes darted around, frightened. He was scared to death.

Jaq's pulse thrummed in her head. *Finn.* She didn't know

what was happening. "What do you mean?" Jaq stepped closer to the boy with the ax.

"Stop. Jaq, don't move." Craig held up a hand. "Finn, put that down."

"You'd love that!" Finn spat. He didn't look at all like the elf Jaq knew. He looked furious, freaking loco.

Jaq turned her flashlight on Craig. He cringed in the light. "What's going on here?" Jaq felt herself go very still. Like she was standing in the eye of a storm.

Craig hunched his skinny shoulders up, his brow pushed down. "There are search teams out looking for all of you."

Finn chuckled. "Surprise. Here we are." His laugh turned to weeping, and he sank to the ground, letting the ax thunk beside him.

"Let's get him." Craig shook his head at Finn's pathetic heap.

"Yeah, come and get me. Get it over with. Sick of hiding," Finn moaned.

Jaq wanted to scream. Finn, a killer. Not sweet, likeable Finn. No words came to her.

Craig scuffed over to where Finn huddled with his arms around his knees. When Craig reached for the hatchet, Finn's hand darted out, grabbing the handle. He peered up at Craig. The two locked eyes, bodies tensed.

Jaq advanced, her knife held out in front of her. Finn's blue eyes glossed over, shining in the flashlight beam. "*Et tu*, Jaq?" he whispered low and sad.

Wait. Something wasn't right. She raised her arm, knife pointing at Craig. His black eyes widened in surprise.

"Jaq?" Craig held up his hands.

"Finn, you say you got the ax out of Erica's body?" Jaq wished her voice would stop shaking.

"Her face," he croaked, covering his eyes with stained hands.

"Did you put it there?" Jaq pushed.

Finn's head jerked up, a look of revulsion on his face. His lips sputtered for a moment. "No!"

Jaq didn't know what to think—what to believe. Everyone seemed crazed!

Craig pulled out a knife. "Don't trust him."

"That's probably my knife," Finn said, focusing on Craig.

"It's mine," Craig said as he pointed it at Finn.

"Show me the handle. We all carved our initials into the handle." Finn had calmed by degrees, his breathing still rough. He looked to Jaq with hope in his eyes. "You aren't part of this, are you?"

"What? I don't know what's going on! Craig, show me the knife." Jaq watched Craig turn to granite.

"You gonna help me stop him or what?" Craig bit out.

"Stop him? I don't think he killed—" Jaq's mind couldn't keep up.

"From talking... from stopping us." Craig broke in.

Jaq blinked, a cold fist clutched her beating heart. "Us," she whispered, flat.

"Jaq, look—you're free. You can go home whenever you want now. And I'm free too. We can go wherever we want." His intense eyes drilled holes into her doubt.

An inner scream shattered like glass, shooting piercing fragments through Jaq's brain, chest, and stomach. "Oh. Lord." Her knees buckled at the realization. "Craig... you don't mean..." She trailed off faint, weak. She knew.

Guilt and horror dropped her to the hard, dirt ground. On her back, Jaq stared, dazed, up at a sky of glittering stars. Each one stung like a spark into her awareness.

"Jaq!" Craig scrambled to her side. "Are you hurt?" He hovered close but didn't touch her.

"You get any closer to her, I'll kill you." Russ jumped down from a large boulder, seeming to appear from nowhere, brandishing his stick.

Jaq sat up. "Russ! It was Craig!"

"I know. I followed him while he followed Finn. I heard everything. I thought you were safe back at the cabin." Russ gave her a grim look.

Craig glared at Russ with pure hatred. He snarled like a rabid dog. "You sick, dirty little pig. I saw you with her—in the lake," Craig seethed.

Finn had risen up, ax in hand. He walked as if in a trance to stand by Russ. The two boys faced Craig, stances ready for something.

"I'm not the pervert who spies on her and molests her in her sleep!" Russ barked.

Craig growled, "You don't understand."

"Neither do I. Explain it." Jaq stood, driven by fury and pointed her light into his eyes.

Craig frowned in confusion, backing up a step.

"Someone beat you with the crazy stick," Russ drawled, gripping his wooden weapon threateningly.

"'Til it broke," Finn muttered, holding the ax in shaking hands.

Craig roared in outrage, his angular face harsh in the white circle of light trained on him. He lunged forward, quick and fluid. The knife in his hand flashed in the narrow strip of light. Just as Russ swung his stick, the knife came down, glancing off the wood sword and slicing into Russ's forearm. The knife fell, skidding through the dirt.

Russ yelled and grabbed his arm, falling to his knees in pain. Craig sprang at him like a wolf on a felled deer. Craig drove his fists into Russ's body as Russ rocked onto his back, blocking with his arms.

"Craig, stop!" Jaq shrieked.

The mangy haired killer turned toward her just as Finn swung the ax. Jaq leaped out of the way, screaming. There was grunting and scuffling as Craig grabbed the handle and wrestled it away from Finn, who flailed and kicked, looking so much smaller than his opponent. Craig raised his knee hard into Finn's crotch. Finn landed on the ground beside Russ, gasping for breath, red faced with agony.

"Hey!" Jaq stepped toward Craig and held up her knife, willing her hand to stop trembling. Craig watched her, chest heaving, ax in hand. She was the only thing between the injured boys and the murder in his eyes.

"Please don't hurt them." Jaq stood firm but her voice quavered with tears.

"They're trapping you here." Craig lowered his arms, the ax dangled from his hand. His face crumpled in frustration.

Russ pushed himself up, limping to Jaq's side, now holding the knife Craig had dropped. Blood ran down his arm and streaked across his face. Finn wheezed and groaned from behind, still on the ground.

Craig looked at each of them and then back to Jaq as tears ran down her cheeks. His long dark hair hung in his face. He brushed it aside, a sad expression pulling down his harsh features as he eyed the two knives pointed at him. Jaq had a sudden memory flash in her mind, of her and Russ facing off with that last coyote. Craig's look of defeat as he backed away a step, assessing the odds, was just like that.

Then he darted into the brush, swallowed by the night.

CHAPTER 22

THE FIRST AID kit lay open on the table beside the white glow of the electric lantern. Russ sat by the fire, his arm newly bandaged, eating ash cakes and stew. Jaq and Russ had dragged the tall cabinet, pinning the door shut. They were as safe as they could be.

For now.

Finn lay on the bottom bunk with his head in Jaq's lap. She ran her hand through his snarled, dusty bangs, humming low. He still hadn't said a word. He'd lain still while Jaq used a t-shirt and water to wash the blood from his hands and face. His blue eyes stared blankly past her, his body sometimes shuddering.

"Please eat something," Jaq said, tracing the sharp hollows of his cheeks with her finger. Finn had started out skinny at the beginning of the program, and now he was frail.

He swallowed and licked his lips. "I could drink," he whispered.

Before Jaq could ask, Russ had jumped up and came toward them with one of the bottled waters. Russ's face was tense with concern as he held the water out to his friend.

Finn lifted his head and took it, taking deep gulps, letting water run down his chin. He gasped for air when he'd finished. "I was thirsty," he said.

"Can you sit up now? Try some stew?" Russ cocked his head as if encouraging a child.

"I haven't had any real food in forever. No food at all for a couple days."

"It's amazing canned stew. You won't believe the flavor bomb," Russ tempted.

"My mouth is totally watering," Finn admitted with a weak smile.

"C'mon." Jaq slid a hand under his bony back and helped him sit up.

They all made their way over to the fire together. Each took turns taking bites out of the can of beef stew with a carved wooden spoon. The ash cakes went down easy, too. Jaq felt a vague peace, having survived another crisis—but she knew it was temporary.

He was still out there. Craig. She cowered away from the guilt wrapped around that name.

Finn brightened a bit after eating. His body stopped shivering and he leaned back on his elbows, legs extended toward the fire. "Better," he said.

"I was worried." Jaq patted his knee.

"I'm just kinda freaking out." Finn sat up and cupped a protective hand over his crotch. "And then that near sex change rendered me a bit taciturn."

Jaq glowed a little to see his humor returning. But he sobered quickly.

"Tell us what happened after you left with Katie." Russ sat forward.

Finn nodded and took a deep breath. "Yeah. You know— about her?"

"I saw." Russ pressed his lips in a line.

A silent communication passed between them. They'd both seen.

"And... Jock?" Finn's voice dropped.

Russ closed his eyes and shook his head.

"Oh. Sheesh Jock." Finn ran his hand through his bangs, his face lined with regret.

Jaq blinked back tears. "Tell us what happened to you, Finn."

He brought his knees up to his chest and stared at the fire for a minute. "Okay... So Katie and I... we hiked all day. Got to that cabin of doom in the middle of the night. Nobody was there—no walkie-talkies. Then she went out to pee or something and didn't come back. I got worried. Went to check and—there she was." His Adam's apple bobbed a few times. Finn shut his eyes. "My kingdom for a new set of eyeballs."

It was witty, but nobody laughed. "How did you get here?" Jaq said, feeling his trauma. She imagined Finn all alone dealing with something so horrible.

"There was a map—Katie had it and a compass in her pack. It was crazy, but I panicked and just took off. I didn't sleep. I got here by morning and found Erica."

"Dead?" Russ asked.

"Not yet. It was yesterday. She was here waiting for Craig. Told me they'd planned some escape together—she had the walkie-talkie. You know how she is—was. Kinda crazy and shrill. It was hard to get the whole picture."

"Was that your fire tonight?" Jaq asked, uneasy with where this was going.

"Yeah. I'd been in here with her, but when she told me all this crazy stuff, I decided to camp on my own. When I heard the four-wheeler earlier, I thought it was Craig and stayed away."

"Then she must have seen us and hid. But Craig found

her." Russ made a face like he was putting a mental puzzle together.

"And she had Mick's ax with her." Finn looked pale and a shadow passed over his blue eyes.

Jaq got the chills. Erica had used it on Daniel and then Craig had killed her with it. Talk about karma.

"What did they think they were doing?" Russ shook his head.

"Not sure. She was jabbering on and on." Finn stopped and his gaze turned to Jaq. "But Erica said you were somehow in on it."

Jaq blanched. Finn and Russ had their eyes glued to her. "No—I just—I wanted to run away and go home—but I didn't!" The whole truth ducked behind Jaq's guilt.

Finn continued. "She was freaking out, saying Craig would be mad because she was supposed to bring you."

"She—did ask me to go—the night before she ran." Jaq wrung her hands together, a smothering distress rising inside.

"W-why didn't you say anything? She t-took the walkie-talkie..." Russ seemed incredulous and almost angry.

Jaq shrunk. "And it caused a horrible chain of events," she whispered. Cold shame crashed down on her like an avalanche. Her hands flew to her face and she sobbed. "It's all my fault that people are dead! It's all my fault! Everything is— I'm so selfish—I never think!" She came apart, her insides caving in.

Someone grabbed her wrists and forced her hands down. "Look at me," Finn ordered, his voice hard, unlike him. "Look. Listen to what I'm saying."

Jaq pulled away from his grasp and wiped her face.

"Erica attacked Daniel because he woke up—she stumbled over him. She did that without you. Understand?" He held Jaq's chin and waited for her to look into his eyes. "She wanted to—bragged about it. Whether you'd said anything or not, she would have taken her chance."

"But-but—"

"No buts, Jaq. She was psycho—hated men." Finn dropped his palm from her face and took her by the hand.

"And Katie? Patti?" Jaq squeaked as fresh tears spilled from her eyes.

Finn gasped. "Patti too?" He blinked at the floor. "Oh."

"Yeah. We found her," Jaq choked out.

"Patti was such a nice lady." Finn's shoulders sunk, his face grim.

Russ spoke up. "I'm guessing Craig got them both—afraid of being followed."

Jaq gazed with sorry eyes at Finn, wanting his forgiveness for Katie's and Patti's deaths. Finn sat up straight.

"We don't know his history with them... Craig is their problem. You understand? Before you ever showed up," Finn reassured Jaq, squeezing her hand.

Jaq sniffed and hung her head. "Craig told me... he was a student here once. That things were messed up in his life and R.J. kinda adopted him."

"Finn is right. Even if you did tell him you wanted to run—there's a history here that has nothing to do with you. Craig was a ticking time bomb." Russ scooted until he sat beside Jaq.

"And I was the detonator," Jaq muttered, miserable. She wanted to scream.

Russ put his arms around Jaq and Finn did too. They curled together in a group hug until Jaq started to laugh through her tears.

"Somebody needs sleep. Can we say delirious?" Finn pulled away, half smiling at Jaq as she rubbed the tears out of her eyes.

"There's no way I can sleep tonight," Jaq moaned.

"I meant me." Finn pretended to swoon.

"We're all going to sleep. We're safe now—the door is blocked, it's three against one. He's not bugging us tonight. And in the morning, we'll take the four-wheeler as far away as possible with whatever gas is left." Russ took Jaq's hand and they walked to the beds.

"That sounds good—there's bound to be something near-by," Jaq hoped.

"I call top bunk," Finn said.

"We'll take the bottom, then." Russ spread out the blankets.

"We? Ah. So that's how it is, huh? What else happened these last couple of days?" Finn gave them both a sly look, then pretended to be bashful.

"I'll tell you all about our adventures as a bedtime story," Jaq said, sounding like a weary mother.

"Oh, goody!" Finn clapped, but his clowning lacked sparkle, his smile seemed forced. Trying to be a good sport and Jaq appreciated it.

Snuggled in the dark, Jaq retold everything that had happened—the coyote attack, Daniel's body in the tree, the other outpost, finding Katie and then Patti... a little relieved to purge it all out. Filling the still, black room with words that only these two boys could decipher. They were united in this experience—the unlucky few with the good fortune to have each other.

When she'd finished, Finn let out a long breath. "Dang, Jaq. It's like we're all trapped in some slasher movie. I choose to believe none of this is happening." He was trying to be funny. His coping device. "I'm glad we all found each other. I love you guys." He yawned. "Goodnight."

Jaq's broken heart warmed. "Finn—you're the best. Love you. 'Night."

Russ hadn't spoken and Jaq realized by his breathing that

he'd given in to his exhaustion and the lull of the pain pills. She nestled into his side and whispered into his ear.

"I love you."

Russ pulled Jaq closer, mumbling something in his sleep. And Jaq closed her eyes.

———

Russ and Finn shoved the cabinet away from where it blocked the door. Jaq eagerly pushed it open and fresh morning air glided in. She peeked outside, cautiously scanning before she stepped out onto the porch. Jaq took a deep breath and faced the sun. Last night seemed unreal—like a nightmare.

"Ah. Oxygen," Jaq said.

Finn coughed a few times. "Is that what that is?"

"No, you're coughing from your own fumes. I demand that you bathe. I have soap and shampoo." Jaq waved a hand in front of her nose.

"I second that." Russ folded his arms across his chest.

"Okay, I can take a hint. And actually, that sounds really good." Finn grinned. He looked at Jaq. "You look good in my shirt."

"Oh, yeah. Want it back?" She glanced down at the plaid.

"Nah." He winked.

Russ went over to the four-wheeler and walked around it. "We have a problem."

"We didn't before?" Finn scratched his head.

"Well, I knew we were probably almost out of gas—but now the tires are slashed too." Russ kicked one of the wheels.

"Craig. That creep." Jaq swallowed her disappointment.

"Wasn't much hope we would've gotten far anyway. At least here we have shelter." Finn forced a positive tone. "A little disturbed, though, that he's sending the signal that he doesn't want us leaving," he added with a grimace.

"Alive, anyway. Dead men tell no tales." Russ stomped back to the porch, his mouth in a bitter twist.

Jaq's stomach dropped. "Great. Now I'm freaking out again. We have no plan and he's still after us."

"Someone will come along soon. Our parents are going to wonder where everyone ended up, if not R.J.," Russ said with confidence.

"If he isn't dead. Thank goodness for our parents then, huh?" Finn stroked his chin.

Jaq thought of her dad. She wondered if he knew that she was missing yet. "Craig said there were search parties. Think that's true?"

"Well, if not yet, then soon." Russ's voice was gentle. He patted Jaq's arm.

"So he's running out of time..." Finn said softly.

It was chilling. Jaq remembered the wild look on Craig's face—thought of the things he'd done. He was a killer. Stone cold. They would have to watch each other's backs.

Jaq left the door open and followed Russ inside. He sat on a chair, checking his bandaged arm.

"How's that doing?" She had to change the subject or go insane.

"Hurts. But it isn't too deep." Russ busied himself with the cut on his arm, putting more antibiotic cream over the wound. When he picked up the roll of gauze, Jaq took it from him.

"Let me do that." While her hands tended to Russ's arm, she cleared her throat. "Um, I'm so sorry about... making you mad last night."

"What?"

"With the whole me not telling everyone about Erica's plan to run. I blame myself for so much."

Russ reached out and cupped her face with one hand. "Hey, guilt is my job. We talked about this last night. It wasn't your fault. Other people's choices. And I wasn't mad."

Jaq examined his sincere brown eyes. "Looked like it."

"No. That was me freaking out that you could've gotten involved in the whole crazy scheme—that you might have run away with Craig." He rubbed his thumb back and forth on her cheek. "That you considered leaving the group—me. I was upset. I'm sorry." His eyelids lowered.

"You're why I didn't go," Jaq admitted, feeling a blush coming on.

"Yeah?" A slow smile spread on Russ's face.

"Yeah." Jaq welcomed his soft kiss.

Finn cleared his throat. "So, that's what you guys have been doing the last few days."

"Etcetera," Russ muttered, pulling away from Jaq.

"Etcetera?" Finn's eyes grew huge.

Jaq laughed. "Meaning, as well as the hiking and surviving and terror."

"Oh." Finn wrinkled his nose, disappointed.

———

They all hiked together to where Finn had set up camp on the other side of the lake. Finn retrieved the bedroll he'd left beside the small fire pit. Jaq couldn't help it—her eyes darted around constantly, and her ears were perked. Craig might be tracking them.

While Finn bathed, Jaq and Russ collected more wood and set a couple traps—just in case—always staying in sight of one another. Jaq knew their "herd" was small, but with a lion hunting them, it was best to stick close to each other. She could hear Finn singing as he bathed, but she glanced toward the water often to check on him.

"It's weird just... waiting. Surviving until someone shows up to save us." Jaq squatted on the ground, testing the cordage trigger on her deadfall trap. She wasn't sure if it would even work. Russ looked up from his trap—it was perfect—and gave Jaq a sympathetic look.

"I know. This whole thing is surreal. But we know there'll be people out looking for us soon, if not already. And wandering in the badlands would just make it harder for them to find us. They'll check all the outposts, and at least we're at the one with a good water source." Russ was really putting his man-voice to work. But Jaq saw the worry in his eyes. "They'll come, Jaq."

"I hope so." Jaq turned her head so that he wouldn't see the tears that stung her eyes.

"Hey. Come hug me," Russ said gently.

Jaq went to him. She needed to feel his arms around her. And she knew that Russ needed her too.

Finn sang a loud Italian opera song in the lake. His comical voice echoed across the water. Jaq and Russ went down to the shore, arms full of gathered wood.

"We're headed back to the cabin," Russ called out to the dripping redhead.

Finn's eyes went wide. He stopped singing and splashed frantically toward them. "Not without me!"

"Well, come on." Jaq smiled, waving him in.

Finn emerged, his thin, wiry body buck-naked, dripping with water, both hands blocking his crotch.

"Whoa!" Jaq spun away, a giggle rising in her throat.

"Finn, man. Have mercy. I'm not sure I can take the competition." Russ chuckled.

"Well, if ya got it, flaunt it," Finn said. He pulled on his dusty clothes and picked up his bedroll. "Eew. I should have washed these too," he muttered, sniffing at his shirt.

As soon as they entered the dimness of the cabin, the hairs on Jaq's arms rose before her eyes even adjusted. Something was wrong.

"Oh, sh—eep dip." Finn clapped a hand over his mouth.

"No," Russ breathed.

Jaq gasped.

It was a mess. The cabinet had been chopped into pieces as well as the table and the chairs. The bunk bed was thrown on its side, the thin mattresses shredded to bits. Russ circled the room, exclaiming to himself. He put his hands in his hair. "All of our stuff is gone."

Jaq's heart dropped. "The food? Everything?" Her eyes scanned the small room and she knew it was true. Even their blankets.

"Dudes. Look." Finn's face was pale. He pointed to the ground, using his foot to shove away some of the debris.

On the floor was a small pool of red liquid, like an inkwell. Beside it was a smiley face and the words "Hi Jaq," turning brown, written in blood.

CHAPTER 23

RUSS KICKED one of the broken chairs across the room. The clatter made Jaq cringe. He was furious. Dark eyes snapping, he gritted his teeth. "I'm n-not gonna l-let"—he swallowed and took a breath—"him win."

"What will we do?" Finn still stared at the bloody message on the floor.

"K-kill him first," Russ growled. The light coming in from the door shone like a spotlight on the veiled threat scrawled on the floor. Russ pointed at the words on the ground and angrily shook his head. Russ stepped to her side and grabbed her hand, his grip almost painful. He looked into Jaq's eyes. "Don't w-worry."

Jaq shivered. His anger was oddly comforting—it made him look bigger, ferocious. But she suddenly feared what Russ would do. He'd take all that fury and throw himself into danger. For her. "I don't want anyone else getting hurt. If I go to him, I can figure out a way to get away—once we get to a town or something. I don't think he'd hurt me. He just wants me," Jaq said, almost convincing herself it was that simple.

"He can't have you," Russ bit out, pulling her closer to his side.

Finn folded his arms, standing straighter. "Can't let you hang out with a psycho, Jaq. There are three of us. We can take him."

Russ's breathing had slowed. He was thinking, glaring at the floor. Jaq didn't want him to feel like he had to solve this. That it was up to him to save her. She couldn't keep relying on other people to solve her problems.

"We'll track him. Hunt *him*," Jaq said.

Russ looked at her with surprise. "Yes."

Finn nodded. "I'm not waiting here, cowering. I'm in. If that moron thinks he can outwit me, he's underestimated my genius." Finn's eyes narrowed. The guys were both alight with testosterone. It was a phenomenon.

"I still have my knife," Jaq said.

Russ rubbed his hands together. "I have a knife now. Finn, we need to get you a weapon."

Finn grinned. "No problem." He untied his bedroll, dug around in the sack and pulled something out.

Jaq's mouth dropped open. "A gun?"

Finn held a small black handgun with a wide barrel. "It's a flare gun. I took it out of Katie's pack. I have five shots."

Russ let out a laugh of surprise. "Awesome. This is great."

"You had that and never shot it?" Jaq's voice rose an octave.

"What, and signal the psychos? I was more afraid of Erica and Craig finding me before some random person who *might* be out here seeing it and coming to help."

"Makes sense except for the fact that you were sending smoke signals with your fire," Russ pointed out.

"Well, I'm a city boy. Okay?" He grimaced. "Back to the problem at hand—let's go find Craig." Finn raised the flare gun up with both hands like some TV cop.

Russ's eyes flickered with what looked like excitement. "The sooner the better. We're out of food, and if he's waiting for us to get weak while he's keeping up his strength. I don't think he's expecting the hunted to become the hunters."

They stood together outside the cabin, looking in every direction. Russ and Jaq scanned the map for a while. "Okay. We'll make a sweep of the area around the cabin and the lake. We should pick up tracks or some sign of where he's camped," Jaq said, knowing that Russ was an excellent tracker.

"Solid." Russ looked at her with a gleam in his eyes.

"Are we fanning out?" Finn asked.

Jaq nodded. "We'll walk in formation. Spread out, but within sight of one another. You see anything at all, you yell. Okay? We'll watch each other's backs. It will be okay." Jaq held up her chin, determined to be brave. She would face this bully, not run or crumble like she always had with Brian. In some ways, this felt the same. But now the stakes were higher. Craig had murdered Katie, Erica, Patti and maybe Mick. She couldn't let anything happen to Russ or Finn. She would never get over that.

As a group, they circled the outpost, in a widening circle.

"Boot marks." Finn pointed to the drying mud on the ground. They each lifted a foot to check the bottom of their boots. The tread, with a herringbone pattern down the middle, didn't match any of theirs.

"Good. We know his print now." Russ took a few steps and stooped to look under a bush. "Huh. Dead mouse." He poked at it. "Fresh."

"Dude. I'm not that hungry yet." Finn scrunched up his nose.

"No. It's just there were a couple dead mice around the cabin. I noticed earlier. All pretty fresh." He stood and scratched his head.

"That's... weird, right? What's killing them?" Paranoia immediately slithered into Jaq's mind.

"If another animal did it—they would've eaten them," Russ said.

They wandered a little further and then arced around the outpost area, tightening the circle, finding two dead jackrabbits, both with large puncture wounds, and a dead grouse, neck broken, it's beak open.

"What is this, a pet cemetery? Freaky." Finn folded his arms across his thin chest and glanced over his shoulder.

Russ stayed quiet for a minute. Then he looked up, his brown eyes lit with realization. "He's chumming." He grabbed his chin and nodded. "Wow."

"What?" Jaq raised her brows.

"Like when you wanna lure sharks—you chum the water with dead fish and blood."

"Okay, I'm taking your word on that. I didn't watch Jaws—way before my time and, well, I'm chicken," Finn said.

"Is there something living in the lake we don't know about?" Jaq grunted in derision.

"No. Coyotes. They're scavengers and opportunists," Russ said in a serious voice.

Jaq had a special place in her heart for coyotes—labeled: *Ahhhh, get away!* "Oh. Crap." She shook off a chill.

Finn and Jaq whipped their heads around, as if the wild dogs were stalking them, waiting to spring from behind every rock and bush.

"They hunt at night. And if they've gotten used to seeing humans or eating their leavings, they'll be bold and aggressive."

"And you know this because?" Jaq stared at Russ like he was a National Geographic magazine.

Finn let out his breath. "It's in the curriculum book, Jaq. There's a section on all the wildlife out here. The gray wolf is king of the badlands, but their population is down, so coyotes are taking over. And there was something in there about making a lot of noise and trying to look bigger if you're confronted by any predator." Finn held his arms out in demonstration.

"I guess I should've actually read the book," Jaq grimaced.

"So you think he's trying to draw predators to our camp?" Finn turned to Russ.

"Yep."

"I think we should try to turn it on him... Can we?" Jaq wondered aloud.

"You're on to something." Russ thought for a moment. "Collect the dead animals and leave them wherever he's hiding. And we should check our traps to see if they got any more."

"Worth a try." Jaq smiled at him.

Using the extra piece of canvas that had held Patti's bundle together, they gathered up the dead animals surrounding the outpost. When they went to check the traps, Jaq's was un-triggered but Russ's trap had collapsed. He pushed at it with his boot, overturning the fall-stone. There was blood smeared across it.

"Caught something, but it looks like either Craig got to it or some other animal," he grunted.

The sun passed its high point as they walked in a diagonal angle several feet apart from one another, searching for signs of Craig. There were prints here and there. As they made a slow circle of the lake, evidence of broken branches and his particular boot print increased. A trail of blood dotted its way on occasional rocks and sometimes in the dirt near some of Craig's tracks.

"I think we're closing in." Russ clutched his knife.

Jaq pulled out her blade, a nervous feeling in her gut. She glanced over to where Finn stooped by a rock, his flare gun in hand.

"I'm seeing coyote tracks and some bits of fur caught in the sage," Finn called, muting his voice.

"There might be a pack nearby—and he's leaving them a trail toward us," Russ said.

"Like Hansel and Gretel but with blood and dead bodies," Jaq muttered.

Russ puffed out a breath, amused. "Yeah. Just like that."

More walking and scouring the ground. Russ still had a limp, but he didn't complain or slow down. They passed Finn's old camp and doubled back, making a larger circle, further out from the lake. The honking of disturbed grouse increased as the sun slid down the blue sky. Gray clouds drifted in, slow and thick. It might rain—it was too warm for snow.

Jaq's body felt weak from lack of food, water, and rest. And the endless hum of adrenaline flowing through her had taken its toll. She trudged just fast enough to keep the others in sight. Drying mud clumped on Jaq's boots, and she stopped to scrape them on a rock. The whisking sound of branches against denim made her turn her head sharply. It was Finn—he'd come closer.

"You okay?" Finn raised his chin at Jaq.

"Yeah." Jaq gave him a small smile.

Russ had stopped ahead, he leaned on a large rock, waiting. Alert.

"The sun's going down soon—earlier than it should because of that ridge." Finn signaled for her to keep moving, and he followed as they continued. They circled again, passing the cabin, seeing no new signs of disturbance.

A gray dusk settled over the landscape. The night insects creaked and the lake rippled silently, reflecting the sun that barely peaked over the ridge.

Russ dropped the dead animals all around the area they'd seen the most tracks. Wherever Craig was, it was nearby and he was well hidden.

"He must've found a cave or something," Russ scowled, disappointed. "But don't worry. We'll get him."

"If I don't at least get a drink of water, I'll faint," Jaq said, licking her lips.

"He took our canteens and bottled water," Russ said. "We could boil lake water to make it sanitary—if we had a billycan. Those are gone too."

"Not mine. I have all my stuff from my camp. I hid it," Finn said.

"Good, it's all we've got. We should head back."

"Anyone else need to use a bush for a second? Been holding it for way too long." Finn made a worried face.

"I could go," Jaq admitted.

"Let's get closer to the cabin first." Russ put his hands on his hips, scanning the area.

"Good idea." Finn threw a glance over both shoulders.

They hiked further as the dimness increased. The clouds pressed in and the temperature dipped. When Jaq saw the cabin in the distance, she breathed out with relief. Almost there. But she wasn't sure how long she could hold it.

"Are my eyes yellow yet?" Finn widened his eyes at Jaq, his eyes shiny and gray in the low light.

"Ew." Jaq stuck out her tongue. "But I'm with you." The pressure in her bladder was almost unbearable.

"One at a time," Russ insisted.

"Me first!" Finn and Jaq said in unison.

"Okay, okay, everyone take a break—but I wanna hear you humming the whole time."

"Any requests?" Finn bowed low.

Russ rolled his eyes. "Yeah. Don't get caught with your pants down."

Finn blanched. "Oh, fine. Star Wars Imperial March it is."

He turned and wandered away humming the Darth Vader theme song, ducking behind a bush several yards away.

Jaq blushed. "I'm not humming while I squat."

Russ grinned. "Neither am I. Besides, I wouldn't want to miss Finn's soundtrack for anything. But stay close." He disappeared around a large boulder.

It was dark enough that Jaq felt less exposed. Finn hummed on, increasing in volume as the song reached a crescendo. Jaq shook her head and snickered. She found a good-sized bush still in view of Russ's rock. After she finished, she pulled up her shorts and started to stand, then stopped. Finn was silent.

She craned her neck, straining her eyes in the direction Finn had gone. A scuffling sound came from over by where Russ was.

"Jaq," Finn whispered through the bush. "You done?"

"Sheez. You scared me," she said back in a low voice.

"Sorry."

Jaq slowly stood; her eyes were riveted to where Russ had disappeared. "I thought I heard something over there. Finn, go check—I don't want to see anything I shouldn't."

Finn stood behind her now. "Shhhh…"

Jaq held her breath, frozen. A shiver traveled up her spine when he laid a hand on her shoulder.

"Damn you, Finn!" Russ shouted. "Get off me! It's not funny!" Finn's laughter echoed up from behind the large boulder where Russ was.

A jolt of confusion followed by terror turned Jaq to ice. In that second, the hand on her shoulder tightened and another hand clamped over her mouth. Hard.

"Jaq! You done?" Russ called. He stepped into view, hands on his hips, squinting in her direction in the dim light.

The mouth by Jaq's ear hissed, "Shhh." Something that felt like a blade pressed at her back.

Finn appeared next to Russ, swinging his arms, pleased with himself for something.

"I got you good, man. You thought I was—"

"Shut up, Finn. Jaq, are you done?" Russ repeated louder. He held a hand up in Finn's face to silence him. Finn went still.

"Uh-huh," her captor answered in a high feminine tone.

It all happened in a few seconds. Jaq's brain switched back on and she thrashed, biting the hand covering her mouth.

"Jaq, are you okay?" Russ took a couple steps in her direction. *So far away.*

She only got out one muffled cry before a solid fist hammered into her stomach, leaving her without air. She crumpled in agony while strong arms lifted her backwards and something rough was pulled over her face, blocking out any light. Deja vu. Her hand flew to her waist, but the sheath was empty.

Finn and Russ began calling her name in panic.

Craig's breath was hot in her ear. "If you want them to live, don't fight me."

Jaq gasped for air. Her feet dragged helplessly on the ground and her mind raced. They could take him. Russ had a knife and Finn had his flare gun. She sucked in for a scream and the hand returned to her mouth, cruel and bruising.

Craig had her. An absurd thought flashed through her mind—her own gravestone inscribed with the words *She Knew It.* Jaq kicked and clawed until a splitting blow on the side of her head clicked everything off.

CHAPTER 24

JAQ MOANED IN PAIN, fading in and out of being in her body. Russ and Finn shouted from far away, branches cracked, harsh breathing in her ear. Jaq's legs scrambled over rocks, getting torn by bushes.

Her head throbbed... hard to breathe. She became more aware. The ache in her head was worse. Jaq's face was covered and arms wrapped around her, squeezing like a boa constrictor.

"We're here." Craig's voice echoed in the enclosed space. He pushed Jaq onto her back on a cold stony surface—pinning her down with strong hands. Jaq clamped her legs together, locking her ankles.

She struggled and pulled as he tied her hands together with coarse rope that chafed her wrists. "Craig, what are you doing?" Jaq tried to speak with force, but the sharp pain in her head and the cover over her face took the power away.

Jaq tried to kick when he tied her feet together, but all his weight pressed down on her legs, his knees pressing into her thighs, bruising. Jaq grunted and whimpered but he seemed not to notice.

When he'd finished binding her, Craig removed the cover from her head. Jaq took a deep breath and screamed. It echoed in her ears, trapped like helium in a tank. It was a small, dark cave, a soundproof room. Cold.

Shaking and sick, Jaq faced the monster she knew she'd helped to create. She clamped her teeth together to stop a sob. Craig leaned against the opposite wall of the narrow space, watching her with black eyes. His pocked face was lit by the upturned red flashlight he'd stolen. It cast deep shadows under his brows and nose. The supplies he'd taken from the cabin lay scattered on the ground. The hatchet leaned against the wall beside him. Jaq strained to sit upright.

"Jaq. What's the problem?" He dragged a hand through his long hair with a confused expression. "Did you change your mind?"

"What's the—problem?" she choked, unable to organize the explosion of fear and fury in her head to form a proper response. Like, *screw you, freaking psychopath!*

"Girls are so confusing," Craig groaned and sunk to a sitting position. "You wanted to get away, and I made sure you did. So why are you fighting me?" His brows pushed down in irritation.

Jaq stared at him. How could he act so normal? It was beyond creepy. "I didn't want you to kill anyone," she heard herself answer, matching his tone as if they were having an argument over a choice of restaurant.

"What does *what you want* have to do with anything?" Craig shook his head. "Teens are so egocentric."

"What?" The dizziness in her head increased to spin cycle as he transitioned from awkward guy to adult therapist.

"Egocentric. It means you think everything is about you and that the world revolves around you," he explained as if she were stupid.

"I know what the word means. I guess what I meant to say

was *what the hell?*" She wondered if he could hear her beating heart.

Craig shoved his hands into his pockets. "You know, Katie would be all over you for saying that. But see—I'm not. You can curse all you want. It's a free country."

Jaq swallowed. Her fear slid silently into shock. It must have. Because she felt a sudden calm. He was nuts, but she could play him.

"You didn't like that about her," Jaq said.

"She was so annoying. Always spying on me—reporting my screw-ups. Told on me for talking to you. She's always been on my case, ever since she got here. She wanted to take my place." There was a small twitch on one side of his face and his hand reached out to touch the handle of the ax.

"Your place?" Jaq swallowed.

"As R.J.'s favorite. Katie, the kiss-up." Craig made a disgusted face, his hand tightening on the ax handle.

"Okay. I can see why that would piss you off." Jaq took a breath. "Is that why you killed her?"

Craig groaned, rolling his eyes. "That and so many other reasons." He let out a puff of exasperated air.

Jaq stared at him. He had no remorse at all. He'd killed her. Killed. Her.

His face hardened. He looked down at the floor between his knees. "If for nothing else, just to see the surprise and fear on her face." A hint of a smile showed in the corners of his wide mouth. Then he froze. "Don't say that," he whispered and shook his head hard.

What the—? Jaq's heart skipped. Was he talking to himself?

"So, what about Patti? She was nice," Jaq said, feeling like she was in a trance or a dream, walking a minefield.

Craig pressed his palms into his eyes. "She made me cry all the time. You should know. She made you cry too." He lowered his hands and stared at Jaq, searching her face for understanding. "And she was against me. Always telling R.J. that I wasn't ready for this or that. But I'm better at this survival stuff than any of them." His voice climbed as he spoke and a shadow of anger crossed his face, a low simmer in the back of his dark eyes.

"Yeah. You really have it figured out." Jaq watched his face change again at her words. Awkward, timid guy was back.

"Patti was gonna come out to find you—with new rations. Nobody knew that Erica had taken the walkie-talkie. And I'd hid all the ones at the outposts. I volunteered to go with Patti. She preached at me the whole ride. About what I should feel— what I shouldn't do. Who I should be."

"Did you understand what she was saying? Was she trying to help?"

Craig scowled. "I'm not as brainwashed as they think. And I was so sick of telling her that I didn't forgive my dad." Craig sneered, frightening in the shadows. Like Brian's mask when Jaq was younger.

"He was bad?" Jaq pressed her back against the jagged wall.

"Famous bad. In jail since I was five, got out when I was ten. Came home. Destroyed everything that mattered... until you. You matter." Craig's eyes softened.

Revulsion turned in Jaq's stomach. "So—you're an orphan?" She had to get the topic away from her.

He folded his arms and shuddered. He bent his head so that his long stringy hair covered his face. "Dad made me an orphan. By hand. In front of me. For the record, foster homes officially suck." His shoulders rose in several rough inhales, and he muttered something to himself that Jaq couldn't understand.

"That must have been horrible." Jaq pulled into herself, feeling like her muscles shrank from her bones. A muted howl sounded to her right. The yelping of coyotes in the distance funneled into the cave. The exit was that way. The way out.

She had to figure out how to escape before he lost it completely.

Craig raised his head, chewing his lower lip. "People just let me live with them for money—and they did stuff." A sudden smile split his face like an open wound "He's—I'm kidding—nothing happened. I got into a lot of trouble and then I came here. My life changed. It's just so beautiful out here. Sometimes I just stare up at the sky and feel so free."

"Oh, good." Jaq tried to play along, but this was insane. Chills raced up and down her back.

"Yeah, and R.J.'s the best. But everyone wants his attention and love." He leaned his head back against the wall, closing his eyes.

"But not as much as you."

"No. He matters too. Like you." Craig reached across the space between them and patted her foot.

Jaq recoiled. How could she reason with a maniac? It was like he was rowing a boat with one paddle, on one side of the boat. Jaq had to navigate this conversation; she had to put her oar in enough to steer it where she needed it to go.

"So Patti... what happened?" She braced herself to hear.

He lit up. "That was kind of spontaneous. I was angry at her. She said Katie told her I was inappropriate with the students. Patti wasn't watching as she steered, I think—we tipped over. We fell. And she sort of lay there like she was dead for a second. And it looked good. I leaned over her, her eyes opened, and I just reacted."

"You stabbed her with the knife you stole."

"I took all of them but yours. I didn't want to worry you." His voice lowered and he glanced away.

Jaq didn't want him to say she mattered again. "Then?"

"Oh, well, Mick saw me do it. He came out of nowhere; I didn't expect him. He knocked me down—he's stronger. But slower. I hit his head with a rock, then stabbed him with the other knife, but it was my last one, so I kept it."

Jaq swallowed her alarm. "Right there—by Patti. You killed him."

"Yeah. I put him next to her. Seemed right." Craig nodded, and his hands started drumming on his knees. "Shhh," he hissed, glowering at his hands.

The killing of the last few days had driven Craig over the edge. Jaq tried to think clearly while her head ached and Craig muttered to himself like he was splitting into pieces.

Had he killed Mick? The big man wasn't there by the time she and Russ reached Patti's body. Maybe he didn't die. Maybe he got away. Or maybe coyotes got him... Jaq's hope deflated. Her eyes met Craig's, and she looked away from the kaleidoscope she saw there.

"My plan has always been to just work with R.J. Mick was okay—he didn't bother me much. He had a temper sometimes." His long fingers reached out and touched the ax again, stroking the handle.

"What happened with Erica?" Jaq somehow forced out the words past the rising terror in her throat.

"That girl is nuts. I knew she was. R.J. told me she was always running. That's when I got the idea. If she ran, she should help you. But she screwed it all up by killing that annoying Daniel kid and not bringing you. So he—I didn't care to help her anymore. And she attacked me. That girl had claws." He squinted, pointing to the side of his face, and Jaq noticed some scabbed over scratches by his ear.

She nudged his foot with hers, hoping her voice sounded sympathetic. She had to be his best friend if she wanted to live. "Erica was awful," Jaq said. "Nobody liked her."

So that accounted for everyone but R.J. But something was wrong—

"We know." Craig clasped his hands together, a spasm rippled through his body. He squeezed his eyes shut. He was fighting himself. Shaking.

Jaq's breath hitched. Her eyes flicked around the cave, trying to determine the exit—too dark. She gulped. *Keep him talking.* "And R.J.?"

Craig looked up, startled, as if surprised to see her. He hugged himself and let out a long breath. "He's on a walkabout. Left me and Patti to mind HQ. He does that sometimes. He loves it out here, in the quiet. No people. The smell of the sagebrush, the call of the coyote. The ridges and bluffs... It's like a second home to him. And to me." His hands trembled and a sheen of sweat showed on his forehead and in the dark fuzz above his lip.

"How long will he be gone?" Jaq heard the echo of faraway howls again.

"He might be back there now. I left a note that we were bringing you guys fresh supplies and stuff and spending a Layover with your group."

"Oh." So even if R.J. was back, he might not think anything was wrong for a day or two. A bell of panic pealed in her chest. How much longer until help came? If not for her, then for Russ and Finn.

"Hungry?" Craig abruptly stood and Jaq cringed against the wall. He disappeared into the shadows, his feet scuffling on stone, echoing sharp in her ears.

He reappeared with a protein bar and bottled water in his hands. "So, I didn't fail you. I *am* helpful." He knelt beside her and unwrapped the bar. The crinkling made Jaq wince. He noticed. "Aren't you grateful?" he said in another voice, mocking.

"Yes."

"Say it," he growled.

Jaq couldn't meet his eyes. He seemed to suddenly vibrate with aggressive energy.

"Thank you, Craig. Really, you're so thoughtful. Can you untie me—so I can eat?" Jaq held up her bound hands.

Craig sighed, his eyes clearing. "Of course. You're free. Tomorrow we'll leave here. Go get your sister—wherever you want. I could live off the land for years, if you like it, or we could try a town." Nice voice again.

"Won't you miss R.J.?" Jaq didn't want him to mention her sister again—she looked down at the rocky floor to avoid his stare. Sunflower seeds were scattered all over. Naturally.

"He'd want to join us, once I explained everything."

He was totally out of touch with reality. "Oh, good."

Craig balanced the unwrapped protein bar on her knee and worked the knots at her wrists. "You had a bad father too. I won't let anyone else hurt you. R.J. would be good to you."

"Thank you. I don't know what I'd do without you." Jaq felt sick. But she knew she had to keep the nice-voice version of him here.

Craig blushed and pulled the rope free. "You're so beautiful. So soft. Nothing ever felt so soft—except maybe... this light blue robe my mom used to wear." Craig's voice cracked.

Jaq rubbed her wrists then reached out and patted his shoulder, bile in her throat. Craig flinched. His eyes were watery, haunted.

"It's okay," she whispered.

He wiped his face and gawked at Jaq. "I've never had a girlfriend before."

Jaq hid her revulsion at the implication that she was his first. She was not surprised he hadn't had a girlfriend... Craig was weird even before he was a serial killer. He'd lived in this strange wilderness world since he was a teen himself. Not a lot of dating options. Just the occasional groping of sleeping students.

"But I know stuff. I'm a man. I want you to..." He looked down. "Well, I saw you with Russ. I want that." His gaze swept over her body.

Nausea. "Okay," she said, concealing her disgust. She knew a bargaining chip when she saw one. "But I want my feet untied and I want to be able to leave the cave if I want. It's freezing in here."

For a moment, an angry, suspicious mask flashed on his face. A low growl sounded in his chest. But he shook it away, turning his head to the cave wall. "Not Jaq," he said in a harsh whisper, his hands clenched into fists. "No." It was like he was commanding a badly behaved dog to leave a guest alone.

Jaq's blood turned to slush. She was so close to madness. To death. Craig was barely hanging on—she had to convince him to keep that thing inside him chained.

"I told you. You're free." He untied her feet and crawled toward her, sitting with folded legs beside her. Jaq picked up the protein bar and shoved it into her mouth. Forcing herself to chew and swallow the flavorless mass to buy time. Nobody would rescue her. She had to play this out—save herself. Jaq swallowed and almost gagged.

He watched her eat, head drifting slowly to a cocked angle, fascinated by her. The flashlight behind him made his black eyes gleam in the dark against his shadowed face. He waited, like any predator, intent, patient.

Jaq took a drink of water, but her breathing was so uncoordinated she ended up in a coughing fit. Craig patted her back and laid a wool blanket over her lap. When she'd wheezed out the water in her windpipe, there was nothing left to stall. She prayed for strength to do whatever she had to do. To live. To get back to Russ. Had to see Flower again. She needed to hug her dad and tell him she was sorry—wanted to start over. Even her brother and Mom deserved another chance. She'd do anything to make everything right with the people she cared about.

Anything.

Craig took the water bottle from Jaq's hands and set it on the ground. He scooted closer until his knee pressed into her hip. Slowly, his hand lifted. Jaq stiffened as he touched her cheek with his cold fingertips. Her jaw tightened to hide the fact that her teeth clicked together. He let out a low breath and traced her cheekbone to her ear. Jaq kept her eyes focused past his shoulder, aware of the dark holes of his eyes aimed at her.

With his other hand, Craig reached behind him and pulled her knife out of the back of the waistband of his jeans. Jaq gasped and pulled back.

He chuckled softly, flashing that crooked front tooth. "I won't hurt you."

Craig pointed the knife to her chest. "I've imagined doing this..." The knife's tip poked lightly at her flesh. He flicked his wrist and a button popped off her plaid shirt. Jaq's insides trembled. She had to think about something else as his hand lowered to the next button.

She shut her eyes.

CHAPTER 25

ONE TIME JAQ and Flower made a picnic and walked down to the nature park. It was a sunny day. Flower was twelve but had brought bubbles. They lay on a blanket, looking up at an impossibly blue sky, watching the clear orbs drifting up and away. Light, shiny, clean. The bubbles would thin and then burst, twinkling like daytime stars. Their mom had shown up with Brian. He blew bubbles for his sisters, and they all laughed together and chased them. Then Mom read aloud to them from a Winnie the Pooh book they were too old for it, but the sound of her mother's voice, the summer air, and the bubbles made Jaq feel drowsy and safe. Content.

Clatter of buttons. The knife moved down the front of her, until the shirt lay open, exposing the IBSA t-shirt Jaq wore underneath. Craig suppressed a grin. He pushed the plaid shirt off her shoulders and pulled it from her arms.

"I'm cold." Jaq shivered, trying to keep from screaming. And she wanted to punch him. So hard. And maybe never stop.

"Not for long." His brows slanted sympathetically. "I'll make you warm." Craig laid the knife on the ground just out of reach.

His hands rested on the bare skin of her upper arms, his

fingers like icy spider legs. He sighed, an expression of wonder on his face that made Jaq's stomach shrivel as his hard, calloused hands dragged lightly down to her elbows.

Skin crawling, Jaq reminded herself not to flinch. If she played this right, it could be to her advantage.

"Were you ever like this with any other girls—who came out here?" She tried to sound insecure—jealous.

Craig blushed. He leaned in closer, touching her hair. "It wasn't the same. You're the only one who matters. Just you." His voice was urgent, desperate to convince her.

Lucky me. "Oh. Good." She fluttered her lashes, looking down. *Gross, gross, gross.*

He leaned in, inhaling. "You smell like shampoo... so good." His hands moved through her hair, over her arms, down to her waist. He skimmed the perimeters, hesitant, shy.

"I've touched you before," he confessed in a whisper.

"I know. It's okay." Jaq forced a small smile despite the replay of her nighttime molestation. Jaq didn't want to think about it. *Help me, God.* She sent a longing look toward the knife, from the corner of her eye.

Craig's hands froze on her knees, contracting. Breath whistled through his teeth. His chin down on his chest, he rolled his eyes, showing too much white, to meet hers, like a creature from a nightmare. "Jaq."

"What?" she croaked, heart drumming sporadically.

"Can I... kiss you?" His voice shook.

Rising gag. "Of course." Bubbles. Bubbles floating in the sky. Winnie the Pooh.

He breathed out through his nose, relieved. His hands, still on her knees, squeezed when he leaned forward until his face was an inch away. Jaq shut her eyes. He smelled like sweat, dirt, and a metallic tang. Blood. Her eyes flashed open just as his lips collided with hers, hard and quick. He pulled back, flushed, his face shiny with perspiration.

Jaq clenched her hands into fists to keep them from scrubbing at her lips. Craig narrowed his gaze and grunted. He cocked his head to the side and moved toward her again. Her lips tightened as he pressed against them. He pushed harder as if to feel something more. Her teeth stabbed the insides of her lips. Jaq knew she wasn't making it good for him.

An exasperated moan sounded in Craig's throat. His lips stuck slightly to hers when he retreated. A hum filled Jaq's head. She didn't want to pass out—or vomit. But she felt light-headed and sick.

"You"—sharp inhale—"aren't doing it—like you did with him." His hot breath on her cheek was a poisonous vapor. His voice had dropped. *Scary voice.*

Jaq's heart jumped. She had to fake it better. Had to get over her revulsion.

Russ. Flower. Dad. Bubbles and bedtime stories. Sunny days and Oreo milkshakes. Patti's smile.

Don't look down—just jump.

Jaq sat forward and kissed him.

Just a mouth. Jaq went through the motions. *This isn't real. A movie kiss—an act. Going to live. Need to get the knife. Run toward the howls.*

Hot mouth on hers, hungry, rough. Salty.

Not real. Not real.

Craig loved the show. His hands groped and grabbed; his breathing grew ragged. Jaq was crushed against the stone wall, but she continued to kiss him. Hating him. Wishing she had fangs.

"Touch—me—back," he pleaded, biting her lower lip.

Her arms stayed rigid at her sides for a moment. Numb. Then she forced them to reach up to his shoulders. One hand traveled to his greasy, snarled hair. She slid sideways down the wall, slowly—toward the knife. He followed, rolling so that he covered her. His weight pushed the air out of her lungs.

God, help me be strong. Jaq opened her eyes. Craig was too far gone to notice. The knife—right there. He panted and growled, bruising her, infecting her. Hot anger burst inside Jaq.

Now.

Her hand flashed out. She grabbed the knife, gripping the handle like the brake on a runaway train.

Time to stop.

The blade pierced his lower back easily with a squelching sound. Craig roared, rearing away from Jaq, his eyes wide. He flopped onto his side, screaming, and Jaq leaped up. Lightning shot through her body.

Run.

She stumbled on jelly legs through the dark cave, scraping against the walls, bashing her hips and elbows. Craig's bellows reverberated in her ears.

Jaq tripped and fell, tumbling out of the cave and rolling down an incline. She stopped against a large patch of bitter-brush. Everything hurt. She lay still, stunned.

Throbbing pain. Stars glared down, but the moon hid behind a cloud. Jaq couldn't move. The wetness from Craig's saliva cooling on her face sparked her back to reality. She screamed out from her gut, raw and outraged. The sound tore through the silent wilderness and echoed back at her, as if the sky screamed with her. She turned on her side as a tidal wave of disgust rose in her mouth. Jaq spit away the bile. Her shaky hands clawed and wiped at her lips. Still tasted him.

Jaq dragged herself on hands and knees further away from the cave. Coyotes called clear and high. "Russ! Finn!" she shrieked.

Footsteps. Staggering. Heavy breathing.

Jaq curled into a little ball under a bush. Her pulse ticked away the time.

"Ja-aaq." Sing-songy. Taunting.

It was him.

Maybe the knife missed anything important. Maybe it didn't go deep enough. She'd panicked—hadn't aimed.

The bad voice said, "Where are you?" He wasn't far.

Dirt scuffing. A shuffling sound of boots.

Then, horribly, there he was, the killer from her dreams, staring down at her. A dark shape—a wraith.

Her strength was gone, the last of it spent in the surge of adrenaline used to escape the cave.

"You hurt me." His voice was cold. Craig held one hand to where she'd stabbed him.

"S-sorry." She kneeled up, instinct telling her to stay off her back. The moonlight poured down like stage lights as the clouds drifted out of the way.

Craig glowered down at her, angular features like blades pushing through his skin. He grabbed a handful of her hair, jerking her to her feet. She thought she'd faint.

"Despite that, I want you back. More." His eyes gleamed dark and lifeless. Like a shark.

"You said I was free!" Jaq's voice broke.

"*He* said you were free. Not *me*," he said, baring his teeth. Craig shook his fist still clutching her hair—her scalp burned. She couldn't pull away without tearing her hair out in a bloody clump. So be it.

Jaq swayed, summoning the strength to fight. She couldn't go back to the cave. *Never. Never. Never.* He pulled on her hair. Light sparkled behind her eyelids.

"Russ!" she screamed before his other hand, bloodied from his back, clapped over her mouth. The taste of his blood made her gag.

Then there was a flash of red light so bright it hurt Jaq's eyes. A comet hissed toward them, passing only a few feet over their heads, illuminating everything around them. Blinding. Then a loud bang that caused Craig's grip to loosen. Jaq dropped and rolled away, scrambling to her feet she lurched, still blinded, into darkness, through bushes, over rocks.

Pounding footsteps. "Jaq!"

Arms clamped around her waist, pulling her from her feet. She thrashed like a wild animal. "Let go!" she shrieked.

"Jaq, it's me!"

Russ.

"Oh, God! Russ!" Jaq sobbed, her world spinning. She flung her arms around his body, clinging to him. But Russ had freed his own arms—he held a knife.

"You psycho freak," Russ ground out.

Jaq looked in the direction Russ faced. Craig stood only a few yards away, his expression obscured in the shadows.

"I'm going to kill you now," Craig promised in a low steady voice. The knife Jaq had left in his back was now gripped in his hand.

Jaq yelped, her body quaking. She released Russ and tried to be strong, like a child telling the monster in the closet to go away. "Craig. Enough. Stop."

"Never," he spat.

"What she said, Hamlet." Finn appeared behind Craig, pointing the flare gun at his back.

Craig jerked his head around, his hand planted on his wound again. He eyed Finn. Then he looked back at Jaq and Russ holding his blade. Craig was outnumbered and injured. Bedraggled, filthy, zombie-like. He lowered the knife to his side, shoulders drooped in defeat.

"Jaq," he whispered. "I still feel you." Craig stepped out of the shadow into a shaft of moonlight. His free hand floated up to his mouth. He touched his lips leaving a smear of blood and closed his eyes.

Jaq shuddered in disgust.

"Oh. God," Russ murmured, his hand finding Jaq's.

Craig turned and broke into a run away from them, waving the knife in his hand wildly as he fled. Russ leaped after him, tugging Jaq behind him. Finn loaded and shot another flare, and it fizzed diagonally toward the sky, lighting up the path. *Bang.*

Craig was headed for the lake, lurching like a broken robot as he went, his back dark and glistening with blood.

Jaq wasn't sure how her legs kept moving, catching herself falling with each step. If they let him go this time, he'd be back and the nightmare would continue. Her heart pumped hard. Jaq gripped Russ's hand as they ran together.

Another cloud covered the moon and the night turned into deep cobalt glass.

Finn and Russ thundered over the dirt with single-minded determination, huffing and grunting as they ran and jumped over obstacles. Jaq lost Russ's hand and he closed in on Craig who shambled slowly forward.

The ground dropped in a steep plunge toward the water on this side of the lake, and they headed toward it in the dark. Jaq watched as black cutout shapes, like shadow puppets of the three boys, converged. Finn and Russ were almost there when Craig disappeared over the edge. Russ and Finn froze, heads bent to look down where Craig had gone. Jaq reached them, gasping for breath, leaning over on her knees, her whole body on fire. There was the sound of grunting and crunching—she strained her eyes and saw Craig bumping and rolling head over feet before finally sprawling out at the bottom of the slope to lay still.

Nobody moved or spoke. The moon reappeared, parting

the curtain of darkness to reveal what felt like the final scene of a play. Craig lay in a broken tangle on the ground, splattered with blood. He'd fallen on his knife at some point; it protruded from his stomach. One of his legs bent the wrong way.

Jaq collapsed into the dirt. Laughter she didn't recognize as her own shook her body, then turned to sobs she couldn't control. Russ dropped down and held her tight against his chest. She dug her fingers into his shoulder, trying to fill her lungs with oxygen.

"Jaq." Russ gently rubbed her back.

"He was so horrible. And sad! I should never have—I didn't know! His hands—were like sandpaper—and he wanted me— but the other him hated me." From a remote place in her head Jaq realized she made no sense. "I wished he was dead—and nobody ever loved him. He told me everything he did—and he wasn't sorry! I just wanted to get away—no matter what—I let him—I let him..." She babbled until she couldn't breathe.

Russ wept into her neck. "You're so b-brave. It's okay n-now. He c-can't hurt you. I'm so s-sorry, Jaq. I d-didn't find y-you in t-time." He stroked her hair, curled around her like a cocoon of protection.

Jaq wanted to tell him it was okay. That he helped save her. *In time? For what?* Jaq's mind started to sort through the jumble, but before she could make her voice work Finn spoke.

"Guys. Guys. We have company." Finn backed away from the slope.

Jaq stifled a hiccup and wiped her face. Russ went still, ears perked. Then, with one arm still wound around Jaq, they stood, leaning on each other.

Yelps, sniffing, a long canine whine. Emerging from the shadows, four mangy coyotes crept, careful, stealthy. Her very soul sank into her stomach. *Noooo.*

The blackest one, leading the pack, howled, and a painful

vibration traveled through Jaq, reminding her of the sensation of hitting something hard with a metal baseball bat.

"Dead animals did the trick apparently." Finn held up the flare gun, reloaded, and fired it into the air. The streaking crimson light and red-glow flash lit up the pack, giving them a supernatural look. The explosion frightened the beasts. They wove and jumped in startlement, ducking behind bushes. When the light faded, the black coyote circled around, testing the ground with its paws as if it were a hot surface. The others followed, heads bent, eyes up, a rumbling in their throats.

"B-back away from them slowly. Keep your eyes on them," Russ whispered, tucking Jaq further into the shelter of his body.

The three of them took slow steps backward, toward the ledge. "Take it slow." Russ pressed his lips to Jaq's forehead.

The earth and rocks slanted steeply away, and Jaq's feet slid several inches, sending a small avalanche of dirt down the steep slope. Russ steadied her arm. They would be in trouble if this turned into a chase. The coyotes would have the advantage with their four legs on the unlevel ground.

The leader of the pack growled and lunged and retreated, startling Finn backward. He flailed his arms and his legs as his footing disappeared. Finn fell, landing on his elbows with a loud "Ooof!" then tumbled a few feet in a spray of dirt and rocks and stopped with a loud moan, clutching the branches of a bush.

Jaq gasped. "Finn! Are you okay?"

"Ouch," he grumbled from below. "I lost the flare gun." He dragged himself to his knees.

Jaq searched the ground with her eyes. Without the moon, it was impossible to make out the dark flare gun among the rocks and dirt.

The coyotes spread out, coming closer to the ridge. Jaq

balanced herself, one knee bent and the other leg extended further down the decline. Her legs trembled, on the verge of buckling. So tired. So afraid.

"Crap." Russ took a sideways step down closer to Finn.

"Exactly," Finn panted and gripped a large stick, using it to stand.

They carefully descended another few feet. Jaq tried not to think about what was at the top, waiting to attack, or what was below—Craig.

With a sudden lurch, the coyotes came spilling over the edge of the ridge, barking and snarling. Jaq's heart stopped for the hundredth time that night. Covering her head with her arms, she plunked onto her backside and slid down the dirt slide, digging her heels into the loose soil and rocks to slow down. But the wild dogs hurdled past her, scampering down the steep slope toward Craig. That's when Jaq noticed Craig's arm move. He was still alive.

A groan rose up from him as the pack descended, biting and tearing into his body. One strangled yell of agony and terror, then nothing but the sound of the coyotes feeding.

Jaq shut her eyes, swallowing hard. There was nothing left in her stomach to evacuate. She wished she could purge her mind of all the images of torn flesh and blood.

Finn and Russ huddled beside her. "We can't draw attention to ourselves. We need to get away while they're... occupied," Russ murmured, his face white and glossy with sweat.

A low, loud howl soared into the night sky. Outlined in moonlight on the ridge above, a large grey wolf posed, snout in the air, majestic. Threatening.

"You gotta be joking," Finn rasped, staring up in fascination as the wolf gazed down at them. There was nowhere to go—coyotes below and a wolf above. They were trapped.

CHAPTER 26

THE WOLF'S eyes gleamed silver in the dark before it plunged down the slanted ground, beautiful and terrifying. It passed by the three huddled humans as if they weren't there, leaping into the midst of the coyotes, barking and snapping at the smaller, skittish dogs. The mangy pack scattered and then rebounded, their narrow snouts covered in the blood of their find. They wouldn't give it up so easily.

The black coyote hunched low, regarding its superior warily, as the other three flanked him, protecting their meal. The two Alphas faced off, rumbling warnings in their throats. The wolf launched from its haunches, but his enemy sprang out of the way. Hitting the ground, the wolf seemed to bounce, already airborne again, jaws open before the black coyote could turn back around. It latched onto the back of the coyote's neck. In the dark, the blur of teeth and fur, and the guttural growling seemed to go on and on, their bodies churning together in a violent dance.

"Mereth en draugrim," Finn whispered as they all flattened themselves in the shadows further up the incline. Jaq was starting to hear gibberish. Shock.

"It means 'feast of wolves' in Elvish—used to describe a

slain enemy." Finn swallowed, his big eyes taking over his face as he gaped at the fighting canines.

Russ blinked at him. His mouth opened and shut once before he managed to say, "Let's get out of here."

Jaq and the boys crab-crawled backward up the slope, never taking their eyes off the *World's Deadliest Animals* episode below.

The two beasts broke apart. The black coyote yelped and let out a shrill whine and darted away, followed by its three minions. The wolf stood, triumphant and tall, piercing eyes watching the retreat. Then it turned to Craig, letting out another howl, mournful and chilling. It bent its shaggy head over the fallen body, and the sound of the wolf's lapping tongue and whining throat broke the sudden quiet.

Without warning, the gray wolf turned and spotted them. It took a few slow steps toward them and barked a percussion that rattled Jaq's chest.

Jaq felt her insides collapse. "I can't run—I can't fight anymore." It was as if someone had removed her batteries. Nothing. It was finally too much.

Russ grabbed her arm hard, yanking her with him as he scrambled to reach the ridge. "Jaq—t-try!"

Her heavy, aching limbs moved as if through water. They could never outrun that fanged thing. Tears spilled down her cheeks—she had nothing left. She'd survived so much—but the badlands had one too many tricks up its sleeve. It had won.

"I can't. You guys run. Run!" Jaq put a hand to her throbbing head. It was wet with blood, and she knew she was about to faint. If she did, Russ would try to drag her and it would slow him down. "Please. Just go!"

Russ ignored her, pulling, grunting. His feet slid in the dirt; they were getting nowhere. The wolf came toward them, slow and cautious. Russ made another desperate attempt to pull Jaq with him, this time with Finn pushing from below.

"Jaq, don't give up!" Finn begged. But his face was weary too.

"GO!" she screamed as the wolf sped to a trot.

"No. Jaq. No. I l-love you." Russ encircled her with his arms. The bandage on his arm was soaked with blood, and Jaq knew his wounded leg must be a mess. No food or decent sleep for too long, running, fighting—the stress was too great. He sagged in resignation. "I'm staying with y-you," he whispered, breathless with effort and fear. He squeezed her to his chest, planting kisses all over face. "I love you," he said again.

Jaq gazed at him, her heart snapping like a flag in a high wind. They had fought so hard, side by side. And now they'd probably die that way. Russ's brown eyes held hers, intense, resolved. They were in the center of a tornado. Calm. Floating.

"I love you, Russ." She leaned her head back against his shoulder, weaker than she'd ever been. She thought her heart had no more breaking to do. But it wasn't over.

Finn's tender, wide eyes flicked from Russ to Jaq as they clung to each other. His chest heaved. He gripped the long stick he'd found like a spear. "How much can one wolf eat?" A strange smile lit his face. He winked at Jaq and spun toward the wolf, his stick held high. "For Narnia!" he roared, his long, skinny legs striding in a toppling run downhill, slanting diagonally away from the stalking creature—and drawing its gaze. The wolf took the bait.

It leaped almost gleefully after Finn as he plummeted wildly, tripping and yelling as he went.

"Finn!" Jaq lost her breath.

The wolf loped at an angle, closing in, its stride graceful and lightning fast. It barked and lunged, flattening Finn on the ground, landing on his chest.

It happened too quickly. Jaq and Russ gasped and cringed, waiting for the screams of their friend. Jaq shuddered, pressing her face into Russ's chest. His heart hammered as he clutched her tight, crying. "Finn."

Then, barks echoed and a long, high whistle.

"Always! Heel!" a man's voice shouted.

There were several moments of confusion before Jaq realized what was going on. She opened her eyes. A tall man in a duster coat appeared on the ridge, limned by the high moon. The wolf danced away from Finn, its tail lifting and wagging back and forth as it returned to its master. Finn sat up, stunned.

"Always," Russ choked in disbelief.

R.J. rested his machete on his shoulder. His sharp eyes swept over Finn, Jaq, and Russ. "Well... shoot." He raised a walkie-talkie to his mouth. "Lake Outpost. I got 'em."

Jaq's mind toppled, free-falling into black.

———

Everything came in short flashes and sensations. The sound of a chopper beating over them like a giant insect. Lights in her face. Someone peeled her fingers from Russ's shirt. A swarm of hands and voices. Movement, the whipping sound of the rotor taking her away from the badlands. It was over. Over.

Russ. She wanted Russ.

In the back of a large helicopter lifting into the air, Jaq's mind finally settled enough to put together the pieces of the scene around her into one picture. An unshaven guy, who must have been a medic, though he was dressed in a plaid shirt and jeans, gave her a pill with some water.

He talked as he unrolled gauze and wiped her with antiseptic, but she only caught some of it. "You're probably dehydrated, and we'll want them to check out some of these wounds. They're waiting to take you..."

He continued, but Jaq looked past him to the seats on the other side of the helicopter. Finn and Russ leaned on one another, asleep—dirty, gaunt, and covered in dried blood. Her heart surged with relief that they were all together.

Jaq noticed the dog, Always, lying on the floor, his head on his paws. The furry, wolfy dog peered up at her, his tongue hanging out, a canine smile on his face. Jaq smiled back into its icy eyes. After the medic moved on to tend to the boys, Jaq reached down and scratched behind the dog's pointy ears, feeling like she was in a dream.

"Good boy. Brave boy," she murmured. The soft fur, touched with silvery white, was such a contrast to anything she'd felt in weeks.

Always whined and lapped at her hand with a long, wet tongue, then dropped his head back down as if tired... and depressed.

The windows let in the gray light of a predawn. Below, the vast high desert rocked slowly in her view. Had all of that really happened down there?

The badlands. Vast and gray in the predawn.

Daniel was still down there, hanging from a tree like a brown leaf ready to fall. Katie, encased in that outhouse, left alone—her greatest fear. The bodies of Patti, Erica, and probably Mick already decaying.

Craig. Broken long before his fall down that ridge.

The loss and violence left a hollow in her stomach that seemed to drop for miles. Jaq shoved away her thoughts. She didn't want to picture any of them now.

Her muscles ached, her body bruised and scratched. But a pleasant numbness masked the pains in her body. Meds. Shock.

She reached up to her head and touched a bandage, stiff and clean under her dirty fingers.

R.J. made his way toward Jaq from the front of the helicopter and sat beside her, his piercing gaze taking in everything.

"How're you feeling?" he asked in his Clint Eastwood voice.

"Like I—survived."

His smile was sad. "Thank God you did."

Jaq wondered what all this meant for the older man. He'd lost friends. IBSA would most certainly close down. Craig, his protégé, had blown up in his face.

"What about... the others?" Jaq wondered how much he knew.

"We found Katie." His voice broke and he tightened his lips. "The boys told me where the other bodies could be found." He cleared his throat. Stress lined his forehead and around his mouth.

"How'd you know about us?"

"Mick. He found me near the main outpost. He showed up —a mess. He'd been to two outposts trying to find a walkie-talkie or me before he ran into Craig. That was less than thirty-six hours ago. A party searched the area where he'd left you, then split up to check the four outposts. I saw your flares."

"Mick's alive?" Jaq's hope lifted.

"Yeah. Barely. In the hospital—a lot of blood loss." R.J. gazed, unfocused, out the window. He looked as if he'd aged. A container stretched thin to hold all his sorrow and devastation.

Jaq stared at her hands. "I'm so sorry about—everything."

R.J. examined her with mild surprise. "So am I." He paused, running a weather-beaten hand through his salt-and-pepper hair. "I guess... you can't keep your problems in the badlands. Gotta learn to live with them in the real world." He sighed, deep and bitter.

The real world. That's where they were heading. Jaq wondered what would happen now. She knew she'd changed. Nothing to prove, nobody to rebel against. It wasn't a matter of rebuilding herself, but uncovering her true self. She was somebody who wanted to love and be loved. She'd experienced how destructive selfishness was—from her mother, Brian, and mostly Craig. And the things done to Daniel and Erica and Craig—to make them who they were—had been done by selfish people who should have protected them.

Even the relentless taking of the badlands itself, only giving back in stingy, sun-dried scraps, seemed to be an allegory designed to show Jaq a truth she never realized before. She didn't want to be like that, letting those around her wither and die inside while she survived however she could. Not if something she could do would make a difference.

"I just want to be nice—I want to nourish. Nurture," she whispered, hoping it made sense.

R.J. only nodded, lost in his own thoughts and his own pain.

———

As the helicopter descended, hovering over the ground, Jaq saw the waiting ambulances and a gathering of people on the landing strip, their hair blowing wildly in the wind from the propeller. Long, light blond hairs swirled higher than the rest. Flower. Jaq gasped, tears stinging, making everything look fuzzy. Her little sister stood beside her tall dad, both squinting, hands up to block the barely rising sun. Her heart raced.

Russ and Finn woke up, jostling against one another as they touched down. Jaq moved to their side of the helicopter. The three survivors gazed at each other in a speechless, timeless moment. A million unsaid things bound them together forever.

They joined hands, forming a small circle that vibrated with emotions that were difficult to name. Jaq grinned at Finn and Russ, and they smiled back. They all hugged and laughed and cried.

"I love you guys." Jaq leaned in, unashamed if she sounded cheesy. The two boys looked back at her, showing they felt the same.

Russ made a sad face. "I'm sorry I c-couldn't protect you. Are you... o-okay?" he asked, hesitant, guilty, and something clicked for Jaq.

"Russ, he didn't... rape me." She let that sink in. "We've all suffered." This wasn't about just her. They were all hurt—not least of all Russ. Guilt didn't belong here.

Russ breathed out in relief. He closed his eyes. Probably thanking God.

"We'll be okay, Jaq," Finn said.

"It's a miracle we're still here." Russ clapped Finn on the back.

"Couldn't have done it without you, man. Lle naa belego-htar," Finn said, bowing his head to Russ.

"Uh, what's that mean, Legolas?" Russ chuckled, his filthy face lighting a little.

"You are a mighty warrior. And Jaq." He turned his blue eyes to her. "Cormlle naa tanya tel'raa. Your heart is that of the lion."

"I could eat like one right now," Jaq said with a lopsided grin.

"Food, food, food," the boys chanted in unison.

The pilot and three other men, including R.J., jumped out of the helicopter. Jaq, Russ, and Finn were unloaded on shaking legs onto the paved ground—impossibly smooth and clean. The rush of the wind still roared overhead.

Jaq grabbed Russ's hand. He clutched hers back, smiling,

with tears on his cheeks. For a moment, there was nothing else but his dark brown eyes locked on her. Then a cacophony of voices and a crush of people swarmed them.

"Jaq!" Flower screamed. "Jaq! I love you." Her skinny arms reached toward Jaq.

"Flower," Jaq sobbed, hugging her tight. "I love you."

Her father loomed large and sturdy behind Flower. Too eager to wait for his turn, he reached out and held the sisters together. "My baby girl. I never wanted to lose you." His gruff voice broke. "I'm so, so sorry."

"No, Dad. I love you. I'm so sorry." She couldn't continue.

Her father stood back, shaking his head, tears rolling down his cheeks. He squeezed her hand until it almost hurt.

A team of medics approached the survivors, and they were guided onto stretchers to be carried toward the emergency trucks with their blinking red lights. Their families followed along.

Something pulled Jaq's attention away like the echo of a distant call. There was Finn, his stretcher flanked by a full-figured, sandy-haired woman grabbing at him, crying, and a skinny, red-headed man, saying, "My son, my son."

Rescue workers opened the trucks, ready to take them all to the hospital, IV equipment dangling from their hands. Hydration, wound care, and rest awaited. They would be okay.

Jaq craned her neck the other direction until she saw Russ. Relief whooshed through her just at the sight of him. He stared back as if his eyes had been on her the whole time. A short, plump woman with dark, shoulder length hair was bent over him. His mother. The woman sobbed and clutched at him, one hand in his hair. He squeezed his eyes shut, his lips shaping words of comfort in her ear.

Jaq watched Russ with longing, and as they were ushered toward the trucks their eyes met again, a flurry of people blurring around them. She wanted to reach out to him, but they were both surrounded for now. As they lifted Russ into the back of one of the rescue vehicles, he turned his head to find her once more.

"Jaq!" he shouted past his mother's head and through the bustling people. His beautiful, dirty face so tender.

Jaq smiled, crying, holding a hand to her heart as she was tilted up into the back of another truck and the double doors clunked shut, hiding Russ from view. Shut in the back of a vehicle again, on her way to be "fixed." She closed her eyes and took a deep breath.

JAQ STARED as the knife plunged, breaking the surface with a pop and then reemerging shiny and wet. She shivered, clenching her fists as a vague sense of panic rose and gradually fizzled out.

Her little sister frowned, brow creased in concern. "You okay, Jaq?" Flower's hand froze, gripping the knife over the pumpkin she was carving.

"Yeah. I'm fine." She flashed a weak smile, pushing away the images of blood.

Flower caught her gaze, set down the knife, and put her arms around Jaq. "I love you."

"Thanks for being here for me." She melted into the hug.

"We're here for each other."

Jaq blinked back tears. "I'm really trying." She breathed in deep, her sister's shampoo and perfume a reassurance that she was somewhere safe.

"I know." Flower burrowed into Jaq's neck.

The weeks had gone by, full of therapy sessions, long talks, bad dreams, and memories. Jaq was grateful for the chance to repair things with her sister and dad. She had almost lost that chance.

"What's going on in here? Aren't you two done with those pumpkins yet? Don't waste my money—those things were twenty-eight cents a pound." Their father came into the room carrying a tiny pumpkin of his own, a grin on his face.

She released Flower and smiled at her dad in his thrift store clothes and oversized glasses. He was awesome. "So, who's throwing this party tonight, penny pincher? It couldn't have been cheap." Jaq glanced around at the black and orange streamers and balloons. The counter in the kitchen was spread with snacks and drinks. *Food.* It was still odd to have as much as she wanted after starving in the wilderness. But somehow, she was never that hungry.

"Let me worry about that." He shrugged his broad shoulders. "Your friends will be here soon. So, get carving."

Friends. She still had some more repairing and apologizing to do. The friends Jaq had left behind during her freak out were good kids. They seemed hesitant but willing to move forward and support her effort to straighten up. It was more than she deserved. In this new frame of mind, Jaq looked back on some of her behavior with shame. She'd been a real jerk.

The sisters finished their slimy work and put candles inside their jack-o-lanterns. The demonic grins glowed yellow on the dark steps of the front porch, a parody of real terror. Jaq knew.

"You excited to see Russ?" Flower asked as they went back into the house.

"Yes. Very." A surge of excitement went through Jaq's body. The fear that pressed in on her every time he or Finn called had finally lessened. They were no longer just an awful reminder.

Russ had been her lifeboat during her readjustment. Sometimes she had vivid dreams of being curled in the safe circle of his arms, his smell and warmth so real. His kiss like fire. She was more than ready to see him again.

"And how do you feel about Mom and Brian showing up?"

"Processing it but... I think it could be good," Jaq said. Everyone had a reason for what they did. If she could start again and be forgiven, then anything could happen. It didn't have to be perfect to be love.

Her father set a huge bowl of popcorn down on the counter. "It's been rough. But maybe we can all figure out how to get along." He snapped a pirate patch over one eye, which seriously took away from his earnest tone.

"Yeah." After all she'd been through, she knew she could face whatever came next. "Thanks, Dad."

"You bet, sweetheart." His voice rumbled, low with emotion.

A little later Jaq saw the Uber through the window. She glanced in the hall mirror, smoothed down her hair and smiled at herself. Clean skin, a little makeup. He'd never seen her look so good. But it didn't matter. He'd seen her at her worst and had only seen the best.

When the doorbell rang, she opened the door and there was Russ. Time stopped. Jaq felt her face glowing with a brilliant smile to match his. His chocolate hair, still shaggy, was shiny and combed, his face shaved smooth and clean.

Russ stepped inside, dropping a duffle bag on the ground, and still neither one of them seemed to be able to speak. It was hard to even breathe. Jaq held his gaze for a long moment.

He seemed to struggle to speak, and then mouthed silently, "I love you." He blinked his dark lashes and reached out for her.

Jaq lunged into Russ's arms and pressed against him as hard as she could. "I love you," she whispered, a sob escaping. The way he held her felt so good. No danger, no fear... just the two of them and a world of feelings between them. And he smelled amazing. His familiar scent mixed with cologne.

Russ kissed Jaq hard on the mouth. It was all encompassing until Flower cleared her throat from somewhere nearby.

"Uh. Hi." Jaq's little sister giggled and tucked her hair behind one ear.

"Oh. Russ, this is my sister, Flower."

"Nice to finally meet you." Russ nodded, his beautiful smile so genuine.

Flower widened her eyes at Jaq. Her face said it all. She approved. "Totally. Heard all about you. I'm going to ask you absolutely everything before you get out of here—just so you know." Flower laughed. "Well, come in and eat something! People will be here soon." Flower disappeared in the direction of the counter full of food, tactfully leaving Jaq alone with Russ again.

Jaq's father was humming in the kitchen, the house smelled like cinnamon, popcorn, and candy apples, and Russ stood beside Jaq, gripping her hand. She hadn't felt this good in a long time.

"How's it going, Crooked Pack?" He touched her cheek.

"Better now. You?" She felt her cheeks warm.

His hands seemed to move over the skin on her arms on their own. Just happy to be touching her. "You kidding? I'm flying. Life is good."

It really was good. Somehow. Jaq thought of part of that poem Russ had recited to her back in the wilderness about holding life like a face between your hands, staring at the flaws, the lack of beauty, but choosing to love it again. It was as if a tightened fist inside Jaq's chest loosened and opened. Ready to receive.

"I missed you. Every day," he said, his brown eyes soft.

"I'm so glad you're here." She leaned in for another kiss.

"Me too," he whispered against her cheek.

"Come meet my dad." Her father had been so grateful for

Russ's role in saving Jaq's life that she was sure they'd get along just fine.

Russ squeezed her hand and took a deep breath. "Been looking forward to it."

"I have too."

Russ and Jaq smiled at each other. Though the high desert, barren and deadly, was far behind them, Jaq still often found herself in their deep shadow. But with Russ by her side, she let the darkness part just enough to let in the light of hope. Something green and fragile pushed up out of the murkiness inside of her. The future vibrated in the distance, a fertile promise of blossoms to come.

———

ACKNOWLEDGMENTS

Many years ago, in a land far from where I live now, I hit 15 (or maybe it's more accurate to say, 15 hit me). I voluntarily entered a wilderness academy in the boonies of Idaho to search my soul. I liked the idea of getting out of my negative rut by confronting and overcoming something difficult and unknown. Little did I know just how challenging it would be!

Having grown up in the California Bay Area, I was unprepared for the snow and cold of Idaho. It was almost unbearable at first! And yes, I was strip searched like the characters in my story but standing outside in the snow!

The people I met (none of whom were murdered), and the challenges I faced in the wilderness changed the trajectory of my life.

Our large fearless trail leader, the college intern with a heart of gold, the jock with an attitude problem, the mysterious stoner, the theatrical and funny addict, the feral girl ... and me.

The hikes were long, and the hunger never ended (we even ate a dead coyote we found in the snow one night out of desperation--it tasted like lamb). The required skills took hard work to master—I'm looking at you, bow drill fire!

But by the end of the trip, I could do things like make fire without matches, navigate by the stars, build traps, stand barefoot in the snow, and howl with the coyotes at night.

In case you're wondering, the characters in this story are all based on real people—except the killer, he's a metaphor. (I hope that readers will discern for themselves what that might be.) The character of Jaq is very different from who I was at fifteen, but she represents parts of many kids I've known.

The only name I didn't change was Patty's. She was the counselor whose compassion and guidance empowered me to build a bridge over my pain and find a new way forward. She passed away from cancer not many years after I left the program, but I still remember how she made me feel. Understood. Seen. Hopeful.

I'm so grateful for the early readers of my manuscript as it was taking shape. My writing group: Jennifer Jenkins, Lois Brown, Margie Jordan, Tahsha Wilson, and James Lewis. As well as many friends and family: Kathleen and Stephan Seable, Jamie and Maribel Rees, Ali Durham, Sandra Seable, Julia Brown, Katie Shomler, Micah Rees, Jessika Armstrong, Sarah-Noël Lipman and many others who read parts of my manuscript and gave me valuable feedback.

A huge thank you to my editors Olivia Swenson and Hannah Smith at Owl Hollow Press and especially for Emma Nelson for giving my story the opportunity to be in print!

I still think about the other kids who went on that journey with me through the wilderness. I hope they're no longer stalked by their pain, anger and self-destructive behaviors. That they've found peace and empowerment and a way to give courage and wisdom to others who suffer.

Although nobody was *actually* killed on my outward-bound journey all those years ago, I like to think our troubled crew, Les Misérables, left our old selves somewhere out there to die in the Badlands in order to live brighter and happier futures.

—One Who Walks With Crooked Pack

Jo Schaffer Layton is a native of the California Bay Area now living in Texas. She is an author, speaker, screenwriter, TV/film producer, and is a Taekwondo black belt.

In addition *Badlands*, Jo is the author of YA novels *Against Her Will* and the Stanley and Hazel trilogy.

Jo is a co-founder of the nonprofit Teen Author Boot Camp, one of the nation's largest writing organizations for teens, with an annual conference and regular programs that support literacy, authorship, and provide books to underserved populations.

She is passionate about community, travel, books, music, healthy eating, classic films, and martial arts. But her favorite thing is being a mom to her awesome kiddos and wife to her hunky husband.

#Badlands | #BadlandsBook

www.joschaffer.com